UNTIL WE MEET

BOOK 2 - WE'LL MEET AGAIN SERIES

RHONDA FORREST

Valeena Press

UNTIL WE MEET 2021

BOOK 2- We'll Meet Again Series

Published by Valeena Press 2021

Published by Valeena Press

Book Cover Design and formatting by Ethel Beckett and Rhonda Forrest

❀ Created with Vellum

UNITL WE MEET is Part 2 of WE'LL MEET AGAIN SERIES and continues the story of ELIZABETH'S STAR (PART 1)

BOOK 1 - *'A dingo howls, a star falls.*
Don't worry for me, I'll be home soon.'

Based on actual events, *Elizabeth's Star* begins the story of Michael and Joanie, unfolding the lives of their families and friends while following the life of Gracie, a little girl left behind when her father went to war.

A moving tale of love, loss, and separation.

BOOK 2 - *'When you go home, tell them of us and say, for your tomorrow, we gave our today.' John Maxwell Edmonds 1918*

Until We Meet is an epic war saga based on actual events that continues the story of Elizabeth's Star. A tale of survival, love and family, set amidst the backdrop of World War II.

BOOK 3 - *My troubles are all over, and I am at home; and often before I am quite awake, I fancy I am still in the orchard at Birtwick, standing with my friends under the apple trees.' (Black Beauty)*

We'll Meet Again is a story of devotion and family, a connection between those who suffered loss and separation and a sweeping tale of hope, chance and love.

AUTHOR'S NOTE

In early 1942 as Japanese forces strengthened their power in the Pacific, thousands of American troops were sent to Australia in preparation for conflicts in the Southwest Pacific Theatre of World War II.

United States General, Douglas MacArthur, arrived in Australia in March 1942, taking command of the SWPA - South West Pacific Area of Command. All allied land and air forces in the region would be under his command, including the combat units of Australia's defence forces. In July 1942, MacArthur moved his headquarters to Brisbane, ensuring he would be closer to the front line in New Guinea as well as the US troop camps near Rockhampton and Townsville.

Brisbane was home to 80,000 US troops during the war years and in April 1942 when a decision was made to establish a United States Navy submarine base and support facilities at New Farm (Teneriffe), a further 800 US service personnel were stationed in the city.

The US Submarines – which were mostly named after fish - were one of their most effective weapons for the allies, with the aim of halting the ocean traffic lifeline of the Japanese Imperial forces, thereby destroying their trade and transport routes through the Pacific Ocean. The submarines made 1,474 patrols in the Pacific with a total of 52 submarines and over 3,500 submariners lost during the war years.

During the war years and after, as many as 15,000 Australian women married American servicemen, many eventually moving to the United States to be with them. The women waited months, even years for the American government to give permission for them to be married. Although the American servicemen were said to be 'overpaid, oversexed and over here', most Australian women did not rush into the decision to marry and waited sometimes up to four years before sailing to America after the war ended.

The Australian government was also making resolutions and during the post-war years decided they needed to 'populate or perish'. Within twenty years, two million immigrants would call Australia home. Between 1946 and 1964, couples who became known as 'baby boomers' were eager to start families. The world was rapidly changing and was a much safer place to live, the threat of war had eased, and families started new lives in what was regarded as a land of opportunity.

To Terry ~
for your patience, love and friendship.

Map of New Guinea, Australia and South-East Asia

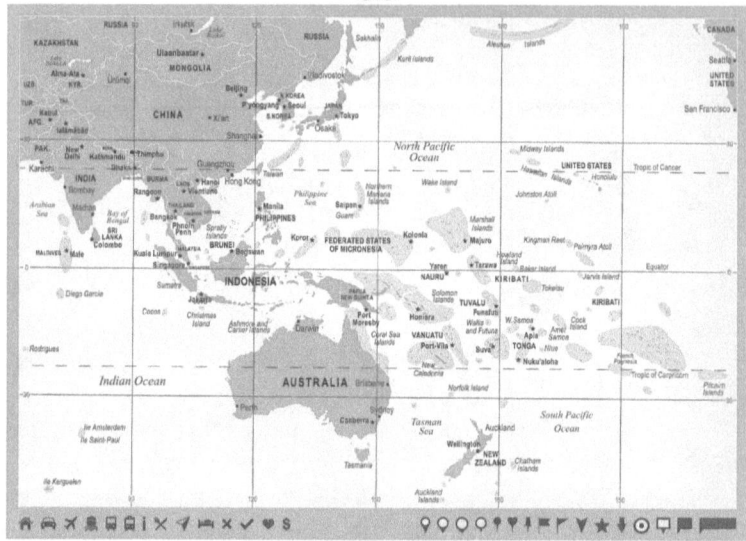

Map of Papua New Guinea and New Britain - Rabaul

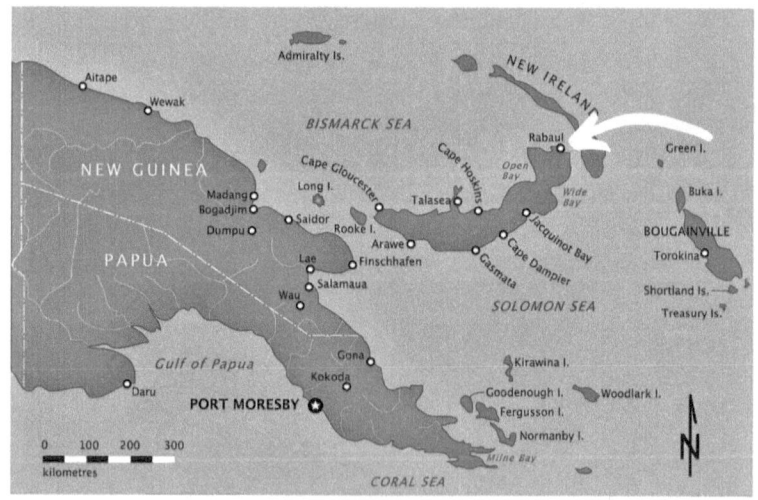

'When you go home
tell them of us and say,
for your tomorrow
we gave our today.'

John Maxwell Edmonds 1918

CHAPTER 1

Oklahoma USA - January 1940

'Rope that one tight for me, Bud. Swing him around this way. Watch him, his ears are back. Yikes, there he goes,' Beth yelled at her brother as the horse flattened its ears, both front hooves striking wildly in the air.

Bud moved quickly, dragging hard on the rope as he pulled the colt's head lower. He talked as he worked; his words calm as he pushed the rope hard in the other direction as the horse swung around.

'Whoa there, Roby.' Bud leaned back, once again just out of the way of the horse's striking front hooves.

Beth laughed loudly from her perch on top of the wooden yard rails. 'You're winning.' She flinched as he narrowly jumped out of the way again.

'Really! If you're so sure then why aren't you here next to me? Maybe you could be putting a ribbon on his tail and getting him ready for the kids' pony rides next week.'

'Hurry up. I can smell Ma's corn pie cooking.' She shielded her eyes against the burning sun that ricocheted off the dilapidated tin buildings, their shapes sinking further and further into the haze. The yard she looked over was a pool of soft feathery powder, the contents sporadically flying through the air and joining the wind that always whistled over these parts of Oklahoma.

Across the prairie, millions of particles whipped from the surface of the plains, joined with dust from their yard, taking off in a swirl and disappearing into the distance.

Bud came closer to where she sat, one hand on the mane of the brown colt, the other firmly holding the rope attached to the halter.'He's gonna be a real good horse once you get him broken in, Beth.'

'I thought you were going to do that. I've got the other three to worry about.' She sat upright, looking across the yards, waiting, watching, for what, she didn't know.

'Well, I sorta need to talk to you about that. Whoa there, that's it, Roby. Take it easy now.'

The horse quietened and although its hooves danced in the dirt, it no longer lunged wildly. Bud talked softly, rubbing his hand up and down its thick, muscular neck, the dust from its coat puffing into the air.

He looked out over the plains.

'What would you be watching for, Beth, out there? There's no one coming. I don't know why you keep looking.'

For a moment he took his eyes off the horse, and she studied his face. There were only two years between them, and except that Bud was a lot taller than she was, they may as well have been twins. Well, that's what their mother always said. Beth's face was the same shape as Bud's, with the same smattering of freckles and piercing blue eyes. Her skin was softer though, and two thick braids of brown hair hung in messy plaits on either side of her face. They wore similar chequered shirts, blue jeans and worn-out, dusty old riding boots.

'At least your hands look like they belong to a woman.' Her

mother had chastised her only last week, concerned about her apparent opposition to adhere to the female niceties that so many of the other young women in the area deemed important.

It took every argument her parents could muster to make sure she attended the final year ball in a dress, and shoes that weren't riding boots. The ball was a one off and since then her attire remained the same; jeans, a chequered shirt and riding boots, finished off with the cowboy hats both she and Bud had received last Christmas.

* * *

Everyone commented on how pretty she looked the night of the ball. Her dark blue dress contrasted against her tanned skin, complementing her blue eyes. Those same eyes now searched beyond the horse yards, across to the horizon.

'So, what are you looking at?' Bud gazed over the yards. 'How long are we gonna be able to survive? Most of the soil from those plains you're staring at has been whipped up and dumped thousands of miles away.'

Beth coughed, clearing her throat which was always sore, due to the fine dust not only in the air outside but also in every space inside the house. 'I'm not sure. I just have this feeling something's coming. Something big.' She squinted into the sun, once again looking out over the plains.

'Like another dust storm?' Bud asked.

'No, I don't think so. This is so big it makes my gut churn every time I think about it.'

'I don't always like your premonitions. They have a nasty habit of coming true.'

'I'm not always happy about them either. Can I tell you something, Bud? You won't laugh at me.'

'I'll try not to, but sometimes the darndest things come out of your mouth.'

'I feel like the war is coming across the oceans. That it's going to come here.'

'Beth, for God's sake, what war is going to bother coming all the way here to dry old Oklahoma? Do you really think the Germans want this dust bowl?' He kicked the ground with his feet. 'They won't come here. You're safe.' He handed her the rope, which was still attached to the colt. The horse stood still, its ears forward, listening to their banter.

'I have a nagging worry.' She rubbed her eyes. 'The other night I had another dream about you.'

'Did I have a beautiful girl on my arm?'

'I'm not sure if it's because you've said that so often, but you will be pleased; yes, you did have a beautiful red-haired girl on your arm. You introduced her as your wife.'

'Jeez, Beth. What did she look like?'

'I just told you, flaming red hair, a few freckles, but very pretty.'

'What else? Did she have a lovely soft voice and look at me with loving eyes? Did I take her in my arms and kiss her passionately, you know, like Rhett and Scarlett in *Gone with the Wind*?'

Beth jumped down, the soft dust flying up as she landed squarely on the ground. 'No, you idiot, she had red hair, Scarlett's hair was black. In fact, her accent was different, like a foreigner and not from around here. Not like Scarlett's accent either. And strangely, the way she dressed and acted, reminded me of me! So, there was definitely no fluttering eyelashes or precious ballroom gowns.'

Beth led the horse back to the sheds, making sure to keep a firm hand on the lead rope. Even though the horse was quiet at the moment, she didn't trust it, not one little bit.

'What was it you were going to tell me, Bud?'

'What?'

'You said you had something to tell me.'

Bud waited until she put the horse back into its stall in the shed. She hung the halter rope on a metal hook and filled the water tank with the red-coloured water that gurgled intermittently out of the pipe.

He waited until she sat down on the metal tin next to him and she smiled fondly at him as they sat side by side. Obviously there was something important to talk about.

He looked straight at her, his words jarring. 'I've joined up.'

Her body tensed. 'You've what?'

'I've joined up. I've enlisted and I leave the day after tomorrow.'

'When did you decide to do that?'

'I've been hankering after a change for a while. There's nothing here for me.'

Her teeth clenched hard together, her chest heaving with anger as he continued.

'Well, nothing except you. And soon enough you'll want to move on. We need to get out of here, Beth. Even Ma and Pa say we should go. I don't want to stay here for the rest of my life.' He picked up a handful of dirt. 'I don't want to live in this dust bowl. I want to see green fields and animals grazing on plentiful grass. I want to feel a fresh wind on my face and look across the oceans.'

'So do I, but I thought we'd do that together.'

'I did too, but I'm ready to move on and if I join up, I'll not only earn money but learn new skills.'

'You don't think we're going to get involved in the war in Europe, do you? I thought our government was going to stay out of it. Remain neutral.'

'Sure, that's what they say, and we probably won't be involved. But then again, if we do decide to back England, I'd already be trained and ready to go.'

'But why join up now? Why not wait and see? The war will probably be over by Christmas.'

'I need to do this.'

'But what if Roosevelt decides to become part of the war and you don't come back?'

'I will. You just said yourself, I'll be around with a beautiful red-haired woman on my arm.'

Beth looked out to the distant hills.

'So, you understand me going, Beth? I'd like to leave with the thought that you do.'

'I do understand, Bud, and I'll stay here with Ma and Pa. No matter what happens, I'll be here. And if things get too bad with this dry, we can always move back down with Pa's brother. Pa's always talking about a smaller place where the pastures are greener and the dirt stays on the ground.'

Bud put his arm around her shoulders. 'I'll keep safe and work hard. I'll be able to come back when I get leave or in between training.'

'For some reason I'm not scared about you not coming back. I feel sure you will, but a lot of people quite close to you will perish.'

Bud dragged his eyes away from the plains stretching out monotonously in front of the ranch and turned to her. There was annoyance in his voice. 'Why would you say something like that? Why say people around me will perish.'

'I didn't tell you the rest of my dream. There was another part of the dream, a part that came before the beautiful red-haired girl.'

'I'm not sure I want to know. You know I only like to hear the good parts.'

* * *

It was a gift Beth had. Sometimes they were short intuitions that came to her during the day. She could be working the horses, bringing the washing in, or just daydreaming. Out of the blue, like a flash, she would sense something; an inkling of what was to come. Sometimes the ideas came to her in her dreams. Like the great dust storms that happened to the west of them years ago and wiped out entire towns, blanketing the landscape for weeks. She was only in her teens when she first dreamed about the storms.

* * *

Beth's mother wrote down the date on a picture Beth drew. It was the tenth of April 1935, and Beth had woken in the middle of the night and gone into Bud's room, shaking him until he woke.

'Bud, wake up. I've had that dream again. The one where the earth is swallowed up by a huge cloud of dust.'

Bud was only half awake and wouldn't even open his eyes when she sat on his bed and shook his arm. 'Go back to bed, Beth, there're always dust storms out there. It's nothing new.'

'This one's big. People will die. Houses will disappear. It's the biggest one ever. You should see it, the cloud is fifty, no maybe one hundred times bigger than the houses.'

Bud rolled over, facing away from her. Eventually, she gave up waiting and went back to her bedroom. She sat at the window for a long while, waiting to see the huge dust clouds she had dreamt about.

The next morning, she drew a picture. 'All the dirt blew off the Great Plains,' she said, pointing to the drawing, called, *Dust Bowl*. 'The houses and farm machinery are covered in sand, and these are people and everything they have left is strapped to their backs.' The picture showed stick people walking in lines away from the cloud. The lines were endless and tapered off into the distance. In the background was the cloud of dust, like a massive wave, stretching to the top of the drawing, taking up three-quarters of the page.

'I think the cloud is out of proportion,' her mother said. 'No storm has ever been that big.'

Beth's voice wavered with agitation. 'This is like nothing you've ever seen before, and the wind will take the ground, and nothing will be able to survive on it afterwards. It will be a black storm and it will bury everything in its path. It will happen,' she waved her hands to the west, to the plains and drought-stricken areas of

Oklahoma, 'out there and then it will move southwards and take everything with it.'

Her mother scrunched her eyes up. 'Will it affect us here?'

'No more than usual. We'll be lucky and just get the edges of it. But those people,' she pointed to her drawings of horizontal stick figures lying on the sides of the tracks where others walked, 'those people, they will die. Children will die, and there is nothing we can do to stop it.'

The picture had been propped up on top of the shelf in the lounge room. Four days later, the family of four stood in front of it after hearing about the calamity occurring to the west and south of them. 'It's the worst dust storm in the United States' history,' Beth's father said, staring hard at the picture. 'Sometimes, girl, I don't know if these premonitions are a curse or a blessing.'

Beth clung to her father's arm. 'I like it when it's useful, but I don't like seeing dead bodies in my dreams. I can only help living people.'

Beth was referring to the night she had dreamt about a small boy stuck down a well. Her father had gone with her to the other side of town, and sure enough, there was a family who were desperate, looking for their young son. Men were out searching, scouring the countryside, looking in dilapidated barns and under rusty cars; any small spaces where a boy might squeeze.

Beth led her father away from the searchers, heading for a farm quite a distance away, the house and yards long ago deserted and no longer used.

The search team had already been over the property, but not down to the distant fields, where they said it was too far for a young boy to walk. Beth, however, was undeterred, and as she and her father came closer to an overgrown section in the far back corner, the whimpering of a small child was audible. The searchers were called in and although it took a long while to get the boy out, he survived. He had a broken leg and cracked ribs, but he was alive and his parents and many of the townsfolk still talked about the young girl called Beth and her visions that came true. It had been that blessing which allowed their only son to survive.

* * *

Now as she sat with her brother, she tried to take in the news that he was enlisting. Bud bumped his shoulder against hers, nearly pushing her off the tin she was sitting on. 'Tell me more about Scarlett, or rather the beautiful girl with the red hair.'

She righted herself and flicked her plaits back behind her shoulders. 'It wasn't just about the girl, although that was the only good part. The rest of it was one of those dreams I wished I'd never had.'

'C'mon, sis,' he poked her playfully in the ribs. 'Tell me.'

She paused and looked down at the ground. 'It was a vivid dream and I felt like I was there. I was in the water, cold and wet, and I could smell the salt in the air.'

'Gawd, Beth, where were you? That doesn't sound like anywhere around here.'

Taking a deep breath, she continued. 'I dreamed of a long grey boat and lots of men around you.' She paused and took another deep breath before continuing. Her voice was raspy, and Bud leaned over towards her. 'There was a large ship, and it was sinking. There were men trapped... they tried,' she took short breaths as if she couldn't breathe properly, 'they tried to get out, but then the ship became heavier. I could feel it weighing down on me, pressing on my body.'

'What happened then?'

'It fell below the waves. It fell to the bottom of the ocean, and then everything went quiet. Like no sound, nothing. It was still.'

'What happened to the men on the ship? Did some get off?'

Beth was firm in her answer, her voice unwavering. 'No, they all drowned. They were locked in below the decks, like the slaves when they brought them out from Africa.'

'Maybe they were slaves?'

'No, they were white men and they all drowned.'

'Did I drown?'

'I don't think so. I didn't see you below the water and then I saw the girl with the red hair on your arm. You weren't on a ship or on the ocean. You were on land, and you looked happy.' She shook her head trying to clear the images from her mind. 'If you died in the ocean with those other men, you wouldn't have been walking down the street with a girl.'

'Great, thanks. I'll carry that thought with me. I wonder what your dream means.'

Beth hung onto his arm. 'It was horrible. Worse than the dust storm dream. I don't want to dream it ever again or feel like I'm trapped under the ocean with all the water above me. The men were nice men, they were sad, but I could tell they were good men.'

'How could you tell?'

'Although it was the edge of death, there was a sense of calm. They nodded at me as if to say it was alright, like they understood I couldn't help them, and it wasn't my fault.'

Bud shook his head. 'I'm always amazed at the clarity of your visions. 'Were there any women there?'

'No, just men.' She looked straight at her brother, their eyes staring hard at one another. 'Who are you joining, Bud? The army?'

'No, Beth, the navy.'

CHAPTER 2

Naval Submarine Base, New London, Connecticut USA – March 1941

o you understand that the requirements for duty as a submariner are far above those for the navy?'

'Yes, sir.'

'Are you aware that life in a submarine does not include the facility of a doctor, and medical services are limited?'

'Yes, sir.'

Bud flinched as the doctor thumped his knee with a rubber hammer, the responsive action of his foot kicking forward, bringing a smile to the doctor's face. 'Great reflexes, and your hand-eye coordination is also good. What did you do in Oklahoma?'

'We have a horse ranch. I broke and trained the horses. That was before I joined the navy.'

The doctor continued his examination. 'I can't imagine living with all that dust. At least if you make it through submarine school the dust won't be a problem.'

'It's real bad out there. There's not much green left, just miles and miles of barren ground.'

'If you're used to those big wide open spaces, how do you think you'll fare in a small confined space with other men? It's very different from the ships you've been on.'

'I'll be fine. I can cope with anything.'

The doctor shook his head. 'You've done okay so far but you still have the pressure testing to go.'

The physical was lengthy, and every part of Bud's body and mind had been prodded or poked, questioned and re-questioned until the tester was satisfied. It took a special kind of navy man to become a submariner, and those selected were trying to find any little crack in his armour, a weakness, either physical or mental, that would strike his name off the list.

The doctor returned to his desk, sitting straight in a tall wooden chair, his pen scratching across a pile of papers in front of him. His glasses perched low on his nose, and he looked at Bud above the lenses. 'Here's your form, young man. You've passed the medical examination. Report to the classroom in the morning for your next set of instructions. Good luck.'

* * *

The next day Bud sat in a room alongside eighteen other men. They all wore the same eager look on their faces, and like him, sat upright and focused as the class was put through the extensive instructions on how a submarine worked. The chief officer paced at the front of the room; his arms clenched behind his back, his shiny black shoes padding methodically over the timber floor. His eyes moved back and forth over the men, his words brusque as he explained what they would be learning over the next couple of months.

'You men are here because you've volunteered to be submariners and you've passed the first part of the testing. You may have done your time at boot camp and with the Navy on the open ocean, but this course will take every bit of concentration and brainpower you possess. Listen, learn, and study every spare opportunity you get. Be here, prepared to learn each morning and we expect you to be alert and ready to take in whatever we instruct. Drink in moderation. Every part of your brain will be required to pass the mental and physical tests. Not all of you in this room will pass the next part. Don't be the one to let yourself down. If this is what you want, then listen hard, remember what you're taught and be on top of the lessons to give it your best.'

Bud wrote down the notes and copied the diagrams, intrigued by the workings of the different compartments that made up the space he would be living in, if he passed the course. Navy life had suited him right from the very first day he had joined up and being on the ocean was as exhilarating as riding a bucking bronco. He had however, been drawn to the idea of volunteering for the submarines, and now that he was here in New London, he was certain this was the path he wanted to follow.

He concentrated hard. To complete the written component of the test, he would need to memorise, draw and explain every working part of the submarine. Further training would also take place in an escape tower. The tower would ensure that the necessary skills were taught in case there was ever a need to escape from a submerged submarine.

The men had discussed the escape tower at length and Bud looked forward to testing his skills in the water. There was a spring in his step as he made his way with the others to the 100-foot high, tower. He peered up at a massive water tank that loomed above him, looking much like a lighthouse with winding stairs wrapping around its exterior surface.

Once inside, Bud changed into striped swimming trunks and listened to instructions for using a Momsen Lung—a breathing apparatus that was standard equipment on a submarine. If need be, submariners could escape using this latest emergency device, which recycled breathing gases. Concentrating hard, he focused on breathing in and out through the mouthpiece attached to the equipment.

It was one thing to be able to use the Momsen Lung in practice and out of the water; however, the next step was for the trainees to be submerged in the training tank before attempting to escape up to the surface. The men learned how to do this by using their Momsen Lung and what was known as a buoyant ascent method. They would start by practising in the shallow depths before eventually moving to deeper and deeper starts, each time following instructions explaining how to breathe and rise to the surface.

At first he was disoriented, taking a while to get the breathing technique correct. The more he used the equipment though, the more relaxed and confident he became. It was just like breaking in an untamed horse. You had to conquer the movements and stay calm, to remain in control.

He repeated the exercises, learning how to pop his ears when needed and staying relaxed while working with the water. If you took your time and worked in a methodical fashion, counting the required numbers, there would be no complications from the bends and you could ascend when required, moving up through the depths of the practice tower.

The confines and narrow area of the tower did not worry him, and he felt sorry for two of the men who were sent away after the first couple of training schedules. Claustrophobia and nerves were a major deterrent for those wanting a career that involved living beneath the sea. If you couldn't cope with the confines of the training tower, then the consistent restrictions of a long metal tube under the sea with no personal space or sunlight, was perhaps not the right choice for your naval service.

Submariner training was rigorous and intense, but so far Bud had been able to understand and remember everything he'd learned. Now that he'd mastered the tower, he would be moving on to the next stage, which actually involved spending time on a real submarine.

* * *

The practice drills and learning came naturally and Bud felt as if he had been born into the world of underwater vessels. He revelled in the procedures and life under the sea, returning from his first submarine trip with a renewed sense of direction and confidence in the path he had chosen. Before he knew it, the two months of training had passed and all that was left was the final test.

He sat tall, his fists clenched, resting on his knees. In front of him were the officers who would pass or fail him on the last part of the course. They drilled him about the different pieces of equipment and the lengthy working procedures of a submarine. Without hesitation, he gave detailed answers. The officers acknowledged his enthusiasm and expertise, shaking his hand before wishing him the best for his new career.

Everything he had worked for fell into place, and the night before he graduated, he wrote a letter to his family.

Dear Pa, Ma, and Beth,

Today I have finished my training with the Submarine School here in Connecticut and tomorrow I will graduate and receive my orders for my first line of duty. The training has been lengthy, but I have never felt so prepared in my life. It is a good choice and I will be with the finest men in the forces. The previous months at sea and training with the navy will stand me in good stead.

Although my conditions will be cramped, smelly and difficult, I know the food is the finest there is, so that will put your mind at ease, Ma. I will be well fed.

I don't know when I'll be in contact again. We aren't told where or when we will set forth, but I want you to know I will remain safe and think of you every day and be back with you once my tour is over or when I get leave.

Beth, keep practising that guitar and look after Ma and Pa. You'll be kept busy with the horses while I am away. Don't turn your back on that brown mare and remember to make sure you exercise Blacky every day. I have the family photo with me and I will look at it each night when I bed down in my small bunk and think of you all. Don't worry about me. I will be safe and wearing my dolphin badge with pride.

Deepest love from your loving son and brother, Bud.

Licking the envelope closed he laid back on his bunk. Tomorrow he'd post the letter. Who knew when he would get to write or when he would see his family again. The world was rapidly changing and although most Americans didn't want to enter the war, at the end of last year, Roosevelt's broadcast had definitively stated that he would help the United Kingdom by supplying them with military supplies. The United States would, however, stay out of the fighting for the time being.

'Give us the tools, and we will finish the job,' Winston Churchill had declared last month.

Bud stared at the ceiling of the dormitory where he had been housed for the last two months. Would Churchill finish the job? Would Germany be stopped from invading the rest of Europe? Would his time as a submariner be spent in peaceful waters or hunting down enemy ships? He was prepared for whatever came and looked forward to this next stage in his career. Soon the ceiling would be closer, the bunks smaller and the rooms confined, but he'd be able to put everything he'd learned into practice and work with other men, as part of a team.

His hands rested on his chest and he closed his eyes. Hitler and his army were on the move and Great Britain and its allies seemed powerless to stop them. How much longer could Roosevelt hold out before he assigned their own troops to stop the Nazi tentacles from spreading across Europe? There was also Japan to consider. Their relationship with the United States grew steadily worse and there were concerns that materials the Americans had sold to Japan were being used in the war against China. A decision had been made and Washington declared that they would no longer allow trade for materials that could be used for war.

He tossed and turned, mulling over the news that he had been following in the last few months. He pictured Beth and his mother and father back home on the ranch. Keep them safe and let the world soon be at peace, he thought, before falling into a deep sleep.

* * *

The next morning the sun shone brightly. The Connecticut sky was clear and blue, the air crisp with the scent of summer days to come. Bud stood tall and proud as he graduated and received his orders for his first duty. He was to take two weeks leave before he began his life aboard a submarine. The submarine he was assigned to, was the SS Sturgeon.

CHAPTER 3

Rabaul, New Guinea - December 8, 1941

Nine months had passed since Michael McTavish and the first group of men from the 2/22nd Battalion, known as Lark Force, had arrived in Rabaul. Michael had joined the Australian Imperial Forces in Melbourne the year before and been surprised to set sail, not for North Africa or the Middle East, but instead heading in a northerly direction, the destination, the Gazelle Peninsula, New Britain, part of the largest island in the Bismarck Archipelago. The crescent shaped island had 1000 miles of coastline that was surrounded by coral reefs, with its rugged spine of mountain ranges giving way to small areas of flat land along its shorelines. The archipelago was part of the region of New Guinea and lay fifty-five miles east of the Huon Peninsula, which was situated on the far eastern side of the mainland of New Guinea. It was a tropical paradise, the name 'Rabaul' meaning mangroves, or 'haul' to the Tolai, the indigenous people of the area.

The township was set out in a grid-like formation with wide avenues, and timber houses that epitomised the colonial era. The graceful buildings were surrounded by exotic birds that flitted in and out of the fragrant frangipani and colourful bougainvillea, neatly contained in well-maintained gardens.

At times, Michael—who had not long turned twenty-five— needed to pinch himself. Coming from Western Queensland and more recently the cold crowded streets of Melbourne, Rabaul was like something in a picture book; a tropical island with an abundance of towering coconut trees and mysterious locations; active volcanoes, dark jungles and a bustling marketplace with unusual produce he had never tasted before.

His life, and that of the other men in Rabaul, was comparatively easy compared to other Australian forces who had been sent to faraway lands to fight alongside the British in the Middle East or North Africa. Other troops had fought in Greece and Crete, and Australian and New Zealand troops from the 6th Division had suffered heavy losses, with many dying in battle or taken prisoner of war. Those conflicts seemed a long way away for the men of Lark Force who had settled into island life, their main job to fortify communications and erect essential buildings for the Australian government.

The social aspect of the small town was a welcome relief from the training and allotted duties, and leave passes were handed out so the men could enjoy a break from military responsibilities. The sports clubs, pubs and trading stores did a thriving business and the idyllic setting with sandy beaches and sweeping bays gave the soldiers a peaceful location where they could enjoy the company of others who also called Rabaul home.

Michael had not only settled into his military duties, but his life had once again taken a different direction when he fell in love with the beautiful Joanie, a young woman who had come to the islands with her father to run the trading store of Burns Philp in the main street of the town. He became acquainted with her father, Reg, and her childhood friends, Peter, and Andrew. Even though he was kept busy running errands for the Sergeant, he managed to find time for picnics with Joanie, long walks with his friend Birri, and dinners and drinks with his new friends.

Like many of the other men who had been sent to Rabaul, he bided his time, certain that in the near future the battalion would be taken back to Australia and shipped out to where they were more needed, near Europe and Great Britain, supporting the Allies in their fight against the Germans. It was what they had all signed up for and they waited patiently, believing that any day now the orders would come through to withdraw and ship out.

* * *

The men from Lark Force were eating their breakfast, listening to the radio when the news about the bombings at Pearl Harbour came through. President Franklin Roosevelt's voice blared through the speakers, the men silent as they listened.

Yesterday, December 7, 1941—a date which will live in infamy—the United States of America was suddenly and deliberately attacked by naval and air forces of the Empire of Japan.

The United States was at peace with that nation, and, at the solicitation of Japan, was still in conversation with its government and its emperor looking toward the maintenance of peace in the Pacific.

It will be recorded that the distance of Hawaii from Japan makes it obvious that the attack was deliberately planned many days or even weeks ago. During the intervening time the Japanese government has deliberately sought to deceive the United States by false statements and expressions of hope for continued peace.

The attack yesterday on the Hawaiian Islands has caused severe damage to American naval and military forces. I regret to tell you that very many American lives have been lost. In addition, American ships have been reported torpedoed on the high seas between San Francisco and Honolulu.

Yesterday the Japanese government also launched an attack against Malaya.

Last night Japanese forces attacked Hong Kong.

Last night Japanese forces attacked Guam.

Last night Japanese forces attacked the Philippine Islands.

Last night Japanese forces attacked Wake Island.

And this morning the Japanese attacked Midway Island.

Japan has, therefore, undertaken a surprise offensive extending throughout the Pacific area. The facts of yesterday and today speak for themselves. The people of the United States have already formed their opinions and well understand the implications to the very life and safety of our nation.

Hostilities exist. There is no blinking at the fact that our people, our territory, and our interests are in grave danger.

With confidence in our armed forces with the unbounding determination of our people we will gain the inevitable triumph, so help us God.

I ask that the Congress declare that since the unprovoked and dastardly attack by Japan on Sunday, December 7, 1941, a state of war has existed between the United States and the Japanese Empire.

*

The quiet morning conversations erupted into loud excited talk. Andrew sat on a long bench seat, as usual, eating all the leftovers he could gather. He was hungover this morning, a consequence of sneaking into town last night and sharing some beers and a bottle of wine with Jean, who had slipped away from the hospital to meet him.

They saw each other whenever they could and Andrew had fallen head over heels in love with the vivacious nurse, who like himself, was high-spirited and up for breaking a few rules.

He stood and stretched before striding towards the pot on the fire, the aroma of the remaining stew, filling the air. 'They must be mad, those bloody Japs,' he quipped. 'Why would they insult the Yanks like that? One of the strongest forces they could reckon with.'

One of the other men, Stanley, shook his head. 'I reckon the Yanks suspected they were up to something. But I don't think that's where they thought they'd hit. I bet the brass hats never counted on it being that close.' He watched Andrew as he helped himself to what was left of the food. 'I've never known anyone to put away food like you. The war just got a whole lot closer and you're still thinking about your stomach. You're a bottomless pit.'

Andrew laughed, using a spoon to scrape the last of the vegetables from the saucepan. 'There was bloody nine of us kids. The trick was to get in quick and fill up. There were never any leftovers.'

One of the other men threw a piece of damper to Andrew, who caught it without even looking up.

'They can't be too great, those bloody Yanks. They've been caught out,' Stanley said. 'According to the radio reports, the Japs zoomed straight in and blew them right out of the water.'

'It'll only be a show of force,' Peter said. 'I don't know how they hit anything. From all accounts, they're the worst pilots in the world and can't see properly to shoot with any accuracy.'

'By the sounds of what we've heard, it appears they were pretty accurate.' Andrew replied, his mouth full of a burnt piece of damper. 'Those other places they've attacked are not far north of us here.'

'Yeah, you could swim there for some action, Andrew. We know how much you love the ocean,' Stanley added.

Andrew shuddered. 'Not me, mate. I'll leave that up to you fellas. I'd say the Yanks have a plan in place to catch them out. They'll know where they're going next.'

'That's where we might get to see some action,' Peter replied.

* * *

In the camp up the road where Michael was, the talk was the same.

No one thought that the Japanese would be so bold as to bomb a base as large as Pearl Harbour.

'Sounds to me like we might need to seriously think about the fact an entire Japanese army is sitting right above us here and perhaps planning on moving down through the islands,' Michael said, peering out through the window of the mess tent, imagining hordes of enemy soldiers advancing towards them.

One of the older soldiers laughed and ruffled Michael's hair. 'I don't think you're going to see any Japs soon, young Michael. Our government will have ships ready to go and an army to scare those bloody Japs off before any of them can even think about island hopping down here.'

'I suppose that's why they've had us here, setting up in case,' Michael replied.

'For God's sake, what's been set up here in Rabaul and around the area by our forces is a token effort. It's a garrison with limited facilities and resources, in a town where life moves along as if there wasn't any war at all,' one of the other men said.

George stood up, his face pale and voice nervous. 'I can't believe they've bombed the Yanks. If they're stupid enough to do that, who knows where they'll go next. My father works down in Canberra. He's got an important job with the government. They'll be working out plans to knock those Japs over.'

'I wouldn't be too worried', a sergeant said. 'I doubt very much they'll come this way and if the Australian government thought for one moment they'd head towards New Guinea, they'd send a huge contingent to re-enforce this peninsula. Menzies knows we're only a small force. You watch, they'll either re-enforce the troops here, or if not, they'll move us out, back to the mainland where we can wait for the entire Australian army to join us.'

Michael sensed George was nervous about what had happened. He patted George's knee and tried to placate his fears. 'Yeah, they'll be watching. Thank goodness we've got a reliable government to back us.'

'What about your friends in town and your Joanie? What will they do?' George asked.

Michael stood up. 'I know they've just ordered that all leave is cancelled, but I've still got supplies to get so I'll go and visit them. I'm hoping Joanie and Reg are already making plans to leave. Even though this may all come to nothing, they need to play it safe.'

'I thought they were booked to go soon,' George replied.

'It's a matter of weeks until they're due to sail, but it'd be better to go straight away. Anyway,' he hopped up from the table, 'I'll take a quick supply run that way now and also find out what the news is down that end of town.'

* * *

Joanie waited impatiently for Michael to visit. He would have heard the radio broadcasts this morning and be worried about the sudden turn of events. She stood on the verandah with Reg. Even though it was early morning, the air was heavy with humidity and dark clouds rested on the mountains. A sickly-sweet aroma from a tree laden with yellow flowers wafted over the verandah and birds flitted back and forth, carrying twigs and leaves in their beaks.

Her father appeared to be contemplating the news and what would happen next, his thoughts broken by the squawking and splashing of a large parrot, taking a swim in the bird bath on the front lawn. 'I'll leave for the store shortly,' he said, his eyes following the movements of the colourful bird. 'I'm keen to talk to the workers and find out any extra information. I'd say your Michael will find his way here as quickly as possible.'

* * *

Michael's army truck arrived in a flurry of dust as he flew in through the gate, screeching to a halt in front of the house. He bounded up the stairs before shaking Reg's hand and kissing

Joanie's cheek. Reg ushered them to sit on the wicker chairs positioned to take in the view of the front garden. The yard boys were already busy; the day the same as any other day for them. The parrot dived under the water again, its head plunging in and out as it cooled itself from the heat of the day.

Michael spoke quickly, the seriousness of the attacks promoting an urgency in his daily life that hadn't been there before.

'You both need to get on the first boat out of here,' Michael said.

'That's exactly what I need to find out,' Reg replied. 'I'm keen to get to town and find out more. I'd say the Australian government will now be on high alert. Who would have ever thought, Pearl Harbour, the bastion of the Pacific, attacked!'

Michael was jittery and paced up and down the verandah, looking out to the road beyond the front yard as if he expected to see the Japanese coming up the other way.

Joanie tried to placate him. She had never thought that the war would directly affect their lives, and besides that, it was less than six weeks until she and her father left. Surely there was no need to go any earlier.

Reg's face was pale, his hands a little shaky as he explained how Rabaul was an important town. The Australian government knew that the garrison was small and he was sure the town would be evacuated if the Japanese were coming this way. They'd either move the units back until they could get a full force to arrive or evacuate the troops back home.

Michael frowned, shaking his head. His theory was that they would get all the civilians and Chinese out first and then take the troops back to Townsville.

'Is it that serious?' Joanie relaxed back in her chair, her eyes following the parrot as it shook itself, droplets of water shaken from its body. 'This island is a paradise and the native people have lived here for hundreds of years, if not longer. Look at the bird there taking a bath. It seems silly that anything would interrupt the way of life here.'

Michael looked at Joanie. Her eyes were a bright green in the early morning light, her blonde hair tousled and messy. He spoke gently. 'The Philippines are just across the water from here. I hate to say it, but the Japs are already close and there's nothing in between them and us at the moment. You both need to get on the earliest boat out of here.'

Joanie sat upright, a puzzled look on her face. 'What about the others who live here?' They can easily evacuate all of us, along with the nurses and the troops, but what about the others, the New Guinea people, and the Chinese? Why, there's more of them than us.'

'That's a good question.' Reg also looked perplexed. 'Surely they'd be safe. The Australian army could easily defend them.'

'What about Mi-Lee and her family?' Joanie asked.

Reg put his hand on her shoulder. 'I don't want you to become too anxious about something that may not happen.' He stood and flicked his hat on his trousers, removing the dust that had settled on it. Placing it on his head, he looked at Joanie. 'My main priority right now is as Michael said. I need to go down to the store and get both of us on the next ship out. I haven't been feeling well lately so it will be good to be back where Edna can take care of me.'

Joanie interrupted, a frown on her face. 'How unwell are you? Why haven't you said something before now?'

'It's nothing serious. I just want us to be away from here and back in the safety of Australia in case anything major happens with these blasted Japs.'

CHAPTER 4

here was a sense of urgency as Michael gave Reg a lift back into town. Their concerns and questions were similar. The availability of a ship to take Joanie and Reg back to Australia as fast as possible was the only solution.

Michael stopped the truck outside the Burns Philp Store and waited on the footpath as Reg gathered his briefcase from the back of the car before coming to stand beside him. They shook hands, Reg's hand clammy in Michael's strong grip. There was fear in Reg's eyes as they bid each other goodbye.

'I'm not sure when I'll see you and Joanie again,' Michael said. 'They've got us busy building gun emplacements and preparing in case there's an invasion. Whatever happens, if you could just get word to me when you're leaving. I won't be able to sleep until I know you're both safe.'

'You're a good man, Michael. Make sure you stay safe and come back to us.'

* * *

Over the next week, Joanie and Reg tried to run the store as usual, however everyone was on edge. Joanie's gut was continually churning, the tension building with each day. Every loud noise made her jump and she continually looked out the windows, waiting for who knew what. Perhaps there would be an order from the government for everyone to evacuate, ten ships appearing, tied up at the wharf to take everyone off the island or maybe an official notice that there was no need to worry, and they were safe where they were.

The store workers and others in town were also waiting to hear what the Australian government wanted them to do. Some fled to the plantations nearby, the sound of them moving furniture and nailing boards across the windows adding to the rising trepidation of what was to come. Peter and Andrew managed to get into town, paying a quick visit to the store. They implored Reg and Joanie to get on the first ship out, hoping they wouldn't be far behind them. Their regiment was too small to fight against the Japs and the word was that the civilians would go first and then all of them.

Once again, Joanie asked the question she had posed so many times that week, but no one had the answer. What was going to happen to the Chinese people, Mi-Lee and her family included? Both boys just shook their heads. They hadn't been told anything more than what Joanie herself knew.

They helped her stack some boxes, packing stock that could be put away in the back room. At least the store looked tidy, and it kept her occupied and distracted from what might be looming for the people in Rabaul.

Peter took an opportunity to speak to her alone. 'I'm not sure I'll get to talk to you again before you leave. Whatever happens though, I'll come back to Woombye and find you.'.

His words carried weight, his tone infused with emotion, and his unwavering gaze never strayed from her face. Her heart thudded loudly in her chest, yet her response was resolute:

Nothing had altered, and all she requested was for him and Andrew to stay safe and watch over each other.

* * *

Joanie made a trip to the hospital to catch up with Jean. They sat on a bench seat under a sprawling tree on the hospital grounds, the shade and seclusion allowing them time to talk.

'Everyone wants me to leave,' Joanie said, handing Jean the sandwiches she had brought.

'I haven't got long for lunch; we're flat out at the moment,' Jean said. 'Of course, you need to get out. I must stay to look after the sick and injured. It's what I signed up for. I'm a nurse, and we're safe all together under the banner of the Red Cross.'

They talked about the war for a while, but soon the conversation turned to romance. The two of them giggled and chatted like schoolgirls, the time flying past. 'Andrew's so handsome and he makes me laugh.' Jean said. 'I wish I could see him more but they're keeping them busy. We talk about everything, and,' she closed her eyes, 'when he kisses me, I feel like I can hardly breathe. I don't want him to let go of me.'

Joanie linked her arm through Jean's. 'I know the feeling. I'm so happy for you and Andrew. You're perfect together.'

Jean gave Joanie a kiss on the cheek, before waving a straw fan in front of her face. 'I swear I'm going to pass out sometimes from these uniforms and these blasted stockings. The uniform is not designed for the climate here.' She looked at Joanie. 'It's time for me to go. That matron has eyes like a hawk, and God forbid if there's even a crease in the wrong place or a hair untucked.'

'I will miss you, Jean, and I will miss Rabaul,' Joanie said as they stood up, their arms wrapping around each other as they hugged each other tight.

'We've both found love.' Jean laughed out loud, re-adjusting her nursing cap that had been knocked sideways from their energetic hugging. 'You and I, Joanie. Who would guess we would come to a remote, steamy place like Rabaul and both find the men of our dreams?'

'We're so lucky,' Joanie's voice was uneven as she tried once again to control her emotions that were so near the surface these days. It was worrying that the nurses weren't being prepared to leave. Jean was young and shouldn't have to deal with the proximity of a war on their doorstep.

The two girls hugged for a long time, Jean whispering in her ear as they parted. 'Andrew and I are sneaking out tonight. He's meeting me out the back of the quarters. Perhaps when you and I meet again, I will be Mrs O'Rourke and living in your little hometown, pushing a pram with Andy Junior in it.'

Joanie shook her head, 'I hope so,' she said. This was not a good time to discuss with Jean the problems that may arise because she wasn't a Catholic. Andrew's mother, Ethel, would have a good fight on her hands if she tried to part these two. It would be an interesting time; because nothing would keep Andrew and the beautiful young nurse he had fallen in love with, apart.

* * *

Joanie kept herself busy with work and organising the house. It had been nearly two weeks since the Pearl Harbour attack and if they were forced to leave earlier, she needed to have the place in order. She was sorting out her personal items when Reg came in through the door, his face red as if he had been running.

His shaky hands clutched at a handkerchief as he wiped the sweat from his brow, his words garbled and loud as he told her she would not like the news he was about to tell. Nothing he said made sense, and she tried to calm him down, telling him to speak more slowly and take deep breaths. Eventually, she got the gist of what he was saying, and he was right, she didn't like it one little bit. The instructions were that all European women and children were to immediately ready themselves to embark in two days for Australian shores. The *Neptuna* would set sail for Australian shores on the twenty-second of December.

Joanie tried to remain calm, but her stomach churned as she asked if he would be on the same ship. Before he spoke, she already knew the answer; the directions were only for the European women and children. There were no instructions or room for anyone else.

Michael slipped away from camp late at night, managing to find a truck to make his way down to Rabaul. The troops had been informed that evacuations would take place on two ships, a cargo of women and children bound for the safety of Australia. An eerie feeling of anticipation filled the air as the truck lumbered through the main street of town. The pubs were quiet, their doors closed shut, and only a few civilian patrons propped up against the bar enjoying a beer. Shutters on houses were closed tight, only here and there a glimpse of a dim light peeking through a gap. The usual gatherings on the wide verandahs were conspicuous by their absence. As he drove further down the street, he watched business owners scurrying back and forth, their arms full of boxes and household items that they stacked high in their vehicles. Some had decided it would be safer in the hills, taking refuge on the plantations, far away from the harbour and military installations.

The hospital was also closed, but inside, the lights were all on as the staff scurried around, looking after their patients but also readying themselves for what might come. Cars overtook him on the road, their lights bright, the drivers speeding past as they transported people and items away from the town. Once the women and children were evacuated, the men would have less to worry about and could concentrate on the safest place to hide their wares or themselves if no help came.

Joanie threw herself into Michael's arms when he arrived at the house. He held her tightly, her heart thumping hard against his own. When she finally pulled away from him, her eyes were red and puffy, her cheeks flushed with distress. Reg shuffled out to say hello and then returned to his bedroom, leaving them alone. This could be the last time they saw each other for a very long time.

They sat on the lounge together, Joanie's arms crossed, her tone resolute. 'I refuse to go without Father.' She turned towards Michael, who was taken aback at her stubborn, angry, words. 'I have said again and again, I will not go without him. They cannot make me leave. Nothing you say will make me change my mind. This is my final decision.'

'Joanie, listen to me. This war is suddenly a lot more serious than two weeks ago. The information coming through is that we may be invaded. They aren't sure when or how and it may not be immediately, but the enemy is aggressive, and these islands are directly in their path.'

'But why are they only evacuating the European women and children? Even Jean isn't going to leave and there is no provision for Mi-Lee and her family. If anyone should be getting evacuated, it should be the Chinese families. They will be the ones in the most danger.'

'It will be only a matter of time before they move all of us out,' Michael said, stroking her arms, wanting so badly for her to understand his reasoning. 'They'll take everyone out in order. You'll find the other nurses and Chinese women will come in ships after you, then the other civilians like your father and finally us. They'll have to get all of us out of here if they believe the Japs are coming.'

Joanie's eyes narrowed. 'Is that what will happen? Do you think they'll get everyone off this island?'

'Of course they will, unless they send an almighty force to re-enforce the troops already here. It's just they want all of you evacuated first.'

'I'm sorry, Michael. I'm going to wait until Father can come. I'm not going without him. We came together, and we'll leave together.'

'Look, Joanie.' He held her arms, his voice stern. 'I'm not sure why they aren't taking everyone, but all I know is you're getting on that ship back to Australia. I don't want to hear any more arguments. I'm telling you that you will get on and go with the other women.'

Joanie leant over and took Michael's hands in hers. 'I can't leave Father. I won't go!'

'You have no choice. Promise me.' He stroked her face and softened his words. 'You must leave on that ship with the others. Promise me.'

She looked into his eyes, her chest heaving.

'Promise me,' he whispered. 'It has become too dangerous to stay. Please.'

She bit her lip, her words barely audible. 'I can't leave Father.'

The next night Peter and Andrew came to visit. Joanie was short with Peter when he also started to give her orders about going, informing him that she wasn't a child and didn't need him telling her what to do. Guilt set in not long after and she tried to make amends for her harsh words before they left.

'I'll think about it some more, but at this stage, I'll wait until Father can go also.'

Joanie's father shook his head. 'Peter has said he will make sure I'm looked after once you leave. You are just being stubborn.'

Her other concern was for Mi-Lee and her family. Surely someone was in charge of looking after all the others who might be in danger if the Japanese invaded.

Even Andrew was sombre. 'It's all happened so quickly. One minute, we were playing tennis and sipping beers, and the next second, it's all become serious. I don't like the thought of being stuck on an island. There's only one way off and that's across the ocean.'

Joanie hugged the two boys as they said goodbye, even letting Peter hold her a bit longer than what was appropriate. He took the opportunity to whisper in her ear that when he was able to return to Australia, they could be together. Joanie smiled and hugged him tightly.

She could sense their apprehension of not knowing where they would end up now that the war was drawing closer. Andrew squeezed her tightly. His final words demanding that she listen to her father for once and get on the ship, resounded in her mind for a long time after they left.

Joanie and her father stood on the verandah, a palpable sorrow lingering in the air, long after the boys left. Silhouetted palm trees stood like sentinels in front of her, the light of the moon illuminating the ominous clouds scuttling across the ranges. High in the sky, stars shone brightly, and bats squealed in the fig tree opposite their house. An owl hooted in the tree next to the stairs, its haunting call sending a shiver down Joanie's spine. Her father placed his arm around her shoulder as they both turned to walk back inside.

CHAPTER 5

Rabaul Harbour - December 22, 1941

Michael visited again, arriving in an army truck he admitted he had taken without permission. He would deal with the consequences when he returned to the barracks. Joanie was unwavering as she stood on the verandah arguing with him. The rumbling of an approaching thunderstorm provided an angry background to the heated discussion taking place. Michael spoke tersely, his voice raised and opinion unbending as he sternly lectured her about her decision not to leave. He refused to sit and talk sensibly and instead paced up and down in his muddy boots, stopping every so often to turn and glare at her. His hair was uncombed, his shirt untucked, his appearance so dishevelled that he looked like he hadn't slept in days. His words flowed fast and furious over the top of hers, and when he'd finished his tirade of instructions, he turned his back on her and told her he did not want to hear another word from her about staying.

She argued back, but his retaliatory words became harsher, his voice deep and angry. He reiterated that she was selfish and only thinking of herself and not her father, who was also desperate for her to leave. How were the men who cared about her going to focus on the job they needed to do and stay safe themselves if they were worried about her? She was acting like a baby, a spoilt girl who had always done what she wanted.

Not since she was a child had anyone spoken to her so harshly, and she lay awake all night after he left, angry, upset and confused. Her father hadn't even come out to see what was happening or to tell Michael to calm down. Her stomach churned when she recalled his words, and the sight of his truck roaring out of the gateway and up the road without so much as a goodbye replayed in her mind. She tossed and turned, sleep evading her even as the first light of the day filtered in through her window.

A heavy sadness pressed down on her as she lay on her bed. Outside, she could hear birds calling out to each other, and she closed her eyes, Michael's angry words resounding in her mind. He was right. She was putting others in danger, and it would make it harder for her father to leave on another ship if she also had to go with him. At least if she left, they would only need to find one more berth for him to fill when the next ship became available.

* * *

That morning, dark, menacing clouds filled the skies above Rabaul, threatening to open up at any minute and drench the groups of women and children gathered on the wharf. Faces were solemn, and the usual chatter and laughter were absent as they waited to board the two ships that would take them back to the safety of Australia. Joanie and Reg walked slowly towards the ships, linking arms, turning frequently to see if Michael had come to the wharf.

They stopped as Birri appeared beside them, his hand clutching an envelope that he passed to Joanie. She thanked him and watched as he turned and made his way back through the crowds, stopping at the edge of the wharf to wave to them.

Her trembling hand grasped the letter, and she closed her eyes, remembering how angry Michael had been. As her father's arm wrapped around her shoulders, she leant into him, grateful that his health seemed improved this morning and he was much happier now that she had agreed to leave.

Reg passed his handkerchief to her and she wiped her face as his arms closed around her. They stood still together as she looked up at him, her voice shaky. 'I was so angry with Michael. I told him he had no say in my life and not to think he ever would. It was a terrible argument.'

Reg moved her forward, keeping up with the line of others who waited to board the ship. 'Now, now, all he wanted was for you to get on this ship and back to safety. I'm sure when you see each other you'll make up.'

Joanie took deep breaths as she looked towards the *Neptuna*. 'I wish you were coming with me, Father,' she whispered. She wanted to turn back, to follow Birri through the throngs of people gathered on the wharf and back to Michael.

'Women and children only,' Reg said, holding her arm and steering her up the gangplank and towards her cabin.

They sat on the small bunk, Reg looking tired and much older than his years. 'If, of course, I'm delayed,' his voice wavered, and he coughed to clear his throat. 'Make sure to look after your mother. I feel responsible for bringing you here and she was good about us coming.'

Joanie tried to cheer him up, wiping her face and taking a deep breath. 'Don't worry about us. I will look after Mother until you come home. I've loved being here with you. What daughter,' she smiled as she kissed his cheek, 'gets to come to such a place with her father?'

She rested her head on his shoulder as they talked for a bit longer, Joanie jumping when a bell sounded, a warning signal for those not sailing to make their way onto the deck.

* * *

Joanie found a space where they could stand together, amidst the crowds of families. Many of the children were confused and crying as they said goodbye to their fathers. Those on board were distracted for a moment as another boat sailed into the harbour. Pulling in against the pier, its decks were packed with women and children who had been brought in from the island of Bougainville.

Wharf workers ran up and down near where the schooner was tying up, yelling out to each other as they tried to work out where to place the bedraggled group now making their way down the gangplank onto the shore.

The women and children clung onto each other, the older children helping to carry suitcases, the smaller ones hanging tight to their mother's skirt. After much discussion, the men on shore directed the group onto *The Macdhui*, which was anchored further up the wharf. The group then moved with a sense of urgency as they were loaded on board. Both ships needed to start moving and take their human cargo as far away from Rabaul as possible.

The noise from the shore was muffled as a loud clap of thunder rumbled across the sky, and large drops of rain splatted on the polished rails in front of Joanie and her father.

Dim light filtered across the valley. The humidity of an approaching storm pressed down as a dense fog crept across the bay, hiding the view of the town and mountains. A clammy damp hung above the families saying their last goodbyes, and a man with a loudspeaker announced that the men were to leave the ship and make their way back to shore.

They hugged one last time, Reg's sad eyes lingering on her face.

'I love you, Father,' Joanie said, 'Come home soon.'

'I love you more than life itself, my dear child. I will be back with you and your mother as soon as possible. Tell her, I love her.'

* * *

Joanie stood on the deck, listening to the clanging of gangplanks being drawn up and the shouts of the wharf workers as they called out directions, signalling that the ship was about to be underway. She pulled out the envelope tucked into her shirt, opening the pages and scanning them as she waited.

Michael's neat handwriting filled the page, and she scanned the words, anxious to know his thoughts.

My Dearest Joanie, 'I am writing this, believing that you will have listened to me and will be on the ship back to Australia. I do not think I will be able to see you off, as we are moving large loads of equipment and every hand is needed. You have made the right decision and I am not sorry that I spoke to you harshly. My main priority is that you leave while you can and hopefully your father will be not far behind you. I would love to hold you close and say one more goodbye, but I fear it will not be possible. My heart is heavy, but you will be safe. I do not know when I will see you again, but I will hold you next to my heart and when everything is sorted, I will be back to you. I love you and whatever happens in the months ahead, hold our love close. My deepest love and thoughts for you, eternally yours, Michael

* * *

Joanie folded the pages back into the envelope and held it tightly to her chest. Her eyes rested on her father, who stood with the other men on the pier, one arm raised, as he waved goodbye. He looked small from where she stood, his shoulders slumped, his hand over his heart, almost as if he found the pain unbearable. She stood still, her body tense as the clammy air pressed down on the crowds on the decks. The familiar putrid smell of the volcano wafted across them and the realisation that she was leaving every-thing dear to her, caused her heart to thump hard, the sound of women sobbing near her heightening her fears. She raised her hand and waved back to her father, her arm held high until his face was no longer discernible.

The *Neptuna's* horn sounded across the waters and Joanie took one last glimpse of the crowd on the wharf and the town of Rabaul. I am leaving behind the two men I love the most in my life and my dearest friends, she thought.

'Keep safe,' she whispered into the darkening skies.

* * *

Michael also watched the ship sail away from Rabaul. He had climbed to a high point above the camp to gain a view across the bay. The *Neptuna* became visible as it broke through the fog and rounded the point, its bow pushing against the dark waters, the decks lined with passengers. He squinted into the fading light, scanning the people on the decks, trying to pick out Joanie. Thunder crackled above, and streaks of lightning flashed across the sky, the forks of light disappearing into the fog. A blanket of white washed over the bay, and the *Neptuna* slowly disappeared. The sky darkened, and he tried to find the star from which he often took solace. But the clouds were too thick. He closed his eyes as large drops of rain fell on his upturned face, the jungle still and silent behind him.

He closed his eyes and took a deep breath. 'Travel safe, my love,' he whispered. 'Until we meet.'

CHAPTER 6

*R*abaul, once a bustling town, now stood eerily silent after the women and children departed. The absence of social events left a void, filled only by the constant activity of the forces, reinforcing defences and gathering supplies. The civilian men, their faces etched with worry, roamed aimlessly, unsure of their roles, waiting for the next communication or direction to break the silence.

With Joanie gone, Reg spent all his spare time trying to find any information he could about other ships available to take him home. Boxes lined the hallway, items they intended taking home wrapped in cloth and stacked neatly inside them. There had only been room for a few precious items in Joanie's travel bag and he had promised her that he would pack the rest and ensure that it came back with him.

He taped up a large wooden crate, looking closely at the address written clearly on the top. Reg Black, Davey Street, Woombye, Queensland, Australia. Pangs of homesickness washed over him, and he envisaged Edna sitting on the verandah, watching and waiting for him to walk up the road, to come through the front gate and bound up the stairs. Surely, there would be plans made for him and the others to evacuate shortly, considering the sense of panic that was pervading the town. An urgency to get out of Rabaul and set sail for that address on the crate overwhelmed him.

Slumping back into a chair, he surveyed the room. It had seemed like an ideal adventure to take on the house and store for Bill and Leila. Despite writing to them again last week, there had been no return mail. He was unsure if they knew what was happening in the town. Some of their more precious belongings had been packed away, the furniture covered in old rugs and cloth that would hopefully protect it against dirt and moisture. The walls were bare; the expensive artwork was also put away for safekeeping. There wasn't much more he could do now except wait. He leant back, the spinning in his head making him nauseous and sapping any energy he had.

The symptoms were a sign of malaria. He had concealed his illness from Joanie and the others, but the sweating and chills had started over a week ago and today, his head throbbed, and it was an effort to stand. Hopefully, if he could get to the hospital, Jean would help him out with some medicine. That's if she was still there. Perhaps arrangements were also being made to evacuate the nurses.

Some letters were still arriving from Australia, and he had written back and consoled Edna that everything was fine in Rabaul. His letters would take much longer to arrive now and would be heavily censored. Edna wrote that Australians back home were also anxious, feeling like the war was almost on their doorstep. People in regional and rural towns like Woombye, were taking in women and children from the city. They offered spare rooms and small dwellings. Anywhere that a family could live for a short while. Many were starting to get worried that the Japanese were planning to invade Australia and felt that it would be safer in small country towns, away from the bigger cities that faced the threats of bombings.

Edna pleaded with Reg to make arrangements to sail back on any of the ships that went between New Guinea and Australia. *'Perhaps try and get a ship back to Port Moresby and make your way south from there. I cannot bear to be parted from you for even one more day. My heart aches when I think of you there by yourself and I will not sleep until you are back by my side. When you return, alas, you will be tormented, as I will not let you leave me, not even for one moment. I love you more than I ever thought possible and hope that when you write next time you will tell me the date you are arriving back to me. Perhaps you will even surprise me and end up on our doorstep unannounced. Even as I write this, I smile. Perhaps you are standing on the decks of a ship, watching the waters widen between you and Rabaul. I hope it is as I dream and when I finish writing this, you will be walking up the path, lingering under the jacaranda tree before arriving at the front door. I hold tight to that dream and know that if I have faith and trust in the heavens to look after us, then it will be indeed the case. Don't knock, my darling, surprise me. Your ever loving, devoted and waiting patiently wife, Edna.'*

CHAPTER 7

January – 1942

As the new year of 1942 rolled in, those living in Rabaul became increasingly apprehensive.

Jean came to visit Reg, aware from his visits to the hospital that his health was suffering and worried because she hadn't seen him for a while. She tried to persuade him to think seriously about other options, rather than waiting for another ship. Quite a few of the civilians who worked in town had already left, heading for the inland plantations or up into the mountains. A basket with food and medicine she brought with her was gratefully accepted, but he declined her offer to travel up to her sister Isabel's place and stay with them.

It was tempting, and he thanked her for her suggestion, aware that others had gone inland. His aim however, was to go directly back to Australia. Considering the condition of his health, a ship home would be the best option. He wasn't alone; there were others in similar situations and some of the men from the post office and the bank, regularly checked on him, their frustration also evident at the lack of response from the Australian government to get them the hell out of there. The window of opportunity was narrowing and they had started to discuss other options in case things became too heated. The word was that if there was any trouble, they'd be safe up in an area behind the town called Refuge Gully.

Jean was perplexed that Reg hadn't left on the *Malaita,* a ship that had been tied up at the wharf during the week. He explained how he had tried everything possible to convince the authorities. The vessel could be a ticket back to safety in Australia, for the civilians, including himself, and the nurses. But his demands fell on deaf ears and the ship was never even unloaded. It sailed in and out, fully laden with its cargo and produce; the only people on board were a small number of Japanese men who were to return to Australia, classed as prisoners of war. Their wives and children had been left to fend for themselves, many of them moving in together, sharing what they had, including food and money.

Jean questioned if he had heard from Mi-Lee recently. The thought of what would happen to the Chinese if the Japanese landed was present in both their thoughts. Reg also knew that Joanie would ask about their situation the next time she wrote to him. The Chinese must be sick with worry, knowing the consequences of an invasion.

Reg paced up and down the verandah, constantly wiping his brow with a handkerchief. His voice was husky and shaky when he spoke. 'For goodness sake, it's 1942 and there are inventions called planes that could land here today and take all of these people, you and me included, away from here.'

'Do you think the Japanese will land here?' There was a hint of worry in Jean's voice. 'I'm starting to feel a bit nervous.'

'I'm sorry, Jean. I'm not myself and I shouldn't worry you with all this talk. The worst that will happen will be that the Japs might drop a few more bombs over Rabaul, just to show they're a force in the area.'

Jean—so young and full of energy—reminded Reg of Joanie. She patted his arm. 'That sounds the same as what we've heard. At least we have Lark Force and the other men here to protect us.'

'We do,' Reg sighed. 'And I hope our government is doing their utmost to get us all out of here and back to Australia.'

* * *

Only four days into the new year, Michael sat with others at the camp. They cleaned their equipment, packed essentials, and talked about the increasing threat of the enemy. He looked to the north, peering above the coconut trees, as a low humming sounded in the distance. The other men also stopped what they were doing as the noise grew louder, the distinct drone of aircraft engines sounding not too far away. They stood together, watching as a perfect V formation of Japanese twin-engine bombers flew high overhead. No one moved or spoke, their minds and bodies frozen by the surreal sight of the bombers winging across the sky. The rumbling of their engines continued, and they flew onwards, closer to the hills. Suddenly the noise of their engines was no longer audible, silenced by the clattering noise of the Australian gunners, who fired round after round of shells to try and stop them. Michael and the other men shielded their eyes against the sun, watching the planes continue with no variation in their direction. The defence put up by the Australians was in vain, their shells unable to reach the height of the bombers' path. The planes continued untouched, and Michael watched until they were no longer visible.

The men stood talking, looking to the skies, waiting for more enemy planes to arrive. But that didn't eventuate. The enemy's mission was completed and loud rumblings along with a cloud of smoke rising in the air from the direction of the airfield, let them know that the Japanese pilots had easily found their target.

Over the next couple of weeks, the number of Japanese planes flying over the area increased and their well-aimed strikes on targets further from the town, set plumes of smoke and dust erupting into the air. Everyone's nerves frayed further as the air raid sirens became a common interruption, along with the sight of huge Japanese flying boats rumbling across the sky. Reconnaissance planes buzzed higher up, well away from the reach of the Australian anti-aircraft guns, making it appear as a simple exercise for the Japanese. Soon Rabaul was a town under siege and everyone was on edge, preparing as best as they knew how and waiting for the orders to come through that would decide their fate.

It was a relief for Michael when he was sent into town to see what supplies he could still muster up. Most stores were already shut, their windows boarded up, and their owners gone to wherever they deemed a safe place to hide. A few other soldiers were also scouting around for necessities, and he was delighted to find Andrew among them. The two shook hands and sat for a moment, a low rock wall under one of the huge trees that lined the footpath, providing a shady spot and time to catch up on each other's news.

Andrew expertly rolled a cigarette, curling the tobacco around in the paper. 'We're getting low on tobacco. If they run out of that, there'll be mutiny.' Michael took the cigarette offered, twisting the end of it and pushing the strings of tobacco down further into the paper with a match, before placing it in his mouth. He cupped his hand around it as Andrew lit it, drawing back and enjoying the heat of the smoke on his throat.

Andrew put the tin of matches back in his pocket and drew back on his cigarette, holding it tightly between his thumb and forefinger. 'Gotta enjoy every bit of this. I don't think the Japs will be handing them out to us for free.'

'Who knows what will happen if they arrive. I'm with you though, I don't think they'll be too friendly. Thank God most of the women have gone. I wish they had taken the nurses off as well though. Joanie will be worried sick about Jean and Mi-Lee.'

'Agh, those bastards down south are only thinking of their

own skins. We're nothing to them up here. Expendable. These air raids are getting closer each time, putting everyone's nerves on edge. Last night they destroyed the fuel dump and the shed where the flares are stored. Seems they know exactly what they're aiming for. Jean told me they also hit the native hospital at Rapindik. Fifteen or more dead and horrible injuries for more than a score.'

Michael and Andrew looked skyward as the sound of aircraft buzzed overhead, their faces tense as they watched a pair of planes flying above. 'Just two of our Wirraways patrolling,' Michael said, another long draw from his cigarette helping to settle his nerves. 'I seem to spend my days looking at the sky, waiting to see what will come over the horizon next. I'm not sure how our defences are going to stand up.' He flicked the ash off his cigarette. 'I hadn't heard about the hospital.'

'I've managed to stay in contact with Jean,' Andrew said as he turned back to Michael, a cheeky grin on his face. 'We're in love.'

Michael smiled. 'I know Joanie was happy that you two found each other. Jean's a lovely girl.'

'She's the girl I want to be with for the rest of my life. We just need this war to be over and then we can get on with our lives. We plan to return to Queensland and live in the north near Cairns. Jean wants to work in the hospital there and I'll find a job.' He winked at Michael. 'I can't believe it, but we're already talking about how many kids we want to have and even what we'll call them.'

'Everything happens here in Rabaul,' Michael said, watching the Wirraways as they circled the bay. 'Who would have known that we'd come all the way to this place to meet the women we're going to spend the rest of our lives with.'

'Your Joanie will be waiting for you. I've known her since we were kids, and it's almost as if she's been waiting for you.' Andrew playfully punched Michael's arm. 'It was meant to be. Don't worry about Peter, he'll get over it. If they were meant to be together it would have happened ages ago. Joanie has always thought of us as her brothers.'

'She does think the world of you both. We've had long discussions about that. You're right, we are meant to be together. As long as this blasted war finishes, and we all get back home. First, we need to get out of this mess and I don't have a great feeling about that at the moment. We're bloody sitting ducks.'

They sat in silence, enjoying their cigarettes as they watched the soldiers trying to deal with one of the Chinese traders, the haggling getting louder, the trader throwing his hands in the air as he tried to hold his price. Most of the Chinese had cleared out, but a few of the older men refused to leave their stores, trying to sell some items before they gathered them up and took them up into the hills to hide.

'They've been hoarding stuff up in the mountains and in tunnels behind the town. The old man should just give it to them. Soon money won't mean a bloody thing here. I don't think the Japs will be interested in it.' Andrew drew back hard on his smoke, making sure he got the most out of the tiny stub he held between his fingers.

'I'm hoping to get out to see Reg,' Michael said, 'I just need to gather a few more items here in town, and then I'll take a run out to the house to see how he's going.'

'He's pretty crook,' Andrew said. 'Peter and I have seen him a couple of times, and I'm worried because Jean said he's been down to the hospital a few times. She managed to get out to see him recently but she's not sure when she'll get there again. She's worried he'll run out of his medicine.'

Michael and Andrew talked for a long while, their faces grim, the reality of the situation, heightened by the continual buzzing of the Wirraways as they circled. They watched as the Chinese trader threw his hands in the air, passing over his goods to the Australian soldiers. The soldiers, in turn, handed over money, shaking the old man's hand and patting him on the back. He bowed several times, and they reciprocated, thanking him loudly and wishing him well.

'God help the Chinese,' Andrew said. 'No wonder they've nearly all headed for the hills.'

The truck with the men in it pulled up alongside, the driver waiting as Michael and Andrew shook hands and wished each other well before chugging slowly up the street.

Andrew stood on the running board, looking back and waving until the truck rounded the corner and disappeared from sight.

* * *

It was strange for Michael to drive to Reg's knowing Joanie was no longer there. Thank God she had left, as the thought of her being drawn into a situation that seemed to be intensifying every day made him feel ill. He clenched the steering wheel tighter, the road empty of vehicles and people, the silence deafening as he pulled up in front of the house. The grass was already long, and the gardens neglected. The house meris and yard boys had been paid out weeks ago, with only a few male staff remaining. The others had not hesitated to leave, heading for the mountains and the villages that hopefully would provide them with some safety.

Chickens roamed around the yard and a pig scratched in a garden, its nose pushing the soil around, the leaves and plants thrown across the lawn as it destroyed the once pristine flowerbeds. The animals didn't take long to realise that most people had gone. The once busy yard was now devoid of workers, the vegetable garden gate carelessly flung open, and the fruit and produce were there for the taking. Michael shuddered, wondering what would become of these beautiful old homes and splendid gardens with their trees and shrubs meticulously shaped and trimmed. If the Japanese did invade, would they spare all this? And what about the native people?

He had caught up with Birri a few days ago. His friend was busy helping some of the traders hide their wares further up behind the town, biding his time before he also made the journey further inland. They squatted in the dirt together. Birri's words and conversation were solemn and sad, his concerns for his people filling his mind with worry. He was also worried about Michael and the other Australians, suggesting that Michael should leave now, before it was too late.

It was difficult for Michael to fully explain the nature of the army job, that they needed to stay together, like a team, like a tribe. Only with their forces joined as one would they have any hope against an enemy. Active service was his job and what he had trained for.

Birri questioned why more Australian men hadn't been sent. The wind told him that larger and stronger forces were coming from across the seas and the skies. The small group of men Michael was with, would not stand a chance. He used hand gestures and his broken English to explain his predictions, his eyes wide as he demonstrated the bombs he had seen fall from the planes earlier in the week. The airfield had been targeted and some of his people injured. He asked again for Michael to leave. He would guide him through the hills and over the ranges to distant villages where even a white man like Michael could hide for many months, maybe even a year if needed.

But Michael was firm in his reply. He was part of the military forces, and to leave would mean to desert his fellow Australians. Hopefully soon, more men, maybe even the Americans, would be sent for backup or they would be taken off in a ship or even on planes. After all, they weren't far from the mainland of New Guinea or Australia. Birri realised that Michael's mind would not be changed, and they shook hands. Apart from a few others from his village who would remain, he was leaving that afternoon. He did not know when they would meet again.

* * *

Michael thought about Birri and the other villagers who lived in and around Rabaul. How would they be treated by the Japanese and what did they make of a war that had nothing to do with them? He watched the pig that had been in the garden, push over the bird bath. Joanie had loved to watch the different birds that gathered on the tub to splash and dive under the water. Sissy had taught her the various names in her dialect, and the two of them had laughed at the funny pronunciations of each other's language. Now the bath lay on its side, the concrete broken, the birds nowhere to be seen.

He charged at the pig, arms flailing wildly, shouting for it to leave. With a single glance, the pig tossed its head and trotted to the far side of the yard.

Soon the animals would reclaim the grounds. There was no one here to stop them. Who knew what would happen to the house once Reg left. That's if Reg intended leaving, of course. To leave, you needed to have somewhere to go.

He bounded up the stairs, stopping at the open front door to ring the large bell that hung from the outside wall. Reg called out to come in. The house looked very different from the last time he had visited. Boxes were stacked against the walls, their tops unsealed, the contents pushed untidily into their spaces. Furniture that usually displayed ornaments or vases, stood bare, the timber dull, dirt gathering on its surface. Other furniture was covered in sheets, the walls bare, the mats that usually lined the floorboards rolled up and stacked away. Reg sat at the large dining room table, papers spread in front of him.

'Welcome, Michael. I'm trying to finalise the accounts from the store. I figured it might be safer here than in town.' He looked up, stony-faced, beads of sweat gathering on his forehead. 'Sit down, son. Here, I'll pour a glass of cold water. It looks like you could do with a cold drink.'

'You've packed a lot of things.'

Reg coughed, his voice hoarse. 'How do you prepare for a war?' He waved his hand around the room. 'This all seems pretty futile. But what do you do?'

Michael sat and sipped his drink, listening to Reg, who seemed to have aged years over the previous weeks. Reg's breath was short, causing him to stop every so often, making his words stilted and slow. He had tried to get on the *Malatai*, but orders were that it was only for copra and the Japanese men who were POWs. Now there didn't seem to be any other way out and as the air raids became more consistent, his nerves were frayed even further. His concerns, similar to others, was that the Japs seemed to know exactly what they were aiming for. 'They're just picking sites off one by one. They don't miss very often.'

Michael had also heard the same and a few of the boys from his regiment were doing groundwork, looking into suspicions that someone was lighting flares, guiding the Jap planes in. Quite a few Germans still lived on the plantations and missions, and the rumours flying around made it difficult to distinguish the truth from fiction.

Reg sighed and wiped his brow again. 'We can only be thankful that Joanie has left. God help the rest of us if the Australian government doesn't do something in a hurry.'

'They haven't evacuated the civilians or the Chinese yet.'

Reg spoke slowly. 'I'm not sure what they're doing. There's another Burns Philp ship due in on the fourteenth. I know that because it's on my books to be unloaded. More supplies for you fellas, if that's any consolation.'

'That could be a way back for you.'

'At the moment it's all I've got to aim for and I'm pinning my hopes on it., I'll hound every official and contact I know to get a passage back. If there's a ship and it's going where I need to go then I should be able to be a passenger. I never signed up for a war. It would be a different story if I was younger and in good health. I'd be lining up for my boots and rifle right now, to join up with you boys. But look at me, Michael, I'm not a well man. These wretched bouts of malaria are sapping my strength.'

'Good God, Reg, don't even think like that. Your place is at home with Edna and Joanie. If the war does come to our doorstop, you'll be needed back there. You'll have plenty to do to help the war effort from the safety of Australia.'

Reg looked Michael in the eye. 'What will become of Lark Force if the Japanese do indeed land? It's not such a large force and I know you said the equipment is outdated.'

Michael put his glass back on the table and stood. He took a deep breath. 'We'll be slaughtered. I'm sorry, that sounds callous, but it's the truth. We've had some training, but our equipment and defences are poorly inadequate. This entire exercise of positioning forces up here in the islands has never been taken seriously until now and the government hasn't taken us, or the impending situation seriously either. We were all waiting it out here, having a merry old time until we received orders to take on the Germans.'

'Now you might be up against the entire Japanese army.' Reg stood, clutching the railings, his knuckles white, matching the colour of his face. 'And if that happens,' he looked towards the ocean, 'God help us all.'

CHAPTER 8

22ⁿᵈ December 1941 – 6ᵗʰ January 1942

*J*oanie stood on the decks of the *Neptuna*, her skirt billowing in the warm gusts of wind that pushed across the decks. This home-bound voyage was completely different from when she had optimistically set out with her father in the opposite direction less than two years ago. Back then, every day had been exciting, and she and Jean had spent much of their time leaning over the rails, delighting in the dolphins that sped alongside the boats or spotting the exotic islands that appeared on the horizon. The men had passed the time reading, smoking, and playing cards, the children running along the decks playing hopscotch or throwing hoops onto sticks. Now the decks were empty, most of the women and children below in their cabins, either nursing their seasickness or lying on their beds, worrying about those left behind. The stifling heat of the cabin was too much to bear this afternoon, and lying on the bunk, berating herself for leaving her father behind, only making her mood worse.

She ran one of her father's handkerchiefs over her forehead as she looked to the west. Salty spray kicked up from the ship's side as it cut through the swell, wetting her face and arms as she leaned out further. The spray was cool, and the distinct outline of the Queensland coast emerging in the distance lifted her spirits a little.

Dark ranges rose above the horizon, puffy white clouds floating above them. She continued watching, even when the sun's golden rays faded and then finally disappeared. The sun and light dipped behind the land, throwing the view into a dim, blurred landscape, the shroud of inky blackness enveloping the surrounding ocean. The ship plunged and moved with each swell, and she stared into the dark, thankful that the coast was nearby.

Her chest tightened as her thoughts turned to her father and she took deep breaths, trying to remain calm, yet feeling like a limb had been torn from her body. Surely Father would soon follow in another ship. Perhaps he was getting ready to set sail or had left already. She breathed steadily, the ache in her chest easing a little as she forced herself to stay positive.

The moon rose slowly above the horizon, a translucent glow shimmering across the top of the undulating ocean. Was Michael also watching the same moon, hoping that his young daughter was somewhere doing the same?

'Gracie might forget me,' he had confided in Joanie.

'A daughter will always remember a loving father. It doesn't matter how much distance or time separates them. It is an eternal bond that can't be broken and I'm sure Gracie thinks about you all the time.'

She closed her eyes, letting the evening air wash over her. She shivered, even though the breeze had a sultry warmth on its wings. When she opened her eyes, tiny lights flickered in the distance, marking the life of small towns dotted along the coastline. In the houses would be families eating their dinner together, revelling in the safety of their homes. Perhaps they might spot the far-off lights of the ship as it hurried down the coastline of Queensland, its passengers torn between seeking the haven of Australia, yet distraught about leaving loved ones behind.

* * *

There was no one to welcome Joanie when she stepped down the gangplank onto the wharf in Brisbane. The absence of men amongst those who disembarked was obvious, re-united families huddling together; the customary excited greetings replaced with long hugs and muffled conversations. A couple of the women and their children walked over to say goodbye, checking that she had a way to get home.

She hugged them back, the forlorn looks on their faces mirroring how she felt as she reassured them that a train would take her home to Woombye.

A knot formed in her stomach as she looked at the children who hung onto their mother's hands. The departure from Rabaul had been rushed for all of them and the older ones were aware that their fathers and others left behind, could soon be in danger. Although many of the women had been born and lived in Australia when they were young, the islands had been their home for most of their lives. Now they stood on the Brisbane wharf, gazing at their surroundings like foreigners, newcomers on distant shores.

Joanie bent down to hug a small boy, his innocent blue eyes staring straight back into hers. For many years, she would remember his face, the uncertainty in his eyes and the desolation of his voice as he said goodbye. It was as if the world he knew was coming to an end.

* * *

As the train wound through green hills back to Woombye, the local railway stops were familiar and the open paddocks and peacefully grazing cows, a surreal sight after the last couple of weeks. The culmination of the journey back and the situation in Rabaul for those left behind was overwhelming and tears blurred Joanie's vision. Thankfully the carriage was empty, so there was no one to notice her crying. Names and faces bounced back and forth in her mind. Jean, Isabel, Mi-Lee and her family, Peter and Andrew, Sissy and the other local people. She tried to calm a rising fear of panic. Father and Michael. Where were they, and when would she see them all again?

CHAPTER 9

January 1942

*E*dna had hardly smiled since Joanie arrived home. Her mother looked like she had aged ten years in the time they had been gone, and the sight of her pallid face and downcast eyes reminded Joanie why she was needed in Woombye by her mother's side.

Often at night, she would find her staring out the window, looking at the sky as if seeking answers to her questions. On her lap was the bundle of letters Reg had religiously written every week since he had been in Rabaul.

Worryingly, since Joanie's return, only one letter had come through, dated from before she had left Rabaul. Reg had glossed over his deteriorating health condition and made out that he was doing fine; there were plenty of others stuck in similar situations and sorting out work matters was keeping him busy. Edna wasn't fooled though, and she quizzed Joanie about the ins and outs of life in Rabaul and the consequences of illnesses such as malaria. Joanie reassured her mother that he would be well looked after. Jean was nearby at the hospital and she would check and take care of him if he were to get sick.

Edna questioned why a nurse, a young girl the same age as Joanie, had been left up there. Whatever was the Australian government thinking?

* * *

At the same time as Joanie and her mother sat talking in the safety of their house in Woombye, a Burns Philp ship docked at the harbour of Rabaul. Reg was in town to speak to Harold Gear, a resident of Rabaul who had been pestering Canberra and doing everything in his power to get instructions for the remaining Australian citizens to leave on the ship lying in the harbour.

'I've bloody requested that the men left here in town be allowed to sail back on that ship, the *Herstein*. She's sitting in the harbour. I've tried everything I can, but the bloody high-arse officials sitting pretty and safe in their bloody offices down there in Canberra won't hear of it.'

'Are you saying we can't leave on it?' Reg's heart sank. He had a feeling that the ship he'd been watching unload and now load back up with copra, was going to be their last chance to leave Rabaul.

'I received official word this morning, just before you started loading down there. The orders are that the ship is to be fully loaded with copra. No civilians are allowed to travel back and no passengers will be on board. Only bloody coconut!'

Reg sighed and shook his head. 'It's unbelievable. It's been over a month since Pearl Harbour. They should have put as many of us on that ship that could fit and high-tailed it out of here while there's still a chance. Instead, they'll leave it there tied up and take their time loading it. We could have been halfway home and well out of the way of the Japs. The way they're dawdling along, that ship is a sitting duck. They need to get it moving, with us included, and not let it sit there for too long. Those Japs aren't stupid; they'll be onto it, and you'll see it will be an easy target.'

Harold's face turned red, and he thumped his fist on the desk that he sat behind. 'The word is they're leaving the troops here as 'hostages to fortune'. To evacuate them would mean that their forward observations line would be disrupted, and they want to concentrate on tasks that are of a higher priority.'

'It's bullshit.' Reg nearly spat the words out.

'Bloody bureaucracy!' Harold said. 'Not a brain between any of them.'

* * *

That week, the last of the house staff had been dismissed. Their usual wide grins were replaced with serious, concerned expressions, as they shook Reg's hand and took the packets containing their final pay. There was confusion in their eyes, their understanding of the situation less than his own. Trying to quell his rising fear, Reg waved the last of the workers off before filling his car with provisions for Mi-Lee and her family.

The streets of Rabaul were quiet and only a few local people scurried along the footpaths, frantically trying to sell or buy whatever they could before retreating to their villages higher up the slopes. Reg made his way into Chinatown. Most establishments were closed, their signs taken down, their verandahs empty. The windows of Mi-Lee's store were boarded up and Reg peered through the gaps. The shelves and tables were empty, and it was obvious from the silence that the family had moved somewhere else.

As Reg made his way back down the street, a few faces looked out at him from other buildings. He knocked on the door of one of the smaller trading houses. The Chinese sign that had once hung with pride from its doorway was now burning in the fire in the middle of the road, along with other items that the Chinese did not want the Japanese to find.

An old man with a wispy moustache and thin-framed glasses sitting on the end of his nose stared through the doorway.

'I am looking for Mi-Lee and her family,' Reg said.

'They left. They all gone further.' The man gestured with his hand, signalling beyond the town. 'They take all the children and other families go with them. They cannot stay here; no help will come for them or me.'

Reg pushed the supplies he had brought for Mi-Lee into the hands of the old man, who bowed and nodded. Three small children appeared behind him, taking the baskets before disappearing out the back.

'Good luck, old man, and may God be with you all,' Reg turned away, his shoulders slumped, his feet moving slowly as he looked back down the street. Only a month ago, the street had been a hub of activity. The people of Rabaul, old, young and of different nationalities, had gone about their business, waving and greeting each other as they passed.

Now, numerous small fires dotted the wide avenues, and only a few Chinese people rushed back and forth, moving belongings to different hideouts or adding something they didn't want to be found to the embers. Reg spoke out loud, looking at the steep mountains that rose behind the town. 'Thank God you're safe, Joanie, because I have a dreaded fear for anyone left here, including me.'

CHAPTER 10

Rabaul January 20 - 1942

*R*eg's sense of foreboding was heightened, and his body ached, not only from the malaria but also from the anxiety that filled every moment. The atmosphere in and around Rabaul was tense, with nothing to do but wait. Sleep came intermittently, the eerie silence of the night, a menacing threat of invisible danger not far from their shores. The house felt empty, his steps taken softly on the worn floorboards, as if he didn't want to make any noise for anyone who might be nearby to hear.

His fears were realised when Rabaul became a town under siege within days. The Japanese forces had arrived. Reg took refuge at home, the empty rooms and silent grounds, a constant reminder that he was on his own. He stood on the verandah, leaning against the railing on shaky legs. Tilting his head to the side, he listened carefully, shielding his eyes as he looked skyward. The faint drone of aircraft engines sounded in the distance and soon the humming grew louder. He gripped the handrails to steady himself as he looked straight up at a perfect formation of planes flying above, the distinctive red circle vivid on their wings.

Before long, the skies were dotted with Australian planes, flying out to intercept the formations of enemy planes that had been spotted to both the west and east of Rabaul. The Australian anti-aircraft battery was pushed into action for the first time.

In town, frenzied civilians hurried back and forth between their businesses and houses, boarding up windows, stashing food and money, and gathering belongings to hide in secret locations away from the town. A sense of panic pervaded those left behind and heated conversations were about abandonment, lack of care and even betrayal. On the wharf, men worked quickly to remove equipment to a safer area, re-locating vehicles and dashing around in army vehicles loaded up with supplies and anything deemed essential. Along with others in the town, Reg waited nervously, unsure what else he could do as he faced the reality that leaving on a ship was no longer an option.

Australian military men who had spent the previous months practising their skills were now thrown into real-life action, and they fought back valiantly, cheering loudly when they brought down the first Japanese plane, which spiralled into the side of the volcano. Their excitement was short-lived, and the reality of war sunk in as the enemy responded, their bombs dropping onto strategic sites around Rabaul. Men stationed higher up the slopes could do very little but dig in and watch as the Japanese planes looped and dived over the bay, teasing the Australians with their acrobatic displays.

***

Reg stood with Michael, gazing across the bay from a safe area near the house. The smouldering remnants of the *Herstein*, floated in the water. The ship Reg and the others had wanted to leave on, had been hit by three enemy aircraft, and not only had the copra burnt but also the oily cargo that had been in its hold. Its mooring ropes had been cut and what was left of it drifted in the greasy water.

Several men had been burnt and it was said that eleven others had died on the ship when it was hit. Reg shielded his eyes against the sun as he stood with Michael, looking out over the bay. Houses on Namanula Hill and on the outskirts of town had been hit, the smoke rising in black clouds in the sky, the buildings destroyed, the yards and road scattered with the remnants of their structures. The runway had also been an easy target. Planes that had been targeted, smouldered where they lay, the runway littered with bomb craters.

Michael was angry, his voice low. 'It's like the Japs are playing. Picking off targets, one by one.'

'If this is playing, I hate to know what's coming next.' Reg sat down on the grassy slope. His legs throbbed and his head spun.

'I can see you're ill. What are you going to do? We're all taking up positions outside of camp. Mind you, they're telling us it's only an exercise drill, but I'm not swallowing that.'

'Why would they say that if it wasn't true?' Reg looked puzzled.

'Because I'm pretty sure the bloody entire Japanese fleet is about to come into this bay and if they tell us the truth, I reckon some of the men might take off.'

'It doesn't appear to be an exercise down there.' He nodded towards where the burning ship was. My worry is, where are you going to go if it really heats up?'

Reg looked at Michael, envious of his youth and strength. At least the younger men stood a chance. He felt weak and ill and wanted only to put his head down on a pillow, to alleviate the spinning and aching in his body. 'Peter and Andrew have also been to check on me. You're all doing your best, but I'm afraid I will have to go with the others and take safety in Refuge Gully. There are some basic huts there and we'll be out of the way until the orders come through to evacuate. Perhaps those reinforcements will arrive tonight. The Yanks might even come and help us out.'

The two men stood and shook hands before embracing each other. Reg's voice was shaky. 'If something happens to me...'

Michael interrupted, 'Nothing is going to happen to you.'

'Just in case, Michael. I want to give you a letter to take back to them both.'

Michael took the letter from Reg. 'What makes you believe I'll get back and you won't?'

'You're young and if you need to, you'll survive in that bloody jungle.' They both looked towards the mountains.

'Goodbye, Reg. I will see you back in Woombye.' Michael grasped Reg's hand, shaking it firmly before they embraced again, neither wanting to let go.

'Goodbye, Michael. Look after my girls for me.'

* * *

Peter and Andrew were dumbfounded that Reg was still in Rabaul. Hopefully he would be safe in Refuge Gully with many other civilians who'd been unable to leave. Peter was angry, knowing that Reg would not go against the bureaucrats. He should have taken matters into his own hands weeks ago and let the bastards in Canberra rot. 'It makes me sick to think of them down there sprouting their bullshit and sitting in their fancy rooms, while men like Reg are left here with no way out.'

'I can't believe the nurses are still here also.' Andrew was worried about Jean if the Japanese invaded.

'Have you seen her?' Peter asked.

'They've moved them out further. I snuck in the other day, but she was flat out and I tell you, it looked like something ... I don't know, something I can't explain.'

'What do you mean?'

'They'd brought in the bodies of our airmen who had been shot down and also there were injured people everywhere from the bombings.'

'Jesus,' Peter rubbed his hands through his hair. 'Why the hell didn't they evacuate those nurses? We've got to try and get her out. Thank God Joanie left when she did.'

'Jean won't go now. They're all sticking together and hoping the red cross on their uniforms will save them if the Japs come to town.'

'I reckon we make a deal, you and me. You look out for Jean, and I'll look out for Reg.' Hopefully, that plan would work, Peter thought, not saying what he was thinking, and that was, who was looking out for them?

CHAPTER 11

Rabaul January 22 - 1942

In anticipation of what was about to descend upon the shores of Rabaul, the volcano, Tavurvur, decided it was a timely moment to gather its forces and burst forth from its crater. Flaming embers and sparks spat upwards, the flashes lighting up the moonless sky.

Michael and his group were ordered to take their place in the trenches they had dug behind barricades made from coconut trees. They squatted together, passing cigarettes to each other, talking and joking as they tried to ward off their nerves.

The sky sporadically lit up with sprinkling embers, and an occasional burst of flame spewed from the volcano, reminding Michael of fireworks he'd seen at the circus. It was unfortunate timing because even though the Japanese might be familiar with the area, the bright flares would also be visible and guide them to where they wanted to go.

George puffed his chest out and tried to sound confident. 'Don't forget my father works for one of the important government departments in Canberra. They'll have men ready, maybe even the Yanks, right behind the hills and gathering to come by sea. It won't be us that will get the surprise, it'll be those stupid Japs. They reckon they're blind anyway and can't see past their noses to hit their targets.'

'They did a pretty good job on the *Herstein*. They didn't miss that by much, or the other targets,' Michael said sarcastically. 'If your father and his department are doing such a good job down south, they wouldn't have left Reg and the nurses to fend for themselves. Not to mention the poor old Chinese.' He brushed off the volcanic ash that continued to rain down onto his uniform as he looked across the bay, waiting for the unknown, the danger heading towards them.

The volcano continued to spit out its wrath, the roar of its furnace filling the night air as Michael sat and waited, his skin crawling, his nerves stretched tight in anticipation of what was to come.

George whispered to Michael, his bravado suddenly disappearing. 'Mate, I'm bloody scared.'

'Stick with me. We'll look out for each other.' Michael patted his back. 'You'll be right.'

* * *

As the night progressed, the volcano behind them calmed a little, and the men lapsed into an anxious silence as the darkness cloaked the area around them. Michael's nostrils filled with the smell of ash and smoke, and he took a swig from his water container, his throat dry from both the polluted air and his uneasiness. He crouched low behind their barricade, his body tense, flinching at any noises nearby, every sense heightened as he waited.

He straightened to gain a better view, before looking down the line of men huddled near him. Holding his hand up to gain their attention, he put his finger in the air, signalling that he had heard something. The men looked towards him before moving into position. Michael tapped his ear and pointed to the beaches below.

A tense silence shrouded the men as they tried to catch any movement in the area below them. Michael listened hard; every muscle in his body clenched as the eerie silence surrounding them was broken by the scraping noise of metal passing over the coral reef. A boat had entered the bay. There was silence again. Eventually, a slight breeze that fanned across where the men hid, also brought forth the chatter of the Japanese, who had navigated a large barge straight into the harbour. Michael peered over the top of the barricade, the surreal scene of the Japanese landing party coming alive under the illumination of a flare that lit up the beach, exposing the sheer numbers of those who had disembarked.

The men in the trenches readied themselves, their machine guns and rifles poised and ready to go. Michael looked towards George, a reassuring nod of his head, in direct contrast to how he was feeling.

It appeared that the Japanese had not expected a hail of fire to rain down upon them as they landed in the dark. They tried to move forward, but the disarray that ensued and the firepower that continued to blast down upon them caused them to retreat. Michael and the line of men in the trenches also moved out and away from the security of the palm trunks, stealing back up and into the jungle behind them.

Over the next few hours, more Japanese forces landed, and the activity and noise from lower down the mountain left the men with no doubt that their initial victory was short-lived. The group crouched together, waiting for the sergeant to give further orders. There were many Japanese men on the beach from that first landing and Michael was apprehensive about how their own small force would fare against such a large enemy contingent. He sat silently with the other men and waited.

Before long, the sound of gunfire penetrating the bushes around them motivated the sergeant, who had earlier appeared confused. He seemed to gain confidence and ordered the men to move further along the ridge. Michael's heart thumped hard as they tramped quickly along the trail, the sounds of a fierce battle below rising through the jungle, gunfire and the anguished yells of men, reverberating off the sides of the valley around them.

* * *

It was a relief when daybreak came and they could see what was going on below. Michael was part of a group who followed a well-worn wide track down towards the town, stopping when they came to an area where they could view the bay. They took turns with the binoculars, peering through the bushes at the scene below.

It was hard to comprehend what he was seeing. On the beaches there were a multitude of different landing crafts, groups of Japanese soldiers on their decks and swarming in clusters on the beach. Other Japanese boats swiftly approached the other beaches to the north and south of the town.

Four huge destroyer ships lined up at the dock, their looming presence complete with menacing red flags flapping in the wind. The entire bay was full of Japanese ships, and when Michael shielded his eyes against the rising sun, he could see a convoy of support ships further out to sea. George looked over his shoulder. 'Any Yankee ones out there?'

'Not a one,' Michael affirmed, his voice shaky, his hands trembling as he passed the binoculars to the next man.

Rounds of gunfire sounded not far below and the men sprang into action. Michael's nerves stretched in fear as he dragged his eyes away from the horrendous sight of what seemed to be the entire Japanese flotilla in Rabaul Harbour.

* * *

Five of the men, including Michael, were given an order to make their way down to a larger unit positioned nearby. The sergeant in charge wanted to find out what the orders were now that the Japanese had landed. He appeared confused and unsure where those orders would come from, but his directions were for them to keep their heads down, make their way to the next unit, and then return with the orders.

Michael moved with the other men to where they thought the other unit would be, but it wasn't long before they were stopped in their tracks, a round of machine gunfire pelting down on them from higher up the mountain. Bullets smashed through the foliage next to them, ricocheting off tree trunks and shredding the nearby bushes and plants. Michael grabbed George's shirt, dragging him into the cover of the jungle before diving into a ditch filled with leaves and ferns.

The other three men jumped and ran through the jungle on the other side of the track, ducking and weaving as they went. Further gunfire reverberated through the trees and loud yells from the men sent waves of panic through Michael's body. He pulled George down lower, both crawling under branches and leaf litter that lay across the bottom of the ditch. Michael pressed his face into the mud, a cool dank scent, mixing with the smell of their sweat and the clamminess of fear. More gunshots sounded behind them, and then there was silence.

* * *

Hooked barbs of gnarly vines ripped at Michael's clothes and he flinched as thorns and jagged rocks dug into his skin. He clambered out of the ditch and heavy undergrowth, staying low as he waited for George to follow. Together they crawled through the dense layers of leaves, sliding on their stomachs through the mud as they moved tentatively down the slope.

George whispered, 'We should try and get back to the main group. What if those Japs come looking for us?'

'Don't move. Let those bastards move on or find other targets. From the sound of the gunfire there was probably more than ten of them. We aren't moving anywhere while it's light. Someone further up the hill is watching for movement in this area.'

They waited until darkness covered the mountainside, crawling slowly back up onto the track before entering the jungle on the other side. They didn't have to go far before they came across the three bodies of the other men. Michael squatted next to them, checking for pulses, but there were none. The shocked look on George's face mirrored how Michael felt, and neither spoke as they looked at the lifeless bodies of their mates.

'We need to bring them back to town for burial,' George finally said.

Michael tried to keep his voice calm, his skin tingling with fear. 'I'd say there's a shitload of Japs between us and the town, and besides, the town would have been the first place they occupied. I don't like it either, but we have to leave the men here for the moment. We'll cover them with leaves and when we get a chance, we'll come back and recover them. But for now, we have to get back to the unit and let them know what's happened and also find out where we're supposed to be.'

Like the night before, there was no moon, and Michael used his instincts to follow the track back to where their unit had been the previous day. Reaching the spot, they found no trace of any of them, nor an indication of where they had gone. George sat on the ground, defeated. He wrung his hands together, scanning the area for a sign of where the men might be. Michael assured him that if they could get back to the road near the *Three Ways*, they might be able to organise some support.

They moved off again, following the same track they had taken away from the area last time. Gunfire below and the sound of explosions made them stop intermittently, forcing them to crouch low. 'That sounds like cars being blown up,' Michael said. 'God knows what's happening to those left in the town.' He waited for just a short while before continuing.

A muddy track snaked through the jungle and he gestured to George to keep up and stay close behind him. The track would cross over near the Junction and perhaps if the Japs hadn't reached that far there might be other Australians making their way along the road. Every muscle in his body tightened as he continually surveyed the jungle, preparing for a Japanese soldier to spring out from the jungle next to him. Gunshots rang out further down the valley and he feared they had been sighted. He signalled George to get down low as they crept through the bush that brought them nearer to the road. Sliding down an embankment into a gully, they listened carefully, the welcome sound of Australian voices drifting up to them.

* * *

Michael called out to the group, letting them know they were Australian. The men stood silent, staring hard as Michael and George emerged from the jungle. The sergeant questioned them before detailing the events of the past hours. The Japs were coming from all directions and the Australian forces were scattered, with men down and the situation helpless. A few other men milled around, listening to the conversation, hungry for any news.

'We've lost three of our men further up the hill. Their bodies need to be retrieved,' George said.

The sergeant's voice was panicky. 'There are others lying in the bush also. At the moment there are no plans to safely extract the bodies. It's a bloody mess.'

'Where do we go from here, sir?' George asked.

The sergeant blinked hard.

'What is the next order, sir?' Michael asked, glancing from the officer to the men standing around him. Their dirty faces wore the same expression of shock, confusion, and exhaustion. They all waited for a command, a sign of leadership.

The sergeant spoke gruffly. 'The order has been given to withdraw.'

Michael's retort was sharp, his mind seething. 'Withdraw? To where?'

'Wherever is safe. Join with us or go back to your own unit.' Michael watched as the other men were directed into the waiting vehicles. The sergeant looked back at him as he loaded supplies into a taxi that appeared from further down the hill. 'It's your choice, there're no directives to defend, and to try and fight would mean certain death. The order is to withdraw.'

George looked at Michael. 'Do we go with them?'

Michael jumped into the back of a truck that only last month he had used to get supplies from the stores in town. Now it was packed with men, their faces anguished, eyes filled with confusion. He held out his hand to George, heaving him into the back of the truck as it started chugging up the road.

The truck had just started to pick up speed when the entire area was strafed with enemy fire. The roar of planes above them forced the truck to grind to a halt. Michael jumped out of the truck and along with the other men, took safety in the ditches on the side of the road. He lay low, his face pressed into the mud, George's body half on top of him.

When the sounds of the planes faded, Michael tried to wriggle out from under George, whose body was heavy and limp on top of him. He pushed him hard. 'Get the hell off me.' George eventually sat up, a dazed and stunned expression on his face. His eyes were wide and he didn't utter a word, not even when Michael pulled him up, brushed him off and pushed him towards the back of the truck, where he took his seat with other men, squashed up against one another as the truck lumbered once again over the bumpy road. Michael perched on the running board. At least there he was in the open and could look towards the sky, yelling out to the driver when enemy planes came their way.

Struggling to take in the turn of events, he tried to keep calm, but his gut continued to churn with fear. He kept an eye on George, who sat in a dazed silence, his bloodshot eyes focused on the rifle in his hands.

When they reached the road that led directly to Rabaul, the truck slowed. Michael ran ahead to make sure there were no enemy vehicles coming their way. He was relieved to see two Australian army vehicles coming up the road. When he looked more closely, he could see every space was filled with men, their faces covered in mud, perspiration, and disbelief, looking like they had also experienced a treacherous journey. Some had makeshift bandages wrapped around parts of their body, blood seeping through wounds. A familiar face, an officer, Errol, jumped down and greeted him, just as the truck with George and the other men, arrived.

The men gathered around Errol, keen to get some direction and hear what the latest order might be.

'Orders are, every man for himself. They're Scanlan's orders,' Errol said, his voice loud and clear so that everyone could hear.

The sergeant from Michael's truck was dumbstruck and he looked around at the men who had stopped talking and were hanging onto every word of their conversation.

'These are direct orders from Colonel Scanlan. I repeat, it is every man for himself,' Errol said.

George came up beside Michael, 'I'm going to surrender.

There're laws about how they can treat prisoners and I'd rather take my chances with the Japs than with the jungle.'

One of the older men came up beside them. Patrick had been in their camp and had often talked to them at the mess tent. 'I reckon George's right. I'm going to surrender, if you want to come with me,' Patrick said.

'He's not going with you. How do you know how they'll treat you?' Michael interrupted.

'Even the Japs have military laws about how they have to treat prisoners,' Patrick replied.

Gunfire sounded below and some of the men jumped back into the truck, ready for it to take them further up the road.

'C'mon, Michael, I'm keen to go with Patrick; come with us,' George pleaded.

'I'll never surrender and you're not going to either.' Michael pulled his mate away from the truck. 'I'm going to take my chances in the jungle and George is coming with me. What are you fellas going to do?'

One of the men answered. 'We're going to stay on the truck. Once we're up a bit higher, we're also going to make a run for it.'

'Any of you are welcome to join us,' Michael said. The men looked at him, their faces confused as they tried to weigh up the best odds of getting out of the situation alive.

One of the men finally asked, 'What do you reckon about surrendering?'

'There's no way I'm trusting those Japs.' Michael looked down the track towards the south. 'I reckon the best bet is to make our way down the coastline towards the bottom end of the island but keep to the jungles.'

'There are Jap boats everywhere. What do you reckon, you're going to stroll along the beach?' Another one of the men said to him.

'You wouldn't make your way along the beach. You'd use the

jungle behind. Stay high enough up so you can see what's going on.'

'You can't survive in that jungle. There are slopes and chasms that are impenetrable,' Patrick added, 'plus the mossies and the blasted rain.'

'I'd rather take my chances with the jungle than bloody Japs.'

'And how far will you need to travel? They're obviously not sending anyone to bail us out. They would have been here by now.' Patrick shook his head, his eyes bloodshot and red.

Another soldier chimed in, 'We're on a fucking island, there's no way out, unless you're a fucking good swimmer.'

'If we can get as far south as possible, we might be able to get a boat or swim across to the smaller islands. I'm asking if anyone wants to join us.'

The men discussed their options. A few were tempted, but worried they were jumping the gun. Perhaps it would be better to see what the next twenty-four hours brought. Maybe the Yanks would show up and blast the Japs out of the water.

George looked from one to the other, shaking his head. 'The thought of spending even one night in that blasted jungle sends a shiver down my spine.' He turned towards Patrick, who was still waiting for his decision. 'But Michael has been with me since training days and when it comes to finding his way around, he's a good man to follow.' The men looked skywards as planes flying low over the far end of the bay fired their guns, the thumping and staccato sounds making them all jump and crouch down beside the truck.

'I'm not staying another minute,' Michael said, pulling George up with him. They shook hands with the other men, and someone passed them a backpack from inside of the truck. Patrick shook their hands. 'God be with you both, and I hope we meet again. He shook his head in disbelief at the situation. 'It really is every man for himself. I bid you both adieu.'

CHAPTER 12

ichael and George picked up their packs and rifles, making their way further up the road. They followed a trail that would lead them away from the others and into the cover of the jungle. Michael had already decided on the direction they would take. It would be a difficult journey, but he had a gut feeling it was the best course to follow. If they could get down as far as they could go, maybe to Arawe, they would be able to swim short distances to the scattered islands or perhaps get access to a boat and sail across to the mainland of New Guinea.

The local people sometimes travelled that way and he had walked a short section of the route with Birri once when he was on leave. To remain out of sight, they would need to stay high in the mountains and away from the beaches. They would also have to move quickly because the enemy would be searching for survivors and hot on the tracks of anyone they could find.

Behind them, noises of further air attacks sounded along the shore and rifle fire punched over the slopes of the mountain to the north. Michael's chest heaved as he thought about the fate of Reg and the other men who hadn't made it out.

He made his way up the slope, George plodding behind him, their boots squelching in the muddy tracks that crisscrossed each other. He looked back and forth before choosing where to go, eventually spotting what he was looking for; a small clearing tucked between the coconut palms with a few huts huddled together at the end of the cleared section. The area was silent, apart from a bush turkey that scurried into the jungle as soon as it spotted them. The main vegetable patch had been dug over, the soil devoid of greenery, the produce dug up and taken. The verandahs of the grass huts were lifeless, and an ominous silence pressed down as they sat on the steps of one of the larger huts.

Michael planned to camp there for the night, however, he was going to leave George for a while and make his way back to the town.

George sounded panicky when he told him of his plan, but Michael was determined to find out what had happened to Reg. Joanie's father was old and unwell, and surviving the jungle trek would have been almost impossible for him. If he could just get him out, perhaps they could work out a plan.

* * *

Michael headed in the direction of the town. Once he cleared the thicker jungle and emerged onto the wider tracks, he heard voices; Australian men, their voices travelling to him through the scrub. He called out before he approached; a group of six forlorn men were crouching down, resting. Andrew was amongst them, and Michael shook his hand before pulling him into a boisterous hug. Andrew's eyes reflected the shock of the last few days as they discussed what had happened. He confided in Michael that he didn't feel like he was doing the right thing by finding their own way out, or following the order, of every man for himself.

Michael reassured him. 'We were given the same order.'

Andrew spoke quickly, his voice agitated. 'It's been utter chaos, with no plan of withdrawal or what to do if we couldn't hold them back.'

One of the other men added, 'Hold them back. That was the entire Japanese army.' He spat on the ground. 'What a fuck-up!'

Andrew shook his head, the men agreeing on the state of affairs. 'Bloody madness,' he said. 'I got separated from Peter during the retreat. We'd said we'd stay together, no matter what, but in the dark, we ended up going in different directions. I'm not sure where you're headed, because the way you're going is straight back into the firing line.'

'I don't suppose you know what happened to Reg,' Michael asked. 'I'm holed up further on the ridge with George, but I want one chance to get down and try and find him.'

Andrew looked down at the ground. 'They got them. The Japs got those hiding in Refuge Gully. I went back down to try and find, Reg, Peter and...' His voice shook and he squatted down, his legs unsteady, 'and Jean.' He wiped the sweat and dirt from his face. 'The men they rounded up were kept on the oval to begin with and then I'm not sure where they took them after that. I could see them through the binoculars. Reg and Peter were there. I also talked to a fellow up in the bush who had hidden in Refuge Gully. He'd left Reg and the others before the Japs came. Said he didn't have a good feeling about it and had decided to head for Kokopo. He said he'd tried to get Reg to go with him, but he'd come down bad with the malaria and couldn't walk far.' Andrew took a deep breath. 'Peter must have been captured trying to get out. There were hundreds of them on the oval. They're heavily guarded and there's no way in or out.'

Michael squatted down on the ground next to Andrew. Bile rose in his throat, his stomach heaving with dread, not only from the last couple of days but from the thought of Reg and the others, so close by, but now prisoners of the Japanese.

Andrew's voice wavered. 'It's tearing me apart leaving them, but it would be certain death to try and break them out. My plan is to get away from here and once we're rescued there might be a better chance of going back in. The place is crawling with Japs, and until the Yanks or the Aussie reinforcements turn up, we've got no chance.'

'Those bastards,' Michael said.

'Who?' Andrew said. 'The Japs or the Australian government for abandoning us all, leaving us here to face the whole fucking Japanese army. What government leaves their nurses behind? I tried everything to get back to Jean. I crawled around all night in the jungle, trying to find a way to get in and help her. There's no way. The filthy Japs have taken the hospital and set up a main camp in the grounds. It's like a fortress.' His voice broke and he put his head between his hands as he squatted in the mud. 'I can't think about her, it's driving me crazy, but it would be suicide to try and get her out. I can only hope they'll treat them well because they're nurses.'

One of the older men in the group sat down with them, waving his hand towards the mountains behind them. 'You know this entire peninsula is crawling with groups of Australian men. Little groups, big groups, all trying find the best way out of here.'

Andrew drew a line in the mud with a stick. His group's priority was to head to Tol Plantation, hopefully to get picked up by Australian patrol boats and be taken back to Rabaul. With extra forces they could go back in and get the men and the nurses out.

Michael wasn't convinced. He explained to Andrew that Tol was only about ninety miles, situated on the water, and due south of where they were. That wasn't far by the enemy's standards. He intended heading a lot further south and staying high in the jungle. The Japs wouldn't want to venture too far inland. He wanted to get down as far as possible before making their way across to the other islands and then onwards to the mainland of New Guinea.

He encouraged Andrew and the others to come with him and George. He could find food and had a good sense of direction. It was a better option than Tol.

None of the other men were interested, all shaking their heads. Andrew, however, was tempted by Michael's plan.

'Our Tol plan reads solid, but I don't have a good feeling about it,' Andrew said. He screwed his face up, looking up into the canopy of trees, the sun blocked by the dense foliage that hid any sense of direction.

'How are you going to get across to the mainland?' he asked Michael.

'If we can get down to the southern part of New Britain, we're hoping to get hold of a native canoe or a small boat, but if we can't, there are places that Birri has told me about. You can swim across to the closer islands and make your way across so far.'

'What, swim in these waters! You've got to be joking. If the crocs don't get you, the sharks will. Sorry Michael, you lost me there. I'll swim in those muddy rivers back home or a dam, but never, never in the ocean.' He stood up, stretching, a shudder running through his body. 'Maybe it's a sign. I'm going to take that as a warning for me not to take that path. Tol is a better option.'

'I think you should consider coming with us.'

'I'd rather face the possibility of meeting up with a few Japs. That water has crocodiles as long as a house and sharks that can swallow a man whole. I think you and George should come with us to Tol.'

Michael shook his head. 'I'm sticking with our plan. If we can avoid the Japanese and survive long enough, we'll make it out and back to New Guinea.'

Andrew held out his hand to Michael. 'I wish you good luck, and if you ever get back, give Joanie a big kiss for me and tell her I was never going to swim. Maybe I'll see her before you. I'd say the Australian government would be sending a large contingent to win back Rabaul. They won't let those bastards get away with this.'

Andrew walked down the track with Michael to say their goodbyes. They gripped each other's hands for a long while. 'If our government doesn't do something quickly, chances are the Japs will be running all over these islands in no time,' Michael said. 'I'm hoping if we get back to the mainland of New Guinea, there'll be other troops we can join with. We might all be back in Rabaul under some proper orders before we know it. I just hope Reg and the others can hang on for that long.'

As Andrew continued down the track, he paused briefly before glancing back at Michael, who had also turned around. Andrew's face was dirty, his hat torn and muddy. He wore a cheeky grin and held his hand up to bid farewell as he called out. 'You make sure to give that beautiful Joanie a big kiss and hug for me when you see her again. And tell her I'll be there with Jean, to dance at your wedding.'

CHAPTER 13

*M*ichael returned to the clearing during the night, George's face lighting up with relief when he emerged from the jungle. When Michael repeated the information about Andrew, George questioned if perhaps they should also head for Tol with the others. Michael was adamant. With just two of them, it would be easier to hide and find enough food, plus the way they were headed was safer. If they wanted to avoid detection, they needed to go further down the coastline than Tol Plantation.

Together they filled the backpacks with all the available food they could find. There was a small overgrown vegetable garden at the back of the huts, and although most of it had been taken before the villagers left, there was still rootstock to fill their bags with. Michael also picked some leaves from a bush that Birri had shown him. 'Rub these on your bites,' he told George. 'It will stop the itching. Infection is the last thing we need.'

The next day, after a feed of taro and coconut, they began their long journey towards the bottom tip of the island. Reg wouldn't want him to be foolish, and it sounded as if there wasn't any way in or out of the heavily fortified town. They needed to get as far away from Rabaul as possible.

* * *

On the first day, they clambered up steep slopes, heavy rain turning the narrow paths into mud pits. Thick jungle surrounded them, and jagged creepers and spiky bushes grabbed at their clothes, ripping the fabric, wet from a combination of sweat and rain that bucketed down in sporadic bursts. Their boots were sodden and heavy with mud, and their bodies ached with the exertion of every step.

It appeared that no one had been this way before them, and the villages were deserted. Only a few useful items were left for them to gather.

The higher they climbed, the quieter it became. The sun sank lower, the cool mountain air swirling around them, relieving the oppressive heat that had been with them during the day.

When they stopped for a rest, Michael passed George a water bottle, noting the distress on his face and the fear in his eyes. 'It'll be okay, mate. I have a lot to live for, and I reckon I know how to get us off this blasted island and away from the Japs.'

'Thanks, Michael, I'll do my best.' They stood silent as their breathing slowed, the moisture dripping off the undergrowth around them, providing an eerie background sound. George looked upwards, tripping over a branch that lay half hidden in the mud. 'I was trying to find a gap in the trees where I could see the sky.' He muttered to Michael, who stopped to give him a hand up. 'Can you believe that order; every man for himself. What sort of government or army leader gives that as a command? We never covered that in our bloody training!'

Michael spat on the ground. 'They left us here, like sitting ducks. I counted over thirty Japanese boats in the harbour, plus three huge carriers sitting out there on the horizon, like the devil itself. You can't tell me they didn't know they were coming.'

'Where are the Yanks? Where's the plan? Where is the backup?'

Michael twisted the lid back on the water container, standing up, eager to keep moving. 'It's you and me now. We'll make our way to New Guinea, even if we have to swim. Birri said sometimes when the tide is low, you can walk across to some of the smaller islands. The people who live on the islands travel by boat to New Guinea. Surely the Japs won't get that far before us.'

Michael took one last look back along the track they had been travelling on, before moving quietly up into the covering darkness of the mountainside.

CHAPTER 14

*R*eg spent the night of the invasion in Refuge Gully. The small valley seemed like a safe place; however, as the hours progressed the sounds of bombs exploding and the continuous firing of rifles down along the beaches made for a terrifying night. His nerves that were stretched tight made his body ache, and his neck was stiff from looking upwards, waiting for a plane to fly over or a bomb to drop directly on them.

The night passed slowly as those who were left huddled together. The three men with Reg had all worked in businesses in Rabaul. Most, like Reg, did not consider themselves fit or young enough to escape down the coastline or over the mountains. Others planned to take their chances, hiding at the plantations or finding a way to the other side of the island. Both options were appealing and if only he was younger and fit, he would have gone with them.

He clenched his fists, his gut churning, the malarial shivers and pains, ever-present. He had no option but to stay with those who were willing to surrender. When his eyes closed, he thought of

Joanie, the droning sound of planes flying low filling his ears. A shiver ran down his spine. Thank God she had left when she did.

I will get back to them. I will not die on this island, he thought, ducking his head lower as another building exploded further down the hill.

* * *

By mid-morning a few of the men left Refuge Gully to surrender. Their plan was to wave white rags as they made their way into town. They would talk to the Japanese patrols and bring them back to the others. That way they could all peacefully surrender.

Reg and the others sat patiently. Some passed cigarettes around to share and a couple wrote letters to pass the time. Reg wrote a short letter to Edna, not knowing if he'd ever have the opportunity to post it.

My darling Edna,

I'm not sure when I will be able to write again. The Japanese have landed. I am well and with other men, preparing to surrender. Our men are scattered and have been ordered to try and escape any way they can. I will not give in ever, the thought of you keeping me strong through the times ahead. I love you my darling and long for your arms around me, your lips against mine. The years with you and Joanie have been the happiest any man could ever wish for and you have not only been my loving wife, but my soul companion and best friend. I love you with all my heart and I am with you always – Until I return and we meet again - Your beloved husband, Reg.

He folded the paper, tucking it into his pocket. The harsh sounds of Japanese voices filtered up through the gully and he stood as steady as he could, straightening his clothes and standing tall.

The newly-arrived enemy emerged from the trees, this first encounter turning his fear into a hatred he hadn't thought possible

The men were armed with bayoneted rifles and pointed them aggressively towards the surrendering Australians. Orders barked in Japenese cut the air like a knife and they waved their guns in the air, herding the men like cattle, pushing and prodding them into lines, until they were all moving off, back down towards the town.

One of the younger men, Thomas, who worked at the Post Office, took Reg's arm and placed it around his shoulder. He took the weight of Reg on his own body and half-lifted, half-dragged him along the track. Reg tried hard to keep up and not be a hindrance, but his feet would not move in the direction he wanted them to, and his entire body shook, the sweat pouring from his face as he tried to shuffle alongside Thomas. Another Post Office worker called Bert, also came to assist. He supported Reg's body from the other side, the two younger men offering words of encouragement as they stumbled forward.

They stopped regularly as they encountered other small groups of heavily guarded men. Many of them were known to Reg, and they nodded back at him with defeated stares as they huddled together, bewildered and in shock. Thank God, Thomas and Bert stayed with him, helping him up when it was time to move on and reassuring each other to continue moving, one foot after the other.

The Japanese soldiers led them to the sports oval and ordered them to sit on the grassy clearing. Only a few months ago, he had sat here with Joanie and watched a friendly game of football. Now the grounds were scattered with groups of civilian and army men.

Bert had moved away from Reg and now leant over another man whose leg had been shattered by gunfire. He pushed a water bottle to the man's lips, helping to lie him down on the ground, the blood soaking through the makeshift bandages quickly leaving a stain on the dirt below. Bert stood up and argued with their captors. He spoke loudly, proclaiming that some of the men were civilians. They were sick and shouldn't be rounded up as prisoners. His remarks were greeted with a belt from a rifle, his body toppling and falling, his face rammed into the dirt. Bert's blood squirted onto the ground and his head split open from where the barrel of the gun had met his skull. Two men who went to help him were also belted with rifles, their bodies crumpling to the ground beside Bert's motionless form.

Reg looked in horror, the bile rising in his throat. He tried to get up and go to the men to offer support. Thomas, who had been assisting him to sit up, pulled him down, whispering to stay still. Someone else tried to gain his attention, and he peered through the men in front of him. Peter was shuffling on his bottom, back towards him, mouthing at him to sit down. The guards were focused on the three men they had beaten, a heavy Japanese boot finding its spot when they tried to stop the moaning from the injured men on the ground. It only took Peter a few minutes to make his way until he was sitting next to Reg, their shoulders touching. They looked at each other, and Peter nodded, before both looked downwards as the soldiers shouted further orders.

* * *

While the Japanese were rounding up anyone they could find in and around Rabaul, Michael and George climbed higher into the mountains. The air was heavy, the jungle thicker the higher they went, its brooding constant dripping, often the only sound apart from an occasional rustle of a small animal as it scurried out of their path. Steep cliffs rose above, and the tiny track they followed, narrowed. To the side of the track, deep gorges sheared the sides of the mountainside, ferns and other plants hanging precariously to shimmering wet rock walls. Michael tried not to look down, the deep chasms filled with clouds that lay like a blanket of wool, obscuring the view below. When the cloud lifted, the base of the gorge sprung up, a dark green sea of foliage, threatening to swallow and cover them for eternity if they were to put one foot wrong.

Neither spoke much that first day; their thoughts were heavy like the clouds.

When they came to a small clearing, they stopped for a rest. Dark circles hung under George's eyes and Michael bent down to help him pick off the leeches that clung to his legs. In front of them, the edge of the mountain dropped away and they looked through trees that lined the escarpment edge. A cliff face pointed downwards, its steep sides running with water that disappeared into the jungle valley at its base. Beyond that were deep ravines and more hills, covered in the same dense jungle as what they had passed through. Further to the north, the distinct line of the coastline was visible, its waters sparkling in the heat of the day. Through the gaps in the trees, they could see across Blanche Bay, and nestled on its shores lay the town of Rabaul.

They took turns looking through the binoculars, moving them back and forth, from the town to the bay and back again. The harbour was littered with Japanese ships, their large grey bulks menacing in the pristine waters. Minesweepers ploughed methodically across the ocean and smaller craft moved back and forth between the shore and the ships. Numerous vehicles lumbered along the roads. The trucks and armoured vehicles were in convoys, the distinct red circle of the Japanese flag visible even from afar.

'Holy shit,' George said. 'They mean business.'

'Still want to surrender? 'Michael raised his eyebrows. 'Those mongrels aren't going to give you three square meals a day. I pity Reg and those other poor bastards. They don't stand a chance.'

* * *

The following days blurred into each other. Relentless rain fell, the incessant heavy drops from the canopy saturating their clothes and boots. The jungle floor was a thick soggy blanket of rotting leaves and the dank air hung heavy, making it difficult to breathe.

It was rare to find a dry area to sleep, although sometimes Michael was able to locate small, deserted huts that provided shelter for the night. Occasionally they came across villagers who gave them small amounts of food. The groups were friendly, but they were also on the move, heading for more remote areas and carefully guarding their supplies.

* * *

A thin trail that Michael had been following, petered out, ending in a thick wall of thorny bushes and dripping leaves. They had travelled many miles vertically, up and down, crossing ravines and waterfalls, crawling on their bellies under bushes and stumbling through knee-deep mud to progress only one or two miles forward. Michael dropped to his knees, blood oozing from scratches and cuts mixing into the muddy water he crawled through. Behind him, George struggled to follow, his groans suppressed when Michael held his hand up to silence him. He turned back to George, his heart thumping hard, his body aching with exhaustion. He pressed his finger to his lips. Below them, through the thickness of the jungle came the sounds of men talking; Japanese men.

They lay motionless, counting the seconds and the minutes, for what seemed like hours, until the tramping of men's feet and chatter of what Michael surmised to be a scouting party of about four Japanese soldiers faded into the distance. Michael's legs screamed with cramps and he pushed forward, inch by inch, not even stopping to look if George was behind him. Eventually, the muddy pond they crawled along ended, and a narrow tunnel opened up through the jungle on the other side.

He stopped, pulling himself upright and trying to stretch out his legs, the cramps sending piercing pain up through his hips. George appeared behind him, his mouth open but no words coming out. 'Rub my legs,' Michael whispered. 'Rub them.'

George stared, his eyes wide, his mouth open still. He blinked a few times before reaching out and grabbing Michael's leg, which was stiff and sticking straight out, the muscles tense and rigid, as spasms ripped through his leg. His hands began to work, his fingers gripping the skin like a vice, twisting the muscles and pushing into the sinew. Michael groaned softly and closed his eyes. 'Keep going, mate, keep going.'

The muscles in the leg finally loosened and relaxed, and Michael bent it slowly, stretching it back and forth to ease the pain. George crouched in the mud, his head between his knees, his eyes to the ground, and a look of utter defeat on his face.

Although their journey had only begun, they both looked like they had been on the move for months. Their khaki shirts were covered in mud and stains, the material wet and torn. Baggy shorts left their legs bare, their skin covered in bites from the mosquitos that stuck to them like the flies that clung to the cattle back home.

The following days blurred into each other. Occasionally they came across other soldiers, small groups of two and three, all with their own idea of where to go and how to get off New Britain. These men looked similar to what they did, their faces unshaven and muddied, their bodies torn from thorns and bites, a haunted, worried look on their faces. Some were ready to surrender. One of them showed Michael a leaflet that had dropped from the sky. Michael held it in his hand, reading it out to George.

'To the Officers and Soldiers of This Island. Surrender at Once and we will guarantee your life, treating you as war prisoners. Those who Resist Us Will Be Killed One and All. Consider seriously, you can find neither food nor way of escape in this island and you will only die of hunger unless you surrender. January 23rd 1942 JAPANESE COMMANDER IN CHIEF.'

As the men parted ways, shaking each other's hands, George again questioned their decision to continue. 'Some of these men are going back to surrender. They reckon their chances are better with the Japs than in this jungle.'

'I'd rather die out here than go back there and die. At least if we can get out we have a hope of helping those poor bastards left behind.'

George watched the backs of the last group of men disappear back towards the way they had come. His voice was hoarse. 'Everyone's so fucking confused. We're not trained for this.'

Michael turned his back on him and began walking. 'Just put one foot in front of the other. We have no option.'

* * *

As they moved down the coastline, Michael changed direction. He stopped before veering off the track, pushing his way through thick jungle that eventually turned into boggy mangroves. George followed, looking towards the sky as if the answers to the way out were written in the clouds.

In the mangroves, their boots sunk in the thick mud, sapping their strength even further. The quagmire sucked like a vacuum, the maze of thick and twisted roots a continual hindrance, with each step requiring all of Michael's willpower to complete. George flicked away the spiders and insects that clung to their skin and clothing, while fierce sand flies relentlessly attacked any bare patch of skin. 'Rub the mangrove mud onto your bites,' Michael said, 'and use the leaves to relieve the itching.'

'How do you know which way you're going?' George's voice was panicky, the tall mangrove trees blocking any visibility. Noises close by made him stop in his tracks. 'Safer to be with the Japs I reckon. There'll be crocs in here.' He muttered as he crawled through the branches that tore at him, adding to the cuts and deep scratches that crisscrossed his arms and legs.

'Yes, there will be crocs around, so keep your eyes open,' Michael replied, also nervous at the thought of encountering the huge reptiles that inhabited the area. 'Stop here.' He passed George his water bottle as he began to dig in the mud between the roots of the mangrove trees. The horizontal branches above were gnarly and twisted, the limbs reaching out like arms. The roots of the trees pointed downwards, a myriad of organised tubes pushing down into the mud, their tendrils the lifeline of the trees that formed a canopy above them.

'There's shellfish here. Hold out your hand.' Michael said.

'Can we eat them?' George's eyes lit up.

'I've had them before with Birri. I'm not sure we should eat too many to start with, but they're edible.' He held out a large brown shell. 'Look, these beauties are dinner!'

Michael gathered more, his body twisting and, at times, lying across the mud as he dug into the top layer of slush. He pulled out shells that he passed to George as he manoeuvred back from between the roots. They tasted better cooked, but they could also be eaten raw.

The mud pulled at their weary bones, and their progress was painstakingly slow until the ground beneath the mangroves became firmer and the trees above them thinned. Finally, they reached a cluster of low bushes that offered protection from the fierce sun and any aircraft that might fly above. They curled up in the shade, exhausted and silent, resting and waiting for the sun to set.

* * *

When they emerged from the sticky mangroves onto a beach, the feeling of clean sand under Michael's feet was an instant relief. The edge of the mangroves gave them some cover as they headed towards a rocky outcrop, the cliff face pockmarked with small caves and ledges. A cave offered some protection and they removed their boots, their footwear resembling clumps of mud on the end of their legs.

In front of them, visible in the dim light, lay a tiny bay, the small waves lapping on the sand, an enticing sight as they made their way to the beach. No moon was out yet, so it was a safe place to soak their aching bodies and clean themselves.

The cool water was soothing on the insect bites that covered their skin, and Michael wriggled his bloody, blistered feet in the sand. He closed his eyes as the salty water soaked into his battered skin, sinking lower as the small waves brushed against his nakedness, the sandy bottom, like carpet under his feet. He scrubbed everywhere, using his clothes and sand to remove the blood and mud.

George whispered. 'How good is that? Even the stinging of the salt is a welcome relief. I feel alive.'

'It's a great feeling,' Michael said before dunking his entire body under the water again. When he came back up, he looked towards the horizon. 'Scrub your clothes as best as you can and then we better get back up to the cave. At least that will give us some shelter.'

The cave was small but offered good protection. George used his pocket knife to open the shellfish, popping the small pieces of soft flesh into his mouth. 'Tastes good,' he said, reaching over to take some papaya that Michael had earlier wrapped in large green leaves. 'If I close my eyes, I can imagine there's sugar sprinkled on that papaya. My mum used to grow them back home.'

Michael sat next to him, rubbing his own throbbing feet with sand. The granules scratched across his raw skin, scouring every sore and cut, but the sand cleaned away the parasites and mud.

'It would be good to stay in this cave and have clean sand and ocean water each day,' George said. 'I'm going to kiss the ground back in Australia if we ever get back there. At least it stays solid and dry beneath your feet.'

'We're already as thin as rakes, but at least we've managed to find some food along the way,' Michael said, 'Even if it upsets the stomach and goes straight through, at least it's keeping us alive.'

'I reckon those blasted mozzies have sucked all the weight from me.' George swatted one, the blood that it had already sucked from him now splatted over his arm.

'Some of these mosquitos are as big as bats. Tomorrow I'll find that plant again, and we'll work out a way to keep the leaves on our skin. I know the jungle is tough, George, but it has everything we need to survive.'

The two sat silently as the moon rose slowly in the east, its light reflecting on the endless ocean that stretched in front of them. Somewhere across the waters lay the safety of Australian shores, the comfort of family and loved ones and a dry place to put their heads down at night. Michael looked along the deserted strip of sand; the next bay they would come to was Jacquinot Bay. The idea of walking along the beach was far more appealing than the mud and jungle behind them, but even though they were well past Tol Plantation and Wide Bay, he still wanted to stay inland. The fleet of large ships and the aircraft that had dominated the sky when the Japanese landed had stayed with him. The enemy would be looking towards the plantations to try and find anyone who had escaped.

His gaze focused on the sea in front. He was going to follow his gut instincts, which were telling him to continue on the path they were on. They would travel down the entire coastline if they had to, and the best way to do that was to stay inland, out of sight of the Japanese.

George put his head between his hands. 'My gut's churning from the food we've eaten, my skin's on fire, and every muscle and bone is throbbing.'

'You can do it, George.' Michael stood up.

He passed George his boots, trying not to look at the condition of his skinny legs, the blisters, cuts and bites, a festering pussy mess on his skin. 'C'mon, we've made it this far. We can do the rest.' He pulled his mate up by his hands. They were both propelled into action as they heard the distant sound of an approaching plane. 'They're crawling all over this peninsula, air, sea and land.

We've got to think smart and stay away from the obvious places if we want to get out of here alive,' Michael reminded him.

George's reply was barely audible, his breath short as they made their way up a small path. Eventually they disappeared into the jungle, which quickly swallowed them, the thick foliage closing over where they had entered.

CHAPTER 15

Woombye - 1942

Joanie had only been in Australia a few weeks when word came through that the Japanese had landed in Rabaul. The newspaper, dated January 24, 1942, carried a small piece titled 'Rabaul Silent Since 4pm Yesterday'.

She spread the newspaper out on the table. *'Militia Fighting Fierce Battle in Rabaul Hills'*. Edna hung onto Joanie's arm as they leaned over to read the words. The colour drained from Edna's face and she sank into a chair next to the table as Joanie read aloud. *Overwhelming odds, fierce battle, increasing Japanese strength at Rabaul, convoy of seventeen Japanese vessels in Rabaul Harbour.*

There were sentences in between, but it didn't matter. The main words stuck, the information jarring and the sentences conjuring up images that were unimaginable.

Edna sat up straight, biting her bottom lip as she often did to stop from breaking down. 'They left them like lambs to the slaughter. They knew they wouldn't be able to defend the peninsula, against how many vessels? Seventeen? Good God!' She placed her hands squarely on the table before tracing her finger over the map next to the article. 'Look at that, Joanie. Eleven hundred miles from Rabaul to Townsville, and our government couldn't get my Reg or the others back here to safety.'

'It's unbelievable. It's almost like they've sacrificed them. Surely now they'll have to move them out. It's obvious from this information that they're outnumbered and don't stand a chance. Maybe this article isn't telling us everything. Perhaps at this very moment there are ships picking them up and bringing them back,' Joanie said.

Edna took one last look at the front page of the newspaper and folded it over so that they could no longer read the headlines.

Joanie sat down next to her mother. 'I should have prepared you for what was in the paper.'

'It won't change anything.' Edna's voice broke, her words barely audible as her hands came up over her face. 'I want Reg back here with us. He's not a soldier. He's a peaceful man who wouldn't hurt a fly.' She wiped her eyes. 'And what about the boys?'

Joanie held her mother tight, her throat dry, her body aching with fear. Where were they, and how were they being treated? Had they escaped before the Japanese landed, or were they taking refuge at places further inland?

They clung to each other until they both calmed down. Her mother wiped her eyes with a handkerchief Joanie passed her, the letters R.B. she had so lovingly embroidered on the corner, setting her off with a fresh flood of tears.

Joanie held her tightly. 'Just wait, Mother, they'll be home soon. Our government will make sure of it.'

* * *

Any news was of interest and Joanie collected paper clippings, took notes from the radio announcements, and talked to customers, gaining any information she could. The war in the

Pacific was creeping towards them and Japan had not only attacked Australian coastal areas but had also taken control of several areas north of New Guinea, including the British controlled Solomon Islands and Bougainville.

On the 19th of February 1942, the city of Darwin in the Northern Territory was attacked by Japanese forces. The assaults occurred during the day, and the enemy fighters and bombers targeted the port and ships in the harbour. 252 allied service personnel and civilians were killed and the Australian forces that occupied the largest centre in Northern Australia were over-whelmed by the heavy air attacks. Darwin was a city under fire, and many Australians felt as if the bombings and the subsequent attack on Broome in March were precursors to a major Japanese invasion.

As the enemy forces spread south and east, other bases in north-eastern Guinea were captured, with Lae and Salamaua on the Huon Gulf, taken easily by March 1942.

A map of Australia and New Guinea tacked to the wall allowed Joanie to plot the towns and areas that were now under Japanese control. Her eyes lingered over the area of Rabaul and she stared for a long time, as if the answers were written in the curvy lines that designated the many bays and islands close to the coast. Using her finger, she traced the coastline, envisaging the terrain and swampy mangroves a man would have to walk through to move further away from the town. Places where someone could cross to the mainland of New Guinea were a long way away from Rabaul, and now, with the Japanese patrolling the entire area, it would probably be impossible to escape the island of New Britain. She stared at the coastline again, her hope dissipating.

* * *

Bill West phoned Edna later that week. They talked for a long while and he explained that he was doing everything possible to track Reg's location. Other families of his staff were in a similar position and he would not give up until there were answers. He had written to the Prime Minister's department, who had passed on his questions to The Department of the Navy. So far, the only reply he had was, *'At the present moment it is impracticable to contemplate an expedition to evacuate civilians from New Britain.'*

He apologised to Edna, but he had nothing more substantial to tell her. The bombing of Darwin had thrown government departments into further chaos and he was having trouble getting anyone to return his calls. He would, however, continue to harass anyone he could to find out where Reg and the other workers were.

* * *

Two letters from Reg arrived after the attack, but they had all been written and sent before the event. In the first letter, he wrote that there had been some bombing raids and the imminent danger was drawing closer. Although he continued to pester anyone he could about returning to New Guinea or Australia, his requests fell on deaf ears. Life had changed and the town was deserted. Mi-Lee and her family had vanished, to where he did not know. The villagers, including Sissy, had taken off higher into the jungles. Most of his letters were taken up with his feelings for Edna and Joanie and how he longed to be back with them, running the shop and promising never to leave them again.

He mentioned that he had seen Michael, who was busy setting up more defence structures. Peter and Andrew also came to see him whenever they could and Andrew had visited Reg, when he was having a short stay in hospital. *Nothing too serious*, he placated Edna with, *just a little fever for a couple of days and now I'm quite well, thanks to the lovely nursing of our friend Jean. And on that note I'm not sure if it was myself, or Jean, that Andrew came to visit. I did see them sneaking a cuddle and kiss on the hospital verandah late one night. I pray that all the boys remain safe. They are young and have their entire life in front of them.*

Joanie and her mother continued to write letters each week, never knowing if their words reached Rabaul or Reg. Joanie also wrote to Michael, pouring out her thoughts and worries. At night they listened to the radio, waiting for any news or extra information. Each night was the same and they sat in silence long after the radio was turned off, both deep in thought.

* * *

Peter and Andrew's mother, Ethel, was also searching for news and started to drop into the shop on a regular basis. In previous years, she had never been very friendly to Joanie's family, and it was somewhat of an amusement to witness her put on her sweetest voice and kindest words when she called in. She was beside herself about the fate of her boys and one afternoon strode up the path towards the shop, a stern expression on her face.

'Here she comes,' Joanie gave her mother the heads up. 'She's probably been down the church praying or taking some liquor to the priest.'

'Maybe she's been confessing all her sins.' Edna chuckled, watching the small woman hurry towards the shop.

Joanie rolled her eyes. 'I don't think she'd have done anything that she considered sinful.'

The two women straightened their clothes and put on their best smiles as Ethel O'Rourke entered the shop, the metal bell on the door clanging loudly to announce her arrival.

'Good afternoon, Mrs O'Rourke.' Joanie greeted her.

Ethel clutched a newspaper in her hand. 'Have you read the Melbourne paper, *The Argus*? Father McLeod gave it to me. There's a write-up about Rabaul. It's more dreadful news, and I'll warn you before you read it, it's terrible.'

Edna and Joanie came from behind the counter and the

three women huddled together, looking at the paper dated a week ago; April 6, 1942. There hadn't been any official news since the article in the newspaper back in January. However this was new information and the newspaper, *The Argus*, was headlined,

Heroism of Rabaul Garrison in Face of Heavy Odds.
Gallant Beach Fighting and Terrible Retreat.

Joanie put her arm around her mother's waist, all eyes riveted on the pages as Joanie read it out loud.

After more than two months of grim anxious silence that followed the fall of Rabaul, former capital of New Guinea, to an overwhelming Japanese landing force on January 23, the story can now be told of the bloody struggles in which the Australian garrison was engaged, and the almost incredible privations they suffered in making their way to safety. Although it is possible that Rabaul casualties - killed, wounded, missing, and captured, and including certain civilians - number about 700, large numbers of Australian soldiers have reached the safety of Australian bases.

She took a deep breath, looking up at Ethel, whose face was white. Joanie's finger traced the words on the page as she continued.

Unshaven and bedraggled men, with sunken cheeks and lined faces, men wearing only the tattered shreds of uniform, have come through some of the most extraordinary adventures in modern warfare and many of them have brought with them their rifles and equipment to use against the Japanese another day.

It is true that they were defeated, but they fought against odds of ten to one, and they did not give in until the Japanese landing force, comprising between 17,000 and 20,000 men, had suffered at least 2,000 casualties. The total Australian garrison consisted of only 1,300 men in the final decisive action they fought, without any assistance from air or sea, against a Japanese land force, an air armada of at least 150 bombers, fighters, and dive bombers, and against the guns of a formidable naval force.

Ethel clenched her fists. 'God help them. I pray they have survived.'

Edna gasped. 'It may be too late for your prayers, Ethel. It sounds like they were up against the entire Japanese force.'

The article continued with details about the ensuing attacks on Rabaul and the courage and heroism shown by the Australian men. Joanie continued, her voice becoming husky as she read. The others listened intently, the grim stories starting to blur, one into the other.

Three hundred men killed, wounded or captured, Japanese swarming, weary troops retreating into the jungle, Australians covered hundreds of miles through some of the most terrible jungle country in the whole world.

The article was lengthy, and after Joanie finished reading, the women scanned the paper, searching for more information. It was an April paper, printed last week, yet the landing had happened on the twenty-third of January, only one month after Joanie had left.

Ethel also looked closer at the date at the top of *The Argus*. 'Father gets them sent up from Melbourne so he can keep up with the news. This in itself is a week old. That's two and a half months since this happened. Where would my boys and your man be?'

'The last letters we received were dated and written before the invasion. It sounded like it was heating up, but we thought the government would do something.' Edna said.

'I don't understand why they didn't send reinforcements,' Joanie added, her voice angry. 'If they weren't going to do that, why didn't they get them all off?' She stood up and walked over to the window, the light outside starting to dim. The cries of plovers nesting next to the shop were a mournful wailing noise that Joanie felt like she wanted to make herself.

Beyond the green hills of Woombye, the last rays of the sun dipped behind their gentle slopes. The scenery was in stark contrast to the steep cliffs and thick jungles that lay behind Rabaul, and she shuddered to think of her father having to retreat and survive in such a dangerous and hostile area. The younger men might stand a chance, but Reg's age and health wouldn't help, if indeed, that was where he had escaped to.

Edna and Ethel looked at her as if reading her mind.

Edna's voice was stern. 'This isn't the time to be surmising what's going on up there. We need to support each other and remain positive. I believe they'll all be safe. Reg is wise and smart, and your young men are fit and strong. They are probably among those who have survived and, even as we speak, are making their way back to us.

'It's mighty strange that we haven't heard anything from them or that the government hasn't let us know they're on their way back.' Ethel stood up and gathered up the newspaper. 'If you don't mind, I'll take the paper with me. I want the others at home to read it also. If we all pray together, we'll be assured they'll all come home.'

CHAPTER 16

*R*eg's wages from Burns Philp continued to arrive until Edna received a letter saying that due to the contract being officially completed, the company was no longer under any obligation to keep paying his wages. She persisted in trying to get further information, not a day passing without her ringing or writing to someone. She also spoke at length to Bill West.

The most information Bill could garner came from a soldier called Ernest, who had been part of the 2/22nd Battalion and managed to escape during the invasion. Ernest had managed to make his way to the mainland of New Guinea before being flown to a hospital in Brisbane, arriving in a condition so bad that he was still trying to recover.

Bill was shocked when he visited him, horrified by his emaciated appearance. Ernest knew who Reg and his daughter, Joanie, were. He had often visited the store to purchase goods. Ernest described the initial panic and subsequent retreat into the hills and what he had observed from the jungles above Rabaul. From a distance he had heard the screams and seen the harsh punishments meted out to those who surrendered or were captured.

His voice was weak. 'We tried to work out how to help those captured, but the place was crawling with hundreds of Japs. They were also up in the jungle, rounding up whoever they could find.'

Like so many others, Ernest had no choice but to try and find his own way out. He'd spent days and nights walking along mountain tracks, surviving on whatever he could find and enduring the worst conditions imaginable.

'I trekked for hundreds of miles through crocodile-infested rivers, continually sodden and covered in thousands of insect bites,' he told Bill. There were three other fellas and me. We survived on plants and root vegetables we found. Sometimes a native might give us some extra to keep us going. It was hell on earth, the rot, the sickness and the hunger.' He stopped to get his breath, his thin hand shaking as Bill passed him a glass of water. He sipped slowly, his eyes yellow, his body wasted from the months of illness and hunger. He passed the glass back to Bill, looking him straight in the eye. 'What we went through was bad, but from what I heard and the bits I saw, our journey was nothing compared to what those poor buggers who were taken prisoners copped.'

Ernest talked to Bill until his voice was hoarse. He was grateful to offload some of his guilt and memories of what he'd seen to someone who knew the area and had connections to many in the town. Eventually the nurse interrupted, asking Bill to leave because Ernest needed his rest. The two men said their goodbyes. Bill was taken aback by the information about the people and places he had lived in and loved for so many years. 'I wish you a speedy recovery. You have survived through the worst, rest up and get well.'

Ernest tried to sit up but he was too weak and once again reached out to hold Bill's hand in his. He looked straight into Bill's eyes. 'I hope you find your people, for there are men scattered throughout New Britain, and your guess is as good as mine as to where they are right now and if they are alive.'

* * *

Bill had also received a letter written from Reg shortly before the invasion. He read over it numerous times, worried about his friend who had said he'd glossed over the effects of the malaria to Edna and that his health wasn't good and he had needed to visit the hospital for both medicine and overnight stays. His last words to Bill, *'I doubt that if the Japanese invade that those of us left here in Rabaul will stand a chance. Such a small group compared to the might of the Japanese forces.'*

CHAPTER 17

*E*thel O'Rourke called into the shop again on the last day in May. Her face was pale, her eyes sunken and lifeless, and it seemed like she had aged ten years in one month. Joanie closed the door behind her, turning the *Open* sign around to *Closed*. Business was slow these days in Woombye, and shutting the shop a few minutes early would not make any difference to their takings for the week. They needed to be careful with their money, as who knew when Father would be back. The two men who had worked for them previously had moved on, and Edna boosted their income by taking on an elderly gentleman as a tenant in the cottage they owned next door. Joanie had also picked up some bookkeeping work, and Edna kept busy with some extra sewing work.

Edna beckoned Ethel to come into the back room and pulled out a chair for her. She lowered herself slowly into the chair, hanging onto Joanie, her legs barely able to support her.

Her hands shook as she placed two pieces of yellow paper in front of them, laying them flat on the small table. They were Commonwealth of Australia telegrams and had arrived together.

One had details about Peter and the other was for Andrew. Both stated in large letters that they were *MISSING IN ACTION*, the typewritten names and service numbers blurring into the other words.

Joanie gripped the table, the room spinning around her. She closed her eyes, the faces of Peter and Andrew clear in her memory from the last time she had been with them in Rabaul. Her head felt tight, her chest ached, and she closed her eyes, trying to stop the nausea rising in her throat. She reached for a glass of water, sipping slowly as she stared at Edna's shocked expression.

The water was cool on her throat and she took deep breaths, trying hard to stay calm as she joined the other two in reading back over the telegrams. She read them over and over, her fingers tracing the letters, as if they might change and say something different.

Ethel unfolded a large handkerchief and noisily blew her nose, before asking if they had received anything about Reg. Joanie shook her head, her voice monotone as she explained how she had talked to some families when she had been in Brisbane last week. They had told her there were stories of men getting off the island and making their way to New Guinea and then home.

'My boys are strong, and the Lord will be with them.' Ethel stood and wiped her eyes. 'We have our faith and I know our prayers will be answered.'

'Let's hope so,' Joanie said, holding back what she really wanted to say, respecting the fact that the boys' mother was holding fast to her faith.

'I'll say a prayer for your Reg,' Ethel said to Edna.

Joanie spoke for Edna, aware that her mother was also trying to take in the news that the two young men she had last seen sitting at her dining room table, laughing and joking, were now missing in action. 'Thank you, Ethel.'

Ethel paused and moved her right hand from her head to her chest, making the sign of the cross from shoulder to shoulder. 'I'm sure the boys will make their way back here to the family and church.'

With that, the devout Catholic woman folded the telegrams and tucked them into her shirt.

Joanie stood to see her out. 'I hope so. I hope someone is watching over all of them.'

* * *

Although the news that Ethel brought was devastating, it did give hope that Reg was safe and that perhaps the Japanese would leave the prisoners at Rabaul until the war ended.

Joanie closed the door behind Ethel, thoughts swirling around inside her head. She had become obsessed with where her father was and the fate of Peter and Andrew. And then there was Michael. Her chest tightened. Had someone received a telegram saying that he also was missing in action? Were his mother and father, about whom he had talked so fondly, also holding a yellow piece of paper next to their heart and praying that he would survive?

Edna scribbled down what Ethel had told them, placing the piece of paper with the information on it into a cardboard box. Inside the box, she kept every newspaper article and note she jotted down while listening to the radio reports at night. There were also letters from Joanie and Reg from the day they arrived in Rabaul.

She closed the lid on the box, turning to Joanie. 'And when your father comes home, we'll be able to read back over all of these and show him what was written in the newspaper and how precious those letters were to us.'

CHAPTER 18

New Britain - May 1942

By early May, the two men had walked the entire length of New Britain's rugged southern coastline. Michael supported George as they staggered along the trails, his instincts telling him they were nearing where he wanted to go. Who knew what they would find, though? With so much time passed since they had left Rabaul, perhaps the Japanese had also infiltrated this far south.

His shoulder took the weight as George leaned against him, his arm flung around the back of Michael's neck. His friend's face was gaunt and unrecognisable from a few months ago, his clothes hanging off him like shredded rags. Michael closed his eyes for a moment, willing himself to put one foot in front of the other, his legs buckling under the pressure of supporting George. He looked at his friend. 'You look like shit, young George.'

George lifted his head a little, his lips cracked and bleeding. 'You don't look that great yourself.'

They shuffled awkwardly down a narrow path, the sound of

the ocean a welcoming sound. When they emerged from the jungle, Michael looked up and rubbed his eyes. The sun's brightness was blinding, and their bodies heaved with exhaustion and hunger as they stumbled forward. In front of them a beach stretched wide, the water lapping languidly on its sand. The coastline was a welcome scene but even more so was the sight of a group of men carrying spears and fishing baskets, walking towards them.

The group quickened their pace, their worried faces peering at Michael and George. Michael collapsed on the sand, holding his hand out in greeting, the skin on his swollen lips cracking and aching as he attempted a smile.

One of the men spoke in broken English, his words coming out fast, confusing Michael, who tried to still the spinning in his head so he could understand what was being said. He replied slowly, telling the story of how he and George had walked all the way from Rabaul. The group shook their heads in amazement and discussed the situation in their language. They gathered around, eventually helping George up, before two men carried him, their joined hands forming a makeshift seat.

At first, Michael attempted to walk alongside them, his arms wrapped around their strong shoulders. He stumbled along the track with one man on either side for support. In the end, he, too, had to be carried.

As they approached a village, inquisitive villagers emerged from their huts, chatting excitedly at the arrival of the two frail white men. Much like the locals they had met before, these people had a muscular build, their legs solid, their loins covered with only a small cloth or grass skirt. Michael attempted a smile; the sight of energetic, naked children grinning and giggling as they peered from behind the legs of their mothers was a refreshing vision.

They neared the circle of huts that sat on short stilts, their thatched roofs providing a dry cover. The villagers positioned Michael and George on grass mats in the middle of a large room.

Some of the men huddled around, squatting on their feet, their dark eyes flitting back and forth, examining the state Michael and George were in. They started cleaning the men's legs, which were covered in pus and sores, their bones like sticks beneath their sallow skin. Michael had a wide gash on the front of his knee, and he sat still as a village man chewed the roots of a ginger plant before rubbing it into the open wound. Others wrapped paw paw leaves and the skin of the fruit around the ulcers on their bodies, the lacerated openings exposing muscles and tendons. Dazed and sick, they drank and ate what the villagers provided. It had been a long and torturous journey, and they still had a long way to travel. Michael looked at George. Thank God they had help and had reached a point of safety.

Michael could communicate with a few of the men who spoke a language similar to the locals in Rabaul.

They had reached their destination, Arawe, and if they wanted to get to Port Moresby, they now faced an ocean dotted by small islands, the water stretching sixty miles across to the mainland of New Guinea.

There had been two other small groups of Australians who had come through before. Two of the men had died not long after they arrived and were buried further behind the village. The villagers had helped the others, taking them in a small boat across to the mainland.

One of the men squatted next to Michael. His arms and legs bulged with muscles, his hands large and strong as he held Michael up, encouraging him to drink a mixture the women had made. His eyes were as brown as his skin, and Michael could read the concern in them. The man, whose name was Alaka'i, explained to Michael that it was still a long way across the water and once they reached the mainland, the insects were thicker and the terrain even more treacherous than what they had already travelled.

George groaned, picking up on some of the conversation. 'It's going to be okay,' Michael said to him. 'Alaka'i says that they will take us in a boat and then stay with us until we get across to the other side of New Guinea. He gives us his word that they will ensure we make it out. The Japanese have not treated their people well, and they will do anything they can to help us.'

George closed his eyes, his cracked, parched lips barely moving as he spoke. 'We've come to a village of angels, fuzzy-wuzzy angels. At least if I die here, I will be surrounded by angels.'

George's breathing was raspy, his chest heaving up and down as he gasped for air. Sweat poured from his face and body, and three men slept beside him during the night, sitting him up every so often to take sips from a bowl that contained a foul-smelling liquid.

Michael slept soundly once he knew George was being looked after, only waking when the men also sat him up, wiping his sweating body dry and making sure he took liquid from the bowl. It tasted terrible and left a burning feeling in his throat and mouth, momentarily taking the focus away from the other pains in his body.

* * *

Michael lost track of time, the days and nights merging. Fever consumed him and dreams of those he loved plagued his mind when he slept. Sometimes he woke to a villager propping him up, pushing a drink to his lips or wiping his sweating body. At other times his moans roused him from his stupor, his legs and arms heavy, unresponsive when he wanted them to move.

One morning he woke to find George sitting beside him. His friend's face was gaunt and worried, but a smile crossed his face when Michael looked at him.

'You're awake?' George asked.

Michael tried to talk, his lips dry and cracked, his words distant to his own ears. He lifted his head. 'How long? How long have we been here?'

George patted his arm. 'Lie back. Rest up. You've rounded the corner.'

* * *

One night, after the women and children had gone to sleep, the village men carried George and Michael on stretchers to a hidden cove on the coastline. A small boat crewed by some of the men from the village made its way towards them. Alaka'i crouched beside Michael and George, patting their arms and assuring them they would be safe. Alaka'i drew a map in the dirt, gesturing how they would sail across the water to Finschhafen. Then he would guide them across the Papuan Peninsula to the southern side of New Guinea. He would get them to Port Moresby, and once they were there, they could get medicine and help, perhaps even get back to Australia.

Getting across the straits was going to be no mean feat. It was sixty miles across treacherous seas with conditions that could change in the blink of an eye. A calm surface could quickly become one where the waves would threaten to push them back to Arawe and the pounding reefs that sheltered the small bay. Alaka'i said that once they reached the mainland, it would take many more days to cross the ranges that ran down the length of the peninsula. It would be a dangerous journey as the Japanese already controlled the areas around Lae and Finschhafen, so they would need to travel further south by boat, avoiding Japanese patrols.

Michael gathered himself and sat up. They had come this far and there was no going back. He raised his bony hand and shook the hands of the village men. 'We will go. Thank you. My friend gives thanks also. He said you are angels, the fuzzy-wuzzy angels of Arawe.'

Alaka'i grinned and patted George's bony shoulder.

Michael tried to stand, but his legs couldn't move, so he took the offered hand of another younger man. This man spoke his native language, and Michael nodded as he listened.

'What did he say?' George asked, 'The only bit I understood was the word Australia.'

Michael looked at George, whose eyes were puffy slits, the swelling and redness in his face and eyelids making his head look grotesque and large on his emaciated body. 'He said he knows the ocean and the mountains on the other side. He said he is strong and will get us to the town of Port Moresby, the only safe place for us to go. He will not give up until we are safe.'

'You will be safe,' Alaka'i said. 'This is my son, Toby, and he will come with us.'

The crew pushed off from the shore, the darkness closing over them as they made their way across the reefs and into the open ocean. Inky water lapped the side of the boat, and the swell lifted them up and down, their stomachs moving back and forth with the movement of the waves. Michael took one last look up at the sky, a bright star shining, its lustrous sparkle drawing him to its light. He stared hard, his thoughts of Gracie and Joanie, as he recited the words from Black Beauty in his head.

My troubles are all over, and I am at home; and often before I am quite awake, I fancy I am still in the orchard at Birtwick, standing with my friends under the apple trees.

His head grew heavy, and his eyes closed. His last thoughts were of a tiny girl tucked up in bed, her curly hair splayed out under her, and her book resting beside her.

CHAPTER 19

US Submarine SS Sturgeon, South China Sea - July 1, 1942

Months spent beneath the ocean had heightened Bud's senses and he listened to the sounds that alerted the crew of an enemy ship ahead. Along with the other men, he went into operation mode, his body tense, his mind alert as the submarine sank deeper before beginning the chase. The SS Sturgeon had experienced some significant successes, and the crew was keen for more, anticipating further action when the submarine sailed into territory where Japanese ships went back and forth between the islands that dotted the area. Now there was a target. The ship they followed was a large Japanese vessel, travelling at a steady speed, its route showing it was bound for Japan.

The submarine cruised with stealth, its position sixty-five nautical miles west of Cape Bojeador, Luzon, in the Philippines. Bud moved to his battle station and along with the other men prepared to wait for the next round of commands. The creaking and groans of the submerged submarine were by now a familiar sensation, and he stood steady as the submarine maneuvered itself into a position to fire its torpedoes. At 2.29 am, after a four-hour chase, orders were given, and four stern torpedoes were fired. The men were silent, and Bud held his breath, his body tensed. The submarine shook as it continued to move forward before diving deep, its mission accomplished. Two torpedoes had found their mark, hitting the intended target 100 feet behind the funnel, causing the oil tank of the targeted ship to explode not long after. It took eleven minutes for the *Montevideo Maru* to sink, the water of the South China Sea covering any trace of the large ship, its human cargo, and its crew.

CHAPTER 20

Brisbane - 25th October 1942

*B*ud sat in the corner of the small Brisbane café, tucking his legs under the table that was just big enough for one sailor to fit comfortably. Groups of servicemen from the Teneriffe, Capricorn Wharf, talked and laughed noisily, their din joining with the clattering of dishes from the kitchen next to where he sat. He didn't mind the racket. It was a welcome relief from the quiet nights spent alone, squashed in a bunk bed, trying to sleep as the submarine glided silently through the waters where enemy ships traversed above.

He soaked in the atmosphere as waiters bustled back and forth, the extra patronage no doubt a bonus when the American men were in town. Being stationed in Brisbane for a couple of weeks was a reprieve from ocean life. The *Sturgeon* was in for a refit and some maintenance work. God knows, she had suffered her fair share of knocks and near misses in previous rounds of operations.

From Makassar Strait to Balikpapan, the *Sturgeon* had combed the seas for enemy ships, the telltale pings of the vessel's sonar sending men running for their posts as they readied for the hunt. Sometimes the tides turned, and they were the hunted, the nervous waiting causing Bud's heart to thump hard as the submarine incurred lengthy depth charge attacks. Overhead threats would send it plunging with great speed to the depths of the ocean, in the hope that charges wouldn't land on its hull.

As the months passed and the *Sturgeon* continued its deathly game of hide and seek, Bud became more accustomed to the cat and mouse games. There were plenty of anxious moments as depth charges exploded, sometimes so close that light bulbs would break, the metal tube groaning and shaking from the impact. Thankfully there hadn't been any serious damage so far.

Life at sea was everything he had hoped for and the men he worked with had become his family. It was however, a relief to have a break from the lengthy stints at sea and the crew were always happy when they were directed to pull in at a town for maintenance and refuelling. The previous stop had been at the port of Fremantle where they had been kept busy cleaning and re-stocking everything required once they were back at sea.

Once they left the shores of Western Australia, the Sturgeon had travelled safely through Australian waters. They had avoided detection from the enemy and continued on, past the coastline of New Guinea and into the waters near the Philippines. The crew had been jubilant when on the first of July they had sunk a ship off the coast of Luzon. It was a large Japanese transport ship called the *Montevideo Maru* and the sinking of it was followed up four days later when they had another direct hit on a Japanese tanker that had been heading north out of Manila. Their tour had been successful, and the *Sturgeon* once again headed back for the western coastline of Australia. They celebrated their victories in style, the town of Fremantle with its dance joints and bars already becoming like a second home to not only the Sturgeon's crew, but also many other American sailors who loved the social life and the woman who lived in the bustling town.

Now, however, Bud found himself on the opposite side of Australia from where he had been in Fremantle. Brisbane was a similar sized town, the climate warm and the people just as friendly as those in the far western state. Raucous social events had been plentiful in both port cities, but now on his last day in Brisbane he was happy to sit by himself. Some of his buddies had gone off to play tennis for the day, while others were on shift, making sure the *Sturgeon* was ready for their departure tomorrow morning.

He relaxed as he sat alone, watching a pretty young girl place cutlery down in front of him. Her words detracted him from his daydreams.

'Penny for your thoughts,' she said, her Australian accent making him smile.

When he looked up at her, his heart missed a beat. She had green eyes and auburn hair that hung in thick curls, its colour warm against the lightness of her skin. Light freckles were scattered across her nose and cheeks, and dimples on either side of her mouth deepened with her smile.

'You're a long way from home,' she said, moving the saltshaker over into the middle of the table. A small vase filled with fresh flowers was pushed to the side, making room for the meal that was about to be served.

'I am indeed.' He turned his head to look straight at her. An older man came up behind the girl as she finished setting the small table. She moved to the side to allow him to place a plate loaded with steak and eggs in front of Bud.

'Thank you, sir.' Bud nodded. He had seen this man on other days he'd been in to eat, and he reminded him of his father. They were much the same age and his eyes crinkled up in the corners when he spoke. The man placed a glass in front of him, Bud's mouth watering at the sight of freshly squeezed orange juice. This might be his last land-based meal for a very long while.

'You look like you could do with a good feed, young man.

Where are you from?' The man's voice was deep and slow, and Bud let the drawling words wash over him. Even the man's voice was like his father's, just the accent was different.

'I'm from Oklahoma, sir. I'm stationed here on the SS *Sturgeon*. She's down at the wharf for a re-fit.'

'You boys are a long way from home. I guess you've seen a bit of action.' The man's words were wistful, and his eyebrows rose up and down as he spoke, his eyes moving around the room, looking at the other marines who were also enjoying the delicious food.

'Yes, sir, there's a lot going on.' Bud's mouth was watering but he was enjoying the conversation and didn't want to appear rude. 'There's always something to do out there.'

'I can't imagine what it's like for you fellas, being below the water. Not seeing the sun for days. How long do you stay under?'

'Father,' the young girl who had set the table interrupted. 'The food will go cold. Let him eat.'

'No, sir, you're fine. It's nice to talk to a local.'

'I tell you what, get Ruby to write down our address. We don't live that far from here and we've often had some of you boys over for dinner. We'd love it if you could join us tonight. The wife's a great cook and she likes nothing more than to fuss over you young fellas.' The man turned, moving back through the doorway to the kitchen area.

Bud tried to call out but the conversation in the café was noisy. 'Thank you, sir, I'd be mighty pleased to have dinner with your family but—'

Ruby wrote down the address for Bud and she interrupted what he was about to say. 'Six-thirty is a good time. The tram comes all the way down through Brisbane to us. Get off at the Gabba and then,' she drew a little street map, 'it's first on your left and then Chapel Street is the one here on your left.'

'Thank you, Ruby, but—'

'Yes, I'm Ruby, and my father is Jack.'

'It's mighty hospitable of your father to ask. The name is Bud, but I'm afraid I'm going to have to say no. We all have to be back on board by sundown. This is my last day in Brisbane.'

Ruby sighed and picked up an empty cup and saucer. 'That's a shame. My dad often asks you boys over for dinner. He and Mother like to extend the welcome and make everyone feel at home.'

Bud looked up into her eyes again, an ache in his chest at the thought that he could have had dinner with a family that might be somewhat like his own. And this Ruby, well, she was just gorgeous. Fate was a mighty thing though and he obviously wasn't destined to have dinner tonight in Brisbane.

Ruby lingered. 'I wish we had met earlier. You remind me of my brothers. Both are up in the islands of New Guinea with the army. We're not sure where they are, but my parents miss them terribly. That's also why they like to ask you Yankee sailors over for dinner. Apart from the fact that they like chatting, they feel it's payback for your support.' She looked directly at Bud, her voice wistful. 'Enjoy your meal. You need to eat that food before it gets cold.'

* * *

Ruby couldn't work out why she was so upset that the serviceman called Bud was unable to come for dinner. There had been plenty of excitement over the last few months as small groups of American men joined them at home for a meal. Her mother loved nothing more than to cook, and the hospitality offered was graciously accepted by men who were far from home and missing their families and home-cooked meals. She was however a great believer in fate and accepted that sometimes things just weren't meant to be. For some reason though, she couldn't get Bud's cheeky grin out of her mind. It was annoying that she hadn't met him earlier.

* * *

Bud stared at the doorway to the kitchen where Ruby had disappeared, hoping that the pretty girl with the beautiful wavy hair would come back out. After a while the smell of steak enticed him to eat and he put the piece of paper with the address on it into his pocket.

He ate slowly, enjoying the fresh meal as he glanced at the doorway, waiting for Ruby to come back out. The United States government ensured that submariners received the best food the navy could offer; the cooks on board were considered some of the most important men in the crew. Tasty food was served each meal to the crew, who all had insatiable appetites. The submarine was stocked well and there was even a small freezer that kept ice-cream ready for serving as a dessert after dinner. The downside was that meals were always rushed. Men had to pass through the small galley in shifts, with usually about ten minutes to scoff the food down.

Today there was no such hurry and Bud ate slowly, the steak melting in his mouth. He let the food roll around in his mouth, savouring the freshness of the meat and vegetables, trying to hold onto the taste for as long as possible.

It was good to sit alone. Life beneath the ocean wasn't too bad, but it was cramped and the living conditions on board depended on the movement of the submarine. During daylight, the sub remained hidden under the water, invisible to those who sailed above. To surface during the day or at night with a full moon was dangerous and rarely done, due to the number of Japanese ships and aircraft in the areas they patrolled. Most of the time was spent below the waves. Although Bud loved the fresh air and the feel of the sea breeze on his face when they surfaced, their safety was determined by remaining obscured beneath the waves, undetected.

Today, even though the café was in a busy area, the air was fresh and clean, and the room he sat in was spacious. Aromatic cooking smells wafted out from the kitchen, and the scent of a woman's perfume seated behind him drifted across, causing him to wrinkle his nose and close his eyes for a moment. He missed the different smells and the clean air that came with being on land.

When they were submerged, the air in the submarine was stinking hot, and he had become accustomed to the distinct smells around him. Unlike the smell of steak cooking and the woman's perfume, the submarine air was a mixture of cooking smells from the galley, the men's sweat from working the engines and the stink of diesel fuel that filled every nook and cranny of the vessel. When they were in port, they had access to daily showers and freshly laundered clothes, which was non-existent once they were back on the water. Nowhere was immune from the odour, and at times, Bud longed for the dusty dryness of the prairie plains back home.

When he lay on his narrow bunk at night, waiting for the tap on the shoulder to resume a shift, he dreamt about the clear blue Oklahoma skies and the dust that covered everything in its path. He aimed to see the war out on the submarines, but he'd already decided that he wouldn't go back underwater again once his duty was done. His life in the navy and below the surface would revert to a farming life. A man had feet for a reason and that was to walk on solid ground. Even if it was dusty and dry, at least it remained still.

Now he watched Ruby go back and forth from the kitchen, her hands full of meals and drinks as she waited on the tables of men in their sailor attire. Bud gave silent thanks that he had come by himself this morning. Wait until he told the others he had received an invite to an Australian family's house and with a beautiful daughter to boot.

He'd keep the address and next time they docked in Brisbane he would look the family up and visit. He pushed his empty plate to the side, gathered his wallet and coat, just as Ruby returned to clean his table.

* * *

Bud nodded and was rewarded with a beautiful smile in return.

'I would've liked to have spent time with your family and of course to talk to you,' he said. 'Perhaps if I store this address,' he pulled the paper out of his pocket, 'well, Ruby, maybe I'll be back here in Brisbane one day and I may just look you up and come for that dinner.'

'That would be lovely.' She picked up his plate, lingering as if she wanted the conversation to continue.

He dipped his hat and nodded.

Their eyes met and they held each other's gaze.

Ruby's cheeks flushed red as Bud continued to stare, his smile stretching across his face. He jumped when someone from the kitchen yelled out her name.

'I'd better go,' she said, 'we're short-staffed today.'

He reached for her hand, the one that wasn't holding the dishes. He gave it a soft squeeze and then brought it to his lips, kissing it softly before letting it go. 'Until we meet again, Miss Ruby.'

Ruby's face turned a dark crimson, and she giggled, a light, cheerful sound that made Bud's grin even wider.

She laughed loudly before turning and returning through the doorway into the noisy kitchen.

* * *

Bud was pleased with himself. He hadn't bothered maintaining a connection with any of the Australian women he'd met while he'd been on shore. Plenty of the other men had though, and quite a few on the Sturgeon had already promised themselves. Sweet young Australian women were prepared to wait patiently for their new love in Fremantle or Brisbane, destined to be the wife of a Yankee sailor once the war ended.

Although he had danced with some beautiful girls, even sometimes stealing a kiss, none of them had touched his heart and it had not been hard to say goodbye as the Sturgeon left Fremantle. Today though, he felt his heart beat faster, his eyes drawn to Ruby's face and a ripple of excitement through his body as he held her hand. He touched his lips, the memory of her soft skin and a faint touch of perfume lingering.

At times he wished he had his sister Beth's ability to predict the future. What would she say? Would she tell him he would return to Brisbane or would she see something else? It had been a long time since he had seen his family and his thoughts turned to them. They would no doubt still be trying to battle with the dust and to keep feed up to the horses.

How they would love this town. A place with lush green trees and large shady parks, where it stormed most afternoons and rain tumbled down in heavy falls. They could sit with him and watch the lightning displays that streaked across the skies or listen to the thunder that rumbled so loud that sometimes the ground shook. It was a tropical delight, a paradise, with no dust clouds in sight.

Whistling a tune, he bounced down the stairs and onto the pavement, stopping for a moment to take in the view of the street. The sky shone blue, and fluffy white clouds scuttled above the red tin roofs of the timber houses behind the café.

The houses were perched on round wooden posts. Their large casement windows flung open to the breeze with wide front verandahs providing a perfect spot to sit and enjoy the cool. Front stairs led down from the middle of the houses, splaying out to join concrete paths lined with flowering plants. Concrete paths were crisscrossed with cracks and joins, leading to rusty iron gates that opened onto the street.

There was something pleasing about the Queensland homes. Each had a similar style and looked like they were built to cope with the hot summers and heavy rainfall during the wet season. He could imagine them filled with families, parents enjoying meals together and kids running around the large yards, laughing and yelling without a care in the world.

Outside the café, the street bustled with delivery trucks and cars. Life was busy for everyone when there was a war going on. He stood on the narrow footpath, looking up at the purple trees that lined the street. He had no idea what type of trees they were, but they were the prettiest sight he'd ever seen in a city. Their wide limbs stretched out across the streets, the grey bark and purple flowers, a vivid accompaniment to the clear sky above.

Flowers from the trees dropped onto the footpath and blanketed not only the concrete that he walked on but also the front yards of the houses and small shops. Purple covered the rooftops of the buildings, the red of the tin peeping through the thick cover as more flowers dropped, adding to the purple hue that covered everything that lay underneath.

The flowers cast a magical carpet on whatever lay beneath. Beth would have loved this landscape, cloaked in purple. Bud turned around, a familiar voice calling out to him. Ruby's father, Jack, stood beside him, a crate of empty bottles hoisted high on his shoulders.

'It's a shame that you're going,' Jack said. 'Maybe next time you're in town you'll visit us. Ruby said you leave in the morning.'

A lady pushing a pram came up behind them and Bud moved over towards the road to give her room to pass. He smiled at the young boy who hung onto the bar of the pram, the child's big eyes locking with his own. The pram bounced across the uneven concrete of the footpath, and Bud moved back further to give the mother more room. As he stepped back, he saw Jack reach out with one arm to try and catch him, but the pram was in the way. Bud's foot caught the edge of the gutter, the fallen purple flowers making the concrete slippery. The last thing he remembered as he toppled over was the child's eyes opening wider as he watched Bud fall. A loud rumbling sounded as a truck came closer. The noise filled his ears, the sound blocking out everything else, making his head feel like it was going to explode.

* * *

Bud never saw the truck coming. He didn't know it had hit him. All he saw were the eyes of the child in the pram locked with his own, an outstretched arm that belonged to Jack, waving in the air and then purple. Everything was purple. Purple was in his eyes, his ears and his lungs. Purple. Purple. He tried to think what the tree might be called, but his breathing slowed, his chest hurt, and a cold, wet feeling covered his body. He closed his eyes, the purple inside his eyelids keeping him awake. Breathing was impossible. He closed his eyes and found peace. The purple faded in and out until it no longer existed.

CHAPTER 21

Ohio – December 1942

*I*t was early December before a letter made its way back to Bud's family. Beth stared curiously at the strange postmark near the Australian stamp. She held the envelope close, praying there was no bad news inside the crinkled covering that had protected the letter over thousands of miles.

Her parents were away for the week, travelling down to Kentucky to her aunt's place to try and get some reprieve from the dust that filled their fields, houses, and lives. They were also looking at properties in the area, and she felt that her family might soon move away from where she and Bud had grown up.

Although the letter was addressed to them, she recognised Bud's writing. There was no way she could wait a week to open it. Anxious thoughts had been plaguing her for a while, and she knew they were connected to her brother. She had tried hard but couldn't clearly understand what was troubling her.

New visions had taken over what she used to foresee, and as much as she tried to meditate and dream about where Bud was, there was nothing—the last time she had dreamt about him had been just recently, on July the first. The dream was lifelike, and she woke up covered in sweat, throwing back the covers and gasping for air. The visions were disturbing and similar to the one she had experienced long ago, before Bud even joined up.

In the dream, Bud was standing under the water, his face sad, but his breathing steady and slow. Tiny air bubbles came out of his mouth and floated up to the surface each time he breathed. He was safe, and she wasn't worried about him, even though he was standing underwater. What terrified her were the noises that filled her ears: screeching noises of metal pulling apart, men yelling out to each other in stricken voices and then the sight of bodies floating around under the water. Unlike Bud though, the bodies weren't breathing, and their eyes were closed, the expressions on their faces peaceful as they floated lifelessly under the water.

Behind Bud, a large ship was slowly sinking to the bottom of the ocean. Giant, colourful fish swam in front of her eyes, their movements causing the water to foam and impair her view. She had craned her neck to see what was happening. Hundreds of men's voices tumbled in her head. There were voices, words, prayers, and even singing as she tried to see behind where Bud stood, his sad eyes staring into hers.

Voices came to her. They were the voices that had always spoken to her, even as a child. This time though, she couldn't understand what they were telling her. The words were jumbled and whisked away with the echoes of the ocean as it gurgled and moved in front of her.

The ship clunked with a heavy noise onto the bottom, and slowly, one by one, the men also floated down beside it. Although the scene was calm and the men were not in pain, the dream left her with a panicky feeling, and she knew that many men were entombed in the ship. It was one of the most vivid dreams she had ever had, and she had peered hard into the depths of the water, but the sea became inky with black oil. When the blackness disappeared, so did the ship and the men.

Bud stood before her, and they looked at each other for a long time, the bubbles still coming out of his mouth. The weight of the water started to press down, and Beth gasped for breath; the difficulty of breathing underwater and an overwhelming sadness at what she had seen caused her to wake up.

She could not make any sense of the dream, and over the next few months she scoured the paper and listened to the radio, trying to find what ships had been sunk or if any events tied into her dream. Nothing linked and she knew that like previous dreams she would have to wait and see what the visions meant.

An envelope with her brother's writing on the front had arrived. She held it, gently stroking its surface. Bud's hands would have sealed this paper and posted it from who knows where. It didn't matter where he was, as long as he was alive and not resting at the bottom of the ocean. There had been so many submariners lost to the war - young lives shattered, families torn apart. Mothers and fathers grieved for sons who were never coming home. They didn't have the closure that came from a physical burial, not even a spot to commemorate where their son might have taken his last breath. No one was there to close their eyelids or cross their hands on their chest.

Beth reigned in her imagination of men lying entombed in submarines and opened the envelope. She unfolded the paper, noting the date on the top. It had been written over three months ago and the return address told her it came from Brisbane, Australia.

Bud formed his letters in a distinct manner and his familiar handwriting warmed her heart. She held the letter to the light, amazed at the many gaps and words cut out from the sentences.

Dear Father, Mother and Beth - I am safe and well.

I am not sure how long this letter will take to get to you but it won't matter, as I will be in this same spot for quite a while to come. I had been travelling well and keeping safe with _____ duties since we left. Life was below deck with a good crew and we were luckier than many _____.

Beth took a deep breath and looked up, trying to take in the words as she watched a whirly wind pick up the loose soil in the yard and swirl it across the bare paddocks, its spiral winding through a wire fence and out onto the brown fields bordering the property.

She smoothed the paper before continuing, the gaps in it glaring at her, challenging her to figure out what words might have been there.

Our _____stopped for _____ in Brisbane Australia, which is a lovely town on the eastern coast. It is quite large and has all the amenities and facilities that one would want. We were due to leave the _____ when there was an incident. It was my own fault. I stepped out onto a road and an oncoming truck hit me, causing me to fall quite heavily.

Beth put her hand over her mouth, gasping out loud at her brother's words.

I will not gloss it over and say it was a small accident, as it was not, and it is only now that I am well on the road to recovery that I write to tell you this story. Many of my bones were broken and I fear my leg may never recover fully. This is of no concern though, as at one stage if it were not for the skills of the hospital surgeon here in _____, I would now only have one leg. He saved it for me and I am forever grateful for that. It is quite twisted though and I will always walk with a limp. The rest of my body is healing slowly and I will be coming out of hospital at the end of this month. It has been a long road to recovery and I am glad that I was able to spare you the worry of it all. Distance can sometimes be a comfort and I am grateful for that, as I would hate to think of you worrying about me.

The hospital is a way from _____ and is an American _____ set in the bush near _____ The staff treat me very well and there are many servicemen from our country who are around me. Many of them are in a terrible way and I thank God every day that I was spared more serious injuries. I feel lucky when I see what they have to endure. The nurses are kind although the matron is fearsome. The food is good and I have started to put on some weight.

There is a family here who have befriended me. The father of the family is named Jack Smith and he reminds me very much of you, father. The mother also, her name is May, is the same caring soul as you, mother, and loves nothing more than to fill me up with her baking that she brings when she visits. This family has become like my own and I know that they also think of me as a son. Both of their own boys are away at war in _____, so there is a big gap in their lives with their absence. They have asked me to stay with them while I rehabilitate as the process is going to be long and the navy has agreed that I can remain here until I fully recover.

There has been a large amount of paperwork back and forth to put this all in place but now I write with full confidence that I am well and being looked after, both here in the _____hospital and also as I begin my full recovery. Of course it is my wish to re-join with the boys on the _____, however I fear that this may not be possible in the short term. Hopefully this wretched war will finish shortly and I will be back with you all soon. I have seen some dreadful wounds and illnesses here in the hospital and it saddens me to see so many suffering, without taking into account the ones who have never made it home.

I hope that you take solace from this letter and even though I am not on home soil, take comfort that I have a family who have taken me in and medical care that is as good as what I would have at home. Give my love to everyone and all take care until I return home. I have had a lot of time to think while lying in the hospital and my thoughts have been of you all. What a lucky man I am to have such a wonderful loving family.

Love from Bud

P.S. And guess what, Sis, I forgot to add that the Smith family has a daughter who I have become very close to. Her name is Ruby.

Beth smiled as she folded the letter, thinking about Bud's words. She was grateful that her parents hadn't been told about the accident until it was over, and it was reassuring to know that a family had taken Bud in and his wounds were healing. However, it was frustrating not to have known that he had been injured and in an Australian hospital for months. She was annoyed that she could no longer predict the future as she once could.

She gazed out across the plains, a selfish thought crossing her mind. At least Bud was safe and not out on the sea, searching for and avoiding enemy ships. She didn't have to worry about him being suffocated in a submarine. His injuries sounded serious though, and it was possible that he may have to sit out the rest of the war in Brisbane. Maybe they would be able to find a desk job for him back home, or surely the U.S. Army bases in Australia would find something for him to do. She breathed a sigh of relief. He was injured, but safe.

She unfolded the letter again, reading the last line. Ruby. A girl called Ruby. She smiled again, folded the letter up and pushed it down into her pocket. Well, it certainly appeared that Bud had plenty of people to fuss over him.

CHAPTER 22

*T*hat night a full moon rose in front of Beth as she sat on the verandah. She watched the golden glow compete with the glint of the largest star next to it. The air was still; the only sound was a horse whinnying far off in the distance. Light filtered across the paddocks and a metal shed roof, shimmered white. The moon became brighter, and she shivered as a dog howled, the moon rising higher in the Oklahoma sky.

* * *

In Canberra, Gracie also watched a golden moon rise over the trees in the paddocks behind her house. She scrunched her face, trying hard to conjure up an image of her father. As the months passed it was harder to remember what he looked like, and she often looked at the creased photo she kept in her jewellery box to try and keep his face in her mind. She ran her small fingers over the picture, tears spilling down her cheeks and onto the photo.

CHAPTER 23

Woombye - December 1942

The shrill whistle of the postman sounded outside the shop. Every day was the same. Joanie counted the minutes until the mail arrived, waiting for information or a letter from Reg. Today the postman stopped, and Joanie and her mother rushed to see what he was delivering. He was an older gentleman with kind eyes that were often sad these days. He nodded respectfully and handed an envelope to Edna before turning his bicycle around and continuing up the street.

Joanie sat beside her mother on the low stone wall near the shop's entrance, her eyes scanning the words on the letter.

Reg Black

Rabaul

Dear Edna and Joanie

This is a short note to let you know I'm alright. I can assure you that I am in good health and spirits and being very well treated. The Japanese are going to great trouble to see that we all have the privilege of writing this note.

Use whatever savings you need and keep my garden watered as I will replant it when I come home. I do have some company and others are busy in the garden. It is with great relief that I can write this note to you - your anxieties over the last weeks must have been great.

Would you please see that the office and friends are all informed that I am still in the land of the living and intend staying that way.

Don't worry.

Love forever, your beloved

Reg – April 1942

'He's a prisoner,' Joanie said. 'And it sounds like someone else we know is with him.'

'What does he mean about the garden?' Edna took the page from Joanie, holding it closer as if she would find something they had missed.

'These letters would have been censored and he's being careful what he writes.' Joanie thought hard. 'I think he means the others, the boys, are in the jungle.'

'He's intent on coming home. He's telling us that by saying to water his garden.' Edna smiled.

Joanie was confused by the letter, which she showed Bill West when he came to visit. It was unlike her father not to fill them in on every detail of what was happening.

'Bloody propaganda', Bill growled. He didn't hold back on his criticism. 'The Japs got them to write those letters back in April and then they dropped them off in bags over Port Moresby. It makes it look like they're taking care of their prisoners, as if they're treating them well.' He went to say more but stopped.

'It's the first letter we've had since the Japanese took over Rabaul,' Edna tucked the letter away in the box with all the other letters and papers.

'Yes,' added Joanie. 'At least we know he's alive.'

CHAPTER 24

New Guinea - December 1942

*M*ichael watched a full moon, a golden ball rising large and luminous over the silky waters of Port Moresby Harbour. The huts he was staying in overlooked the town that had become a strategic point for American and Australian forces.

With the help of Alaka'i and Toby, Michael and George had made it across the waters from Arawe to the mainland of New Guinea. Men from local tribes on the New Guinea side met them when they landed and supplied their group with food for the long journey that lay ahead—the rugged Papuan Peninsula. Three other men joined them, helping to lead them along secret trails that trailed high into the mountains—trudging through jungles where the mosquitos were twice as thick as they had been in New Britain.

The men supported them through the mud and torrential rain that hindered every movement. They tramped barefoot, without hesitation through the muddy quagmire, avoiding or ignoring the leeches and slithering snakes that reached out to them from the dripping foliage lining the tracks. At times the men carried Michael and George on stretchers, their feet slipping and sliding as they climbed a steep bank or traversed raging rapids and wide rivers. Alaka'I and Toby never left their side and kept them alive, providing them with water and handfuls of berries and other fruit they found along the way.

Sometimes the men cut through dense jungle, forging new paths that met up with older paths leading to villages. The villagers would always welcome them and the dry cover at night felt like the plushest hotel in town, the floor of the hut a comfortable bed to sleep on. Sometimes Michael wanted to keep his eyes closed, to let the fevers and sickness take control, allowing him to drift off into a permanent sleep so he would no longer have to endure the pains that wracked his body.

But Alaka'i was careful not to let him sleep and would gently shake his body, encouraging him to keep going. The men led them higher into the clouds, through tall mountain ranges, seemingly impenetrable barriers running through the middle of the island.

Michael tried to remain stalwart, but his thoughts wandered into self-doubt that perhaps neither he nor George would survive the journey. His head thumped, the pain making him writhe on the stretcher as the jungles closed in tighter, the treks steeper. Days rolled into one another, and he had no idea of how long they had been walking for. He faded in and out of consciousness. The only sense of reality was when, one day, Alaka'i pulled him to a sitting position on his stretcher and pointed out through the trees to the grassy hills below them.

Michael's voice was a croaky whisper as he looked over at the stretcher beside him. 'We've made it, George. Moresby is below us.'

George's eyes sunk into the hollows of his head, his body still. There was no reply from his friend and Michael closed his eyes and lay back down, wondering how on earth they had made it this far.

* * *

Alaka'i and Toby delivered the Australian men right to the entrance of the hospital in Port Moresby. Michael held the hands of the two men who had been with them since Arawe. Words could never express how he felt about them and the other villagers who had supported them and stayed until the end.

'We owe you our lives,' he said through cracked lips. 'One day I hope to see you again and repay your kindness. I wish you and your people, villages, and island all the best. May you keep safe.'

A few weeks later he stood at the front of the hospital, his medical release papers tucked under his arm. He waited to say his goodbyes to George, who was departing on one of the ships filled with sick and injured men, back to the safety of Australia. They looked at each other for a long time. George's eyes still sunk into his head, his skeletal body barely recognisable as the young man who had left Rabaul. 'We'll meet again, I'm sure,' George said, his voice barely audible as they shook each other's hand.

'I'm not sure where this new battalion I've signed up with will go. Once this war is over and I'm back home, I'll be sure to come and find you.' Michael did not want to let go of George's hand.

'We'll go and find the best steak place in town and drink a cold beer together. I owe you and those men from the villages my life. Keep your head down, Michael. Make sure you come home.'

Michael chuckled, some of his former strength returned, his face and legs already starting to fill out. 'I'll come back.' He passed George a letter, the envelope addressed to Joanie. 'Make sure you get this to Joanie for me. At least she'll know I made it out of Rabaul. They must be desperate with worry about Reg and the others, unless they somehow have also made it out.'

The men hugged each other. 'I'll see you when you return.

Don't let those bloody Japs get you,' George said as he hobbled away, making his way to where a truck was waiting to take him down to the harbour. He leaned out of the truck window, waving weakly, a smile across his face.

Michael lifted his hand and waved back, his voice a whisper. 'I'll see you when I get back.'

CHAPTER 25

Woombye - January 1943

Joanie held the letter to her chest. The mailman had just delivered it and she turned it over. The writing on the front was Michael's and the letter had been posted in Cairns. She sat on the garden chair positioned in the front yard, carefully opening the envelope and taking out the pages of paper inside.

She took a deep breath before she began to read. The date at the top of the letter was dated a month earlier, *25th December 1942.*

My Dearest Joanie,

I hope this letter finds you in good health. I am sending this letter back from New Guinea with my good friend George, who travelled with me to this town. It has been a long and difficult journey but we arrived here thanks to the help of the natives, without whom I would not be writing this letter to you. I have re-joined a battalion here in Port Moresby and we are due to move out later this week. I do not know when I will be able to write to you again. I am sad to say I have had no word about your father, Peter or Andrew. We were all separated and I can only hope that they too have made it out or are hidden somewhere awaiting the end of the war.

I ask you to stay strong. Hold fast to the hope that it won't be too long before I return to you. I love you more than I can say in words and this love has kept me going through the long months.

You are forever my true love and I long for the day when I can once again hold you in my arms.

My deepest love and longing,
Michael
Port Moresby

CHAPTER 26

Woombye - January 1945

It had been over two years since Joanie received the letter from Michael, and she had not received any news since then. They had not heard anything more about her father and as the New Year was proclaimed, her spirits sank lower. The days passed slowly, every minute dragging, waiting for the postman or some word about where the men were. Newspapers were valuable items and she collected cuttings of the major incidents that had occurred over the years. Not even in the sleepy town of Woombye did they feel safe, with air raids of towns to the north, including Townsville and Mossman, being too close for comfort.

So many in their town had lost loved ones over the years, both in Europe and in the Pacific. Memories of those missing or lost plagued Joanie's mind. It was hard to push the sadness aside; the grief hung heavy, and often she found it difficult to find anything to be happy about. She looked at a photo she used as a bookmark when she was reading. It had been taken in Brisbane, not long before she left for Rabaul in 1939 and showed her linking arms with her friend Vera, the two of them wearing knee-length dresses matched with fashionable gloves, hats and bags, as they walked down Adelaide Street in Brisbane. A photographer had taken the shot and it had appeared in the newspaper alongside an article about the wonderful shopping and social activities there were to enjoy in the burgeoning city of Brisbane.

The girls held their hats, laughing as they looked at each other. The dresses were pulled in tight at the waist, showing off their tiny waists and slim figures, their blonde hair sitting in thick waves on their shoulders. The elegance of their pose was completed with stylish court shoes that were the height of fashion at that time and completed their chic city look. The photographer commented how they could pass for sisters. He was delighted with the photos and posted a copy to each of them. It was one of Joanie's favourite photos and had travelled with her to Rabaul and back. They were both so happy in the photo, and the years living together in the tiny flat that looked out over the main street held fond memories of carefree days, laughter and dancing.

Back then, Joanie had worked at McDonnell & East, the popular shopfront and office situated in the bustling thoroughfare of Queen Street. Vera was a nurse at the Brisbane General Hospital and was her dearest friend; the two of them spending every moment together when they weren't working. Their spare time had been spent strolling through the city, popping into every dress and shoe shop and meeting up with others in the cafes for tea and scones before returning to their tiny flat to try and cook something for dinner.

The years in Brisbane included a whirlwind of working and social activities. They shared their clothes, their hats, their secrets, and their hopes for the years ahead. The major concerns were what to wear to the next dance or how to politely tell another young man that friendship was all they were chasing and not romance. When they celebrated the new year of 1940, their dreams for the future were about freedom and adventure, both excited about what was to come.

* * *

Joanie closed her eyes as she placed the treasured photo back in her book, a terrible ache pressing on her chest as she touched the figure of Vera. In 1943 she had received tragic news about her dear friend.

After Joanie left for Rabaul, Vera continued to live on her own for a while until joining the army, her nursing skills sought after as the war effort intensified.

That same year, Vera was one of twelve army nurses on duty on the Australian hospital ship *Centaur*. The ship had sailed from Sydney with its crew, medical staff and supplies and had been located off Moreton Island, about fifty miles out from Brisbane, when it was torpedoed by a Japanese submarine. Her dear friend, Vera, had perished along with 268 others. Only 64 others were rescued, including one nurse.

Vera's death, along with the memories of others who were missing kept Joanie awake at night, their faces and voices coming to her in her dreams, their whereabouts undetermined, their fates unknown. She tried to keep strong, throwing her energy into the store and keeping the house and yard the way her father liked it, but darkness permeated her thoughts and as much as she tried, sometimes it seemed like there was no future. There was also the responsibility of looking after her mother, which was a never-ending effort to provide support and ensure she wasn't sinking further into a bottomless pit of misery.

* * *

Joanie's mother had been in bed all week, and her room smelled musty and dank. When Joanie entered, she immediately drew back the curtains and opened the shutter windows wide to the breeze. It would be easy to sleep all day and night, to keep the overwhelming worry of what had happened and what was to come, at bay. She knew the feeling herself and constantly fought the urge to curl up and sleep, closing her mind from everything. But that would not solve anything. The shop needed to keep running, bring in an income, and support its loyal customers.

It was time her mother stopped spending so much time in bed. Today was a good day to rouse her out of this tiresome lethargy. She would make her walk around the yard, perhaps trying to rekindle her mother's passion for gardening.

Despite Joanie's best efforts, Edna lay on her side, her eyes glazed as she stared at the wall. She commented that Reg would sort the gardens out once he returned, to which Joanie agreed, but wouldn't it be a nice surprise for him if they were all neat with no weeds. There was no response from Edna, and Joanie sighed loudly. The conversations had been much the same over the last year as her mother began to lose her previous zest for life.

'Father would not want you to be spending so much time in bed,' Joanie berated her. 'I know he'll be hoping you're keeping everything as normal as possible until he returns. Besides, if you get out of bed, I may have a snippet of news. It's not anything major but it may bring us some hope for Father and the boys.'

Joanie had Edna's full attention and she sat up in bed. Joanie winced at the thin body of her once sturdy mother. 'What is it? Are they on their way back? Are they here?'

Grasping Edna's hands, she pulled her to her feet. 'Let's get you showered and changed, and we'll walk in the garden in the cool of the afternoon. It's a lovely day outside.'

Edna's eyes widened, and she looked pleadingly at Joanie. 'He's back, isn't he?' She looked around the doorway and down the hallway.

Joanie's voice was firm. 'No, Mother, he is not back, but I have been talking to some others who were in Rabaul. I'm not telling you anything else until you get up and dressed.'

* * *

Joanie wanted her mother back to her old self. The sadness and grief that hung heavy in the house intensified as Edna sunk lower and lower, increasing Joanie's struggle to deal with the worry of where everyone was and if they had survived. She clenched her hands tightly, her chest tightening, a familiar ache in her body that she knew was caused by the torment of the unknown. She couldn't go on like this. Who knew how long they would wait for news of where everyone was. Over the years they had tried every avenue to find out what had happened to Reg and the others left in Rabaul. Each week, they would ring the Army Military Board and the Department of External Affairs. Joanie knew the numbers by heart and wondered how many other families were also ringing, trying to find where their loved ones were.

Sometimes she met with women from the New Guinea Women's Association. Although they didn't know much more than she did, there was often a new snippet of information she could take back to her mother.

* * *

Edna emerged from the shower. Her skin was pale, and her cheeks shrunken. However, her eyes had regained some of their brightness, and she wore a floral dress.

'I looked in the mirror, Joanie. Good grief, I look terrible. I need to look my best for when your father comes back. Now tell me your news.'

Last week Joanie had talked to the ladies at the New Guinea Association. Some had been in contact with several men who had made it out of Rabaul. They told how the men had walked through the jungle and then sailed by boat to the mainland of New Guinea. It had been rough going, and most of them ended up in the hospital, their bodies skeletal and covered in sores, their physical and mental being wracked with the ills of malaria. But they had survived to tell their stories. Others had escaped with some hiding out on the plantations. There were men, both soldiers and civilians from Rabaul, scattered in many different places. However, it was difficult to get further information out while the war continued.

Edna sat up, the first hint of a smile for many months on her face. It was similar information to what was in the letter from Michael, and Edna decided it was good news and she should start cleaning and sorting out the house in case Reg was coming home soon.

Although Joanie was not as confident as her mother, it was good to talk to the other women at the New Guinea Club, most of whom had lived in the islands before the war. Like her, they had a direct connection to what they thought of as their home.

The stories that the women repeated were horrendous. Tales of men who had escaped by traversing the mountains, their lives hanging by a fine thread as they avoided the enemy and survived on what little they had. There was dire illness and starvation amongst them, and many men had died along the way from disease or malnutrition.

The information shared was sketchy and the stories traumatic, however out of it shone a glimmer of hope. Some men had made it out. Apart from the stories filtering through, there didn't seem to be any trace otherwise, and families could only assume their men were either prisoners-of-war or hiding.

Joanie and her mother continued to write each week, hoping their letters made it through to Reg. Not once over the years had there been a letter in reply.

CHAPTER 27

Woombye – 1945

'We will keep our spirits high and your father and the other boys will come home,' Edna said to Joanie at breakfast one morning. 'The war in Europe has ended and people in Europe and Great Britain are celebrating. For them, the war is finished. It won't be long until the Japs are also driven back.' Edna had returned somewhat to her previous self during the early part of 1945 and hoped that Reg and the others might soon return.

The Germans had surrendered on the seventh of May and Joanie felt that it wouldn't be too long before the Japanese did the same. She tried to keep her thoughts positive, her anxiety swinging between worry for Michael and her father, as well as Peter and Andrew. Often the anxiety about the fate of Jean, Sissy and Mi-Lee and her family added to this overwhelming sense of dread and she kept herself as busy as possible so that her mind was distracted momentarily.

Edna was also trying to keep busy, tidying the house and gardens in preparation for Reg's return. She had even made a concerted effort to be extra polite and patient when Ethel O'Rourke came to visit.

It had been a few months since they had seen Ethel, who spent most of her days praying at the big church on the hill. She had lost a lot of weight, and her once buxom build was now that of a bent, thin woman, her clothes hanging baggy on her gaunt figure. Hair that was once brown and thick was now grey and wispy, and her hands shook as she reached over to hold Edna's hands.

Her voice, however, was still loud and confident. 'The war is coming to an end. The Allies have beaten the Germans, and it will only be a matter of weeks before the Japs surrender. It will only be a short time before our boys are back. I've cleaned out their bedrooms and ordered some new clothes.'

It was the first time Ethel had smiled in a long time, and Joanie was amused to think what she would make of the steamy romance Joanie had witnessed between Jean and Andrew in Rabaul. She took a deep breath, the tightness in her chest making her panicky when she thought about the fate of the nurses in Rabaul.

* * *

Over the previous years, as the war continued, Joanie had tried to find out what had happened to Jean. There was sketchy information, but it was definite that some of the nurses had been taken prisoners, and the word was they had been transported back to Japan to see out the war. Now that the war was nearing an end, they, too, might be coming home.

CHAPTER 28

*N*ews filtering through declared that although Germany had surrendered, Japan had no intention of taking the same fateful path as its ally. They were determined to fight to the death to serve their Emperor. It would be unthinkable to surrender. The leaders and soldiers of the Japanese Imperial Forces considered it an honour to die, and the disturbing news in Australia was that they were planning suicidal attacks on the Allies.

Hopefully, her mother hadn't heard the reports of the enemy's intentions, stating they would kill all prisoners of war, both in Japan and the Pacific. Joanie's nerves frayed to a snapping point. Every time the gate opened or there was a knock at the door, she thought it was her father arriving home or the postman with a letter from Michael. Perhaps it would be a telegram from the War Office.

As much as she tried, she hadn't been able to find out anything about Michael's whereabouts. She stood on the front verandah, wondering for the millionth time where he and the others were.

Looking up to the night sky, she shivered, a cold August breeze passing across her face.

Wind whistled through tall pine trees next to the house and small animals rustled as they made their way around the garden. Closing her eyes, she pictured her father and Michael leaning on the verandah at the Rabaul house, laughing and sharing a drink together. She could hear their conversation as they tried to work out the names of the different birds that splashed around in the birdbath next to the front stairs. She opened her eyes, hoping one of them, maybe both would be walking up the street, coming home, coming back to her and her mother. But the street was deserted, it was too cold for anyone to be outside, and the only noise was an owl that cooed a lonely call from its perch high up in a nearby tree.

Perhaps all the men would come back on the same ship from New Guinea. Maybe they were already on it, making their way back to Australian shores.

They'd have a massive party. Reg could sit in his big white cane chair, mother beside him, their hands joined. Andrew would be dancing wildly, and Jean would be with him, twirling and cavorting without a care in the world. Andrew, as usual, would have had too much to drink. His mother would be scowling at him, working out how she was going to separate the two lovers. Joanie frowned at the thought; Ethel wouldn't change, not even for a war. Peter would meet a lovely girl and he'd be waltzing with her, putting on his best manners.

And me, she thought, closing her eyes. She would be out on the verandah with Michael, their lips pressed together, his arm around her waist as he kissed her, yes, in front of everyone. Who would care? Their men would all be back; it would be a different world. The world as they knew it would be gone and the war ended. It would be a better place and they would have the rest of their lives before them. The world would be filled with love again and not hatred and fear.

She pulled a blanket around her shoulders, feeling better now she was sure it would all work out. She said the date out loud so she would remember and tell them when they returned, how she had experienced a strong premonition that everyone would be back together soon. 'Sixth of August 1945', she said to the owl and the whistling wind. 'Sixth of August 1945. A night to remember because I'm sure they're all coming home.'

CHAPTER 29

Canberra - August 6ᵗʰ, 1945

oday was Grace's tenth birthday and Henry and Dawn held a party to celebrate. Her friends from pony club and school were all dressed in their finest clothes, and a long table was filled with presents they had brought for her. One had even given her a new edition of her favourite book, Black Beauty. Dawn had made her a new dress for the occasion and Gracie thought it was the most beautiful dress in the world. She didn't want to take it off, but her mother promised once it was washed and pressed, they would let her wear it on any day she wanted.

Now as she lay in bed, she gazed at the beautiful dress draped over the timber chair next to her bed. Her parents had taken photos of her with her friends and sitting on her pony. She wished that when she got the photos, she could send one to her father. Not her Papa, who was Henry, but her father. She could still remember him and the tiny photo she kept hidden reminded her of how he looked. The photo no one in the entire world knew about except her.

She'd been too scared to tell her new parents about her real father, Michael. If she did, they might take her back to Layla and then she would be hungry and cold again, left alone at night and covered in bruises from Layla's temper. She had to remember that one day he would return and find her so they could read books together again. He could live with Henry and Dawn as well; there were plenty of spare rooms in the house.

He'd be surprised at how much she'd grown and how pretty her dress was. He'd told her stories about the horses he'd ridden, and she wanted him to see her pony, Misty, and to watch how good she was at riding over the small jumps Henry had built for her.

Sometimes when her parents weren't looking, she could even stand up on Misty and last week she had balanced on his back and turned all the way around as he walked around the paddock. She'd love to show her father how she could do that. As the years passed, she hadn't forgotten her real father, but Misty and her new parents gave her plenty of other things to think about during the day and at night.

Some nights she didn't think about him at all, but tonight as she lay in bed, she squeezed her eyes hard and tried to remember what he looked like. It was upsetting because she couldn't remember his face. She pulled back the fluffy eiderdown and placed her feet on the thick carpet of her bedroom. It was a cold night and she was dressed in a warm nightie and bright pink woollen socks that Dawn had knitted to keep her warm.

She pulled out her jewellery box and at the bottom under some of her birthday cards from her new parents, she found the crumpled photo of her father. The light from the lamp shone on his face and she bit her lip, an ache in her body that she didn't understand, making her eyes fill with tears.

She had only been little when he'd left, and now, she was ten years old, living in a city called Canberra with her new parents and a pony of her own. Why had he forgotten her and not come back?

Why hadn't he talked to her through the stars and the moon, like he said he would?

She looked out the window at Elizabeth's star, shining brightly, twinkling its light towards her. She held the picture tight to her chest.

'Remember me,' she whispered, looking at the star, searching for her father. 'Remember our books, remember *Black Beauty*. Remember you said for me to read to you.'

She looked for a long time, but there was nothing. The paddocks beyond the house were visible in the moonlight and in the still night she could hear Misty munching the lush green grass. He lifted his head and looked towards her, his shape visible in the darkness, as he gave a whinny, letting her know he was there. Shaking his head, he snorted and then went back to eating the grass.

She clenched the photo and held it up towards the star, wishing with all her might that she would hear his voice on her birthday. He would know it was her birthday. She squeezed her eyes closed and wished harder. But there was nothing—no one to answer her questions.

Tears ran down her face and she closed her eyes, trying the hardest she had ever tried to talk to her father again. Nothing. She focused on finding him amongst the sky, wanting to hear his voice, wanting to read *Black Beauty* together. But there was a gaping silence. She started to cry, tiny sobs that made her body shudder and tears fall, wetting the front of her nightie. She held tight to the picture but did not look at it again, instead pushing it into the pages of the book she held in her hand. She wanted so badly to read it to her father. It always made her feel better to read, and she imagined that he still cared and maybe even sometimes thought of her.

A thick black cloud passed before the moon and Elizabeth's star, blocking any light. She tried to find Misty, but the paddock was cloaked in heavy darkness, not even the munching noise audible in the stillness. Blackness filled the space in front of her. The air felt musty and she wiped her eyes, finding it hard to get her breath. Something heavy pressed down on her body and she found it difficult to stand, as if something was crushing her. Gracie sat on the chair, not even caring that she was creasing her beautiful dress. The air in her room chilled, and she looked at the window, checking that it was closed; it was. She sat still for a very long time, gasping for air. Eventually she crawled into bed, curling up in a ball, her arms wrapped around her legs. Her body heaved and she tried to call out for Henry or Dawn to come, but no sound came. She closed her eyes, a dizzy tight feeling in her head. Finally, her breathing returned to normal and the weight on her chest subsided. She snuggled down under the blankets, her eyes heavy as she drifted off to sleep.

* * *

Even when she was an adult, Gracie would remember that night and how she had felt like something was suffocating her, pressing down and crushing her body, not allowing her to breathe. She would question the meaning of the moment and remember the realisation that the stars and moon were not going to talk back to her. She tried a few more times in the following months, but over time she gave up. Over the years her childhood memories became mixed up and not always clear. Some disappeared altogether or were scattered and vague. That recollection though, the memory of the night she couldn't breathe, always stayed vivid and remained with her as an adult. The date also, was etched in her mind. It had been her tenth birthday, the sixth of August 1945.

CHAPTER 30

Hiroshima, Japan - August 6, 1945

As dawn broke over the western Japanese city of Hiroshima, the citizens who lived within its boundaries awoke, readying themselves for an ordinary day at work, school, and home. After a sleepless night of false alarms, mothers woke children for school, workers dressed for their jobs at the factories and military staff went about their training. Overhead, an American B29 Bomber named *Enola Gay*, flew over the city of 350,000. It coasted steady and slow, the pilots focused on their task. Once it reached the required position, it offloaded its cargo, code-named *Little Boy*. Tibbets, the pilot, who had named the plane after his mother, watched *Little Boy* fall, its gliding path a smooth descent to detonation point.

The Enola Gay flew away from the city, travelling eleven and a half miles before the shock waves from the world's first deployed atomic bomb buffeted the small plane, the crew looking back at the monstrous white mushroom cloud, towering high into the sky.

CHAPTER 31

Woombye - October 1945

As the war came to an end, the names of those released from prisoner-of-war camps were available on lists. Every night, Joanie and her mother listened to the radio. When they could get hold of the printed versions, they read them again.

At least none of the men were listed as "killed in action". The lists were, however, still incomplete and there was always a note at the bottom stating new ones would be published soon. Ethel was also confident her sons had been taken prisoners of war and they too would be returning home soon. She had received some news through a soldier who had escaped from Rabaul. He had crossed the mountains of New Britain and been picked up by an Australian ship. He told Ethel he had talked to Andrew after the invasion, not far from Rabaul. Andrew had been with a small group of men who were headed for the safety of one of the plantations.

* * *

Joanie was visiting her friend Loreen, who two months earlier had given birth to her third son. It was good to focus on a happy event and Joanie cuddled the new baby, enjoying the sight of Loreen surrounded by three healthy boys.

Loreen's husband was at work. He had not been able to enlist because of his eyesight and the girls chatted about how he was torn between gratitude that he was safe in Australia and guilt that he wasn't able to play his part in the war effort.

'Working on the family farm and providing food for the people is also essential,' Joanie reassured Loreen. 'Different people have all played their part without leaving the country.'

'You and I both know that, but it bothers him. Especially when he thinks about his school friends, boys like Andrew and Peter and all those who joined up.' Loreen placed one of the other boys on her lap, kissing the top of his head as he snuggled back into her. 'Do you remember what that gypsy lady told us all those years ago, the night of your farewell party, before you went to Rabaul?'

Joanie touched the brooch she wore, a pink rose, its delicate petals made from china. 'You bought me this brooch that night. I took it with me to Rabaul and always kept it with me. I've always treasured it.'

'Do you remember the lady telling me I'd have three boys? The eerie part is that she said the last boy would be born on a day that would signal a great change for the world.'

Joanie lifted her arms higher, looking down at Loreen's youngest baby, who she held, his tiny hand clenching her fingers as he tried to put them in his mouth. 'His birthday is the sixth of August, isn't it? The day they dropped the bomb on Hiroshima.' She kissed the top of his head. 'The world did change on that day.'

Loreen added, 'She also said that my firstborn would be good at puzzles or put one together. He would like music.' She watched her eldest son, Freddie, as he methodically placed wooden blocks one on top of the other. 'She's right, Joanie. He's so clever at putting those picture blocks together, and he's always dancing when music comes on the radio. Maybe she'll be right also that you'll have two children.'

'Who knows? She also gave me a message. I can't remember exactly what she said, but it was something about me going to Rabaul, even if others thought I shouldn't. Do you remember her words?'

Loreen laughed. 'I don't remember them exactly. I was too concerned that I was going to have three babies in such a short time. At the time I thought it would need to be triplets as we all thought the war would end much sooner. Who knew it would go for that long and what she said would come true.'

* * *

Joanie thought about the fortune teller's words as she walked home. The predictions the lady had spoken of that night came back to her and she stopped and thought hard, talking out loud. 'When they say to leave, you must go.'

* * *

She was in the middle of telling her mother about how the gypsy's prediction had come true for Loreen and how cute the latest edition to her friend's family was when Father Patrick entered the store. It always amused Joanie that his cassock, drawn in by a belt, accentuated his paunchy belly. He was a short, rotund man and the large silver cross that swayed from a chain around his neck appeared oversized. His fingers adjusted his white collar, which was stiff and tight, sitting just under his bulging Adam's apple.

Joanie turned away from the counter and busied herself restacking a shelf nearby.

'Good morning, Father, what can we do for you?' Edna asked.

Father Patrick nodded and took off his hat. 'Good morning, Mrs Black. I must say you two have done a marvellous job keeping the store going all these years. Your Reg would be mighty proud of both of you. Have you heard any news of him?'

'No, Father, not yet, but you know what they're saying, no news is good news,' Edna replied, sending a warm smile the priest's way.

'I'm glad you've kept a positive attitude, Mrs Black.' He looked grim, his eyes looking everywhere as if he didn't want to make eye contact. Joanie came up behind her mother, suspicious of why the priest was there.

'Were you after something, Father?' Joanie looked at him, remembering all the empty alcohol bottles stacked outside his quarters, not to mention the stories Andrew had told her about the goings on between the Father and the young nuns who stayed in his cottage for retreats in the pre-war years. That all seemed like a lifetime ago now.

She wondered if Peter had confessed his lustful feelings for her to Father Patrick, both as a teenager and before he left for the war. Now, however, he looked like he wanted something from them, as if he was about to ask for their help.

He raised his eyes as Joanie gave him a defiant look. 'I know I don't usually call on you and I'm sorry I haven't been able to help with your man away, Mrs Black, but there's been many of my own flock to help over the last four years.'

'That's perfectly fine, Father, we've managed.' Edna kept smiling.

'I'm sorry your man hasn't returned yet. I pray he will.'

Joanie stepped forward, her flashing eyes looking straight into his. 'We don't need your prayers. My father will be returning soon.'

Edna placed her hand on Joanie's shoulder. Both women's nerves were at breaking point and Joanie wanted to push Father Patrick out the door and slam the door behind him.

He looked towards Edna. 'I know Ethel O'Rourke sometimes comes and talks to you.'

'She does,' Edna replied.

'It is good that she has you to lean on.'

'Her boys are very close to our family. They always have been.'

'They are indeed grand boys but I'm afraid some news has come through regarding their whereabouts. I'm asking if you could go and visit her. She's doing poorly and no matter what I say or do or the prayers I offer, I fear she is slipping to the point of no return.'

Joanie came to stand beside Edna. 'What's happened?'

The priest shuffled his feet. 'She's had a telegram.'

The blood drained from Joanie's face, her skin tingly and clammy. Her mother also turned pale. However, she managed to keep her voice steady as she asked the priest, 'What did it say?'

Father Patrick placed his hat back on his head. 'She's actually received two telegrams and I'd rather she told you. She won't even let me pray for her. She ordered me to leave the house. I fear she's lost her mind.'

'Where is Percy?' Edna asked. 'Surely she'll take comfort from her husband and listen to him.'

'He's disappeared. The telegrams came and he left not long after. She's no idea where he's gone and we've looked everywhere but we can't find him. I'm worried about him also. I'd appreciate it if you talked to Ethel. I need her to be well for Sunday mass.'

* * *

Joanie and her mother closed the shop as fast as they could, neither speaking as they drew the curtains over the windows. A warm October breeze met them as they crossed the empty street, twirling gusts sending dry leaves flying across their path as they walked towards the O'Rourke's house. Soon it would be November and over seven weeks since the Japanese had surrendered. They had waited for four years for news, but these last weeks were the longest.

'Hmpph, fancy Father Patrick coming here. I mean we've been battling by ourselves for years and he's never come near.' Joanie was annoyed and pushed her hat down harder on her head. 'He's never bothered with us before now. As if his bloody prayers have done anything anyway.'

'Please Joanie, don't swear. Never mind, he's come to ask a favour. At least he's looking out for Ethel.'

'He's only come to us because he has nowhere else to go. And if she doesn't get better, she won't be able to play the organ for his special mass coming up on Sunday.'

* * *

One of Ethel's daughters opened the door and let the two women in. Joanie recognised her as the second youngest, Maria. She would be about sixteen now, Joanie thought, remembering her as a chubby baby who Andrew and Peter used to carry around on their shoulders. It was clear she had been crying, her eyes puffy and red. They hugged and greeted the teenager who took their coats and hats, thanking them for coming.

'I'm guessing Father Patrick came to see you. It's a dreadful time. Mum hasn't left her bed, not since the telegrams arrived. Dad read them and I haven't seen him since. I've no idea where he's gone. He's disappeared.'

The young girl started to cry, and Edna placed an arm around her shoulders. 'It's okay Maria, we're here to help. Can you tell us what the telegrams said?'

'Mum has them with her. I read them though, before she took them away.' The young girl wiped her eyes. They were dark green, similar to her brothers' and they looked straight into Joanie's.

Her words tumbled out between her sobs. 'The telegram said that Andrew has been killed in action.'

Joanie's legs weakened and she collapsed into a chair nearby. She closed her eyes, her head in her hands. Maria continued. 'We have also been told he died at Tol. We have no idea what that means.'

'Tol is a plantation. It's not far from Rabaul,' Joanie looked up, drawing sharp breaths as her head started to spin.

'Not long after we received the telegram, a man called Philip came here to the house. He asked to speak to my dad. He told Dad that Andrew escaped the invasion and made his way to Tol.'

Edna interrupted, 'So he might be safe then?'

'Philip said he needed to speak to Dad alone and he made me leave the room.' Maria started crying again. 'All Dad would tell us is the man said Andrew went to Tol with a lot of other men. They thought they would be safe there and get picked up by an Australian ship. They wanted to get back to Rabaul to save the others. But Dad said something happened and most of them died. Philip was there with the men at Tol, but somehow survived. He said Andrew had been killed and he wanted us to know for sure he was gone. He saw his body.'

'Wouldn't the government know that? Why is there so much confusion around where the men are?' Edna asked.

'Apparently the men were told to fend for themselves, so they went in all different directions. Philip also said many other Australian men had been lost at sea on a Japanese ship.'

'What about Peter? Did he say where he was?' Joanie asked, her chest tight, her skin clammy at the dread of what may have happened.

'He didn't know about Peter. He said my brothers were separated the night of the invasion and although Andrew wanted to go back to Rabaul and find Peter, there was no way they could. They'd tried but it was heavily guarded. They knew if they went back they would be killed.'

Joanie shook her head. It was hard to imagine the pretty town of Rabaul filled with Japanese soldiers.

Maria kept talking. 'He said Andrew tried to return to Rabaul a couple of times because he was desperate to get to Peter and other friends, as well as a nurse called Jean who he had fallen in love with.'

'That's correct. Jean is my friend.'

'Philip said Andrew had a photo of her he carried with him. He was going to make it back home so he could marry her. He said when it got really bad, Andrew kept them all going with his jokes and stories. He talked a lot about Jean.'

'So, what happened,' Edna's eyes were wide. 'Why aren't Peter and Andrew back home here?'

'Dad won't say. Philip said… ' Her words were broken by sobs and Joanie stood up and wrapped her arms around the distraught girl. 'He said it was definite that Andrew was dead. Dad yelled at Mum when she kept arguing with him and then he wouldn't say any more. After he told us this, he read over the telegrams one more time and then left. We haven't seen him since and Father Patrick can't find him. My other brothers are out looking for him. We need him to come back and help Mum.'

Edna took a deep breath. 'And what did the other telegram say?'

'The other telegram was about Peter. The information on it reported he left Rabaul on a ship called the *Montevideo Maru*. The ship was lost, as well as all crew and men on board.'

'He was on a ship?' Joanie's voice wavered and the confusion showed on her face. 'The name sounds like a Japanese ship.'

'It is,' Maria said. 'It left Rabaul not long after the invasion, June 1942. Father Patrick made some phone calls down to the Presbytery in Sydney and was told that at the end of September, there was a write-up in the *Herald*. The report said a ship carrying Australian prisoners of war was lost at sea.'

'How was it lost?' Edna stood tall, her head held high as if disbelieving the information she was hearing.

'Father Patrick said it had been sunk by an American submarine, the SS Sturgeon. The submarine wasn't aware it was carrying prisoners of war. He said …' her voice quivered, and she looked up at them.

Edna's eyes were wide. 'What, what is it?'

'He said… he said he heard there were—' she paused for a very long time, her voice a whisper when she finally spoke. 'There were over a thousand men, prisoners-of-war, from Rabaul, on board.'

* * *

Joanie propelled Edna into another chair nearby. Her face was as white as a sheet and she struggled to speak. 'Were they all soldiers? Were there any civilians on board?' Edna asked, her voice shrill.

'Father Patrick didn't have any more details at the moment. I'm sorry, Mrs Black, I know you've been like Mum, waiting all these years for information.'

'We don't have anything to go on,' Edna said. 'We've no proper news of Reg, although there are stories of men emerging from the jungles, hidden for all these years.'

Joanie added, 'We're hoping he'll be home soon.'

Maria sighed and wiped her eyes. 'Maybe for you, no news is good news. At least Mum kept praying and hoping when she didn't know. Now she has nothing. Both of my brothers are gone.'

'Could we see your mother?' Edna stood up and straightened her dress.

Joanie's legs and feet were like lead weights, her mind numb, as she followed Maria up the stairs to Ethel's bedroom. The hallway was dark, and a musty smell wafted out from every room they passed. 'Mother won't clean. She wants the boys' bedrooms left as they are.'

Ethel lay in her bed, the heavy bedroom drapes pulled so that no light could enter. Edna sat down in a chair beside her, reaching out and gently taking Ethel's hand. A set of blank glassy eyes turned towards them.

No one spoke until Ethel broke the silence. 'Run downstairs, Maria, there's a good girl. Maybe the postman will have been and there might be letters from the boys.'

'You've already had telegrams delivered, Mum.' Maria spoke gently.

'No, we haven't had any news except to say the war has ended.'

'Maria said you've received bad news about Peter and Andrew,' Edna spoke quietly, wiping her face with a handkerchief, the air in the room, stifling.

Ethel shook her head, as if to clear the conflicting thoughts in her mind. 'No, everything is fine and I'm about to get up and clean their rooms so they're ready for them.' She smiled as she pushed the bed covers back and lowered her thin legs over the edge of the bed. She wore a long night dress, the collar high, the sleeves long, her grey hair hanging loose and matted onto her shoulders. Her bare feet shuffled across the timber floorboards as she moved towards the window, pulling the drapes back to let the sunlight into the room.

Maria stood next to Ethel, whose hands were now clenched tightly to the curtains. The young girl prized her mother's fingers away, releasing the fabric. Maria led Ethel back to a chair.

'Mother, you need to rest. Father Patrick will come and say some prayers for you soon.'

Ethel looked around the room, her thoughts scattered, lost in the specks of dust dancing in the stream of light shining through the window. She reached up and attempted to catch some of them as they dispersed with her touch. 'Do you remember how Peter used to like catching the flecks of dust? Remember when he was little, and he'd pretend to put them into a glass jar and then let them out down there on the grass? We used to call him the magic dust collector.' She looked out the window, the green paddocks stretching towards the hills beyond the town. 'I need to go and wait downstairs.' She looked straight at Edna, 'All our waiting is nearly finished, Edna. They're all coming home. The war is over.'

CHAPTER 32

*J*oanie held Edna's hand as they walked back home. They walked past the church the boys had attended when they were younger, past the school where the three of them had shared their childhood and back past the barn where Peter had tried to steal that first kiss from Joanie so many years ago. Neither spoke until they reached the picket fence that Reg had painted a clean white before he left for Rabaul. 'We will always know which house is ours, Edna. The best painted picket fence in all of Woombye,' he had said.

They opened the squeaky gate, Edna as always stopping at the letterbox which she had already checked this morning. She bent down and double-checked, as well as running her hand around the box before peering inside in case she had missed something.

Standing up straight, she pushed her hair back behind the turtle shell comb Reg had posted back for her the first month he was in Rabaul.

'He will be home soon, Joanie. If he were on that ship that sunk, we would have a telegram, the same as Ethel. Every day they are finding men who have travelled in small boats to escape. They will be hiding all over those islands, in the jungle, on missions and the plantations. Look at your Michael, making his way down the coastline of New Britain. It won't be long.'

Joanie followed her mother up the path, her head spinning and mind jumbled.

* * *

That night, Joanie cried herself to sleep again, memories of Peter and Andrew whirling in her head. They were both so young and strong. Peter would have made it to land; he was a good swimmer. There was no way he would have drowned. And Tol Plantation—it should have been a safe place for the men. Andrew was fit and healthy the last time she had seen him. He would have survived illnesses or whatever obstacles there were.

Joanie cried so much that her pillow became wet, and the front of her nightdress sodden from her tears. And where was her father? Where were Jean and Mi-Lee and her family? What had happened to her friends, her New Guinean sister, Sissy? What had been their fate?

* * *

In the next room, Edna listened to her sobbing daughter, her own tears drenching her pillow. She slept wearing Reg's flannelette shirt. She hadn't washed it since he left and when Reg and Joanie had been together in Rabaul she had always kept it under her pillow for comfort. There was a faint scent of something, reminding her of Reg, and it gave her comfort.

Thank God Joanie had come back when she did. At least she was home safe. A million and one questions rattled around in her mind around Reg's whereabouts, her head pounding incessantly, forcing her to get out of bed and place a wet washer on her forehead. She looked out the window, glimpsing a person walking down the street in front of the house. She pulled the curtains back so she could gain a better view. Her heart pounded and she pressed her hand to the window to open it and call out. But the person never looked her way; instead they continued to walk up the street, pushing open a squeaky gate further up the road.

Edna crumbled, her face pressing hard against the glass. It was Mr Small from up the road, returning home from the night shift at the bakery. Was this how it was always going to be? Whenever she saw a man walking up the road, would she think it was Reg? Whenever the phone rang or the doorbell chimed, would her heart leap into her throat? Was this what it was like to lose someone but not really lose them?

She pressed the wet washer up against her forehead. He would be home. He was somewhere safe, just unable to get back to her and Joanie yet. He was coming home.

CHAPTER 33

*J*oanie was serving a customer when her mother came running into the shop, her hands clutching an envelope addressed to Joanie. Thankfully, the customer left straight away, and Joanie stood looking at her mother across the counter. The letter was from Michael, and the return address was on the back.

Joanie's hands trembled and her heart thumped hard. She ripped the envelope apart and opened the folded paper inside. Her voice was steady as she read the words written neatly on the paper.

To my darling Joanie,

I write this letter with the hope that you still have the same feelings for me as you did so long ago in Rabaul. The war has been long, but my feelings have remained the same and my love is stronger with each passing day. I am ill with malaria in hospital in Sydney. I will need time to recover but as soon as I can, I will make my way to you. I long to talk to you and hear your voice. Please write back and let me know your feelings and any news you may have. It haunts me every day that I was unable to get back to the town to help your father or the others. I hope you will understand what the situation was. I await your reply.

As always, your beloved,

Michael

Sydney

* * *

Joanie replied immediately; her main concern was when Michael would be out of the hospital. It pained her to write that they hadn't received news about Father and that she understood how difficult it would have been for Michael to return for Reg the night of the invasion. She didn't tell him the news about Peter and Andrew. She would wait until she saw him in person.

* * *

It took all her willpower and patience to wait for the following letter. When it arrived, the writing on the envelope was different from the last, and she held her breath as she read the first part of the letter. A nurse had written the letter on Michael's behalf.

To Joanie,

My name is Sister Charmaine and Michael has asked me to write word for word what he wants in this letter. He is unable to write for himself at the moment.

Dearest Joanie

I am recovering still in hospital and your words have made me happy to know that our future is still together. I love you as much if not more than ever and I only need to recover some more before I make plans to travel to Woombye.

I have tried to locate Gracie, however, so far I have been unsuccessful and now because of this wretched malaria, I will have to wait until I am better. I send lots of love and I will be the happiest man in the world once we met again. Until then my dearest love, I sign off – Michael.

The nurse had lovely cursive writing and had added her own postscript at the end. *To Joanie, Your man Michael does not know I have written this part of the letter, but I think you should know that his health is dire and even though your letter has made the colour in his face return a little, I fear his health is not improving. He cried when he read your letter and I feel the need to tell you all of this in case you are running out of time together. Sincere regards, Sister Charmaine.*

Joanie's mind was in turmoil when she finished reading.

'Does Michael have any news about your father?' Edna looked up from the bookwork that she worked on each night. The shop had continued to provide them with a modest income and now the war had ended, business had picked up. They had put on a young man who would be a good offsider for Reg once he returned.

'Michael has no news about Father. I'd like to go to Sydney, Mother.'

Edna put her paperwork down and removed her glasses, listening as Joanie told her what the nurse had written. 'You should pack your clothes tonight and be on the first train to Sydney. I'm sure there are plenty of boarding houses or accommodation where you can stay.'

'Oh, Mother. Really? Will you be alright if I go? What about the shop?'

'Don't be silly. Of course, you must go. The new boy is capable.'

'I could be on the first train out of Brisbane tomorrow. I'll get a lift down with the farmer's produce run. You know, Mr Pitt and his truck. He leaves early each morning for the markets.'

At three o'clock the following morning, Joanie and her mother waited at the front gate. Although it was the end of October, the night air was cool. A curlew sent an eerie call from the yard opposite and a pair of tawny owls, perched in the sprawling branches of the Jacaranda tree looked down at them curiously as they waited for Mr Pitt.

'You know your father planted that tree the day you were born,' Edna whispered. 'He watched you climb it when you were little and said one day, he'd like you to get married beneath it. Maybe his dream will come true.'

'I hope so, Mother.' Joanie looked up at the silhouetted branches of the tree, the limbs stretching out over the yard, the stars and moon peeping out from behind the thick clusters of purple flowers.

The noise of a truck chugging up the road sounded, and Joanie picked up her small suitcase and gave her mother one last kiss and a long hug. 'I will write and ring when I can.'

'Give that boy my love,' Edna replied. 'We'll all be back together soon, your father included.'

CHAPTER 34

Sydney - October 1945

*J*oanie held Michael's hand, resting her arm on the cool white sheet that was a stark contrast against the heat emanating from his feverish skin. His hands were rough and tanned, and she held them gently, his fingers limp in her grasp. Staff came and went, bustling around his bed, their smiles forced as they patted her on the shoulder, or passed her a glass of water.

The nurses avoided her eyes and she knew what they were thinking. She had been told when she arrived, Michael wasn't expected to make it through the night. The malaria he had originally contracted when he escaped through the jungles of New Britain had returned with a vengeance.

The matron had written down Michael's service record, adding snippets that Michael had told her. She handed it to Joanie for her to read, the notes filling in some of the gaps of where he had been.

It showed that after escaping Rabaul he had arrived in Port Moresby. After convalescing, he re-joined another unit before serving in different areas throughout New Guinea. During the next three years he had been forced to return a couple of times, via ship, to Townsville, to recuperate after bouts of recurring malaria. Once he recovered, he sailed back up north and rejoined his unit.

As the war came to a close, he had gone with his battalion and returned to Rabaul for the end of the war and the clean-up. That had been the last place he had been, before once again the malaria forced him firstly into the army hospital in Moresby and then back to Sydney Hospital.

Why did he return to Rabaul? Joanie pondered. He had paid his dues, narrowly escaping the Japanese invasion at the start of the war. He could have used his recurring malaria to remain in Australia. There would have been desk jobs in the army, or work available in the supply units. Anything would have been preferable to returning to New Guinea to fight not only the Japanese again, but to front the illnesses and dangers of the tropical islands.

The nurse, Charmaine, who had written for Michael, told Joanie that he had confided in her that as the war came to an end, he had returned to Rabaul to look for the lost men and particularly Joanie's father, Reg.

Although he escaped from the Japanese, he had not escaped the guilt. He told Charmaine it was difficult for him to face Joanie, knowing he had been forced to abandon the other men.

Charmaine whispered to Joanie as she sat by his bedside. 'It's as if he needed to tell his story. He was exhausted by the end and I kept trying to stop him, but he wanted to talk.'

'Please tell me. I want to know.' Joanie said, her mind wrought with worry.

'Your Michael said that when Rabaul was invaded it was chaos and the men went in all different directions. His group was sent further away from the town and therefore escaped the initial invasion. He wanted to return, and he saw another friend, called

Andrew, who also wanted to go back for his brother and one of the nurses. He said this soldier was also someone you knew. They discussed the impossibility of returning for your father and the others.'

'That's Andrew who I grew up with. His brother is Peter and,' she whispered, 'neither made it back.'

Charmaine glanced at Michael. 'He has a terrible guilt and remorse about those left behind. He spoke about your father and the other civilians as well as your friend who was a nurse at the hospital. He said that you had friends among the Chinese and the New Guineans.

'They didn't evacuate any of them. The Australian government only allowed the white women and children to leave but left the rest to fend for themselves.'

'Against the entire Japanese army, by the sounds of it,' Charmaine said. 'He said the order was, every man for himself, and his exact words were that they were left like lambs to the slaughter.'

'I asked him some more questions,' Charmaine continued. 'He was quite lucid that day, plus I'm also interested in the nurses who were in Rabaul. Last month in the *Courier Mail* there was a photo of some of them captured when the Japanese invaded. They were thin, and some very ill, but it said they were in good spirits despite living through three years in a prisoner of war camp in Japan.'

'I knew some of the nurses in Rabaul.' Joanie sighed. 'Did Michael say any more?'

Charmaine sighed. 'He became upset and stopped talking. He was so weak, although he made sure to ask me to write to you. I thought it best to add those words of my own because he didn't let you know how ill he really was.' She patted Joanie on the arm. 'I'm glad I did. He talked about how much he loved you and I wanted you to know how sick he was. Even the matron had started to worry.'

Charmaine's eyes rested on Michael. 'The army padre visited.

He helped Michael to write to his family. The padre said it would be unlikely they would get here before he passed.'

'I won't give up on him,' Joanie whispered as she turned to Charmaine. 'He was so strong and healthy the last time I saw him, with so many reasons to live.'

* * *

The doctor arrived at the ward and nodded at Joanie. Here was the woman about whom this young man, who now lay in a coma, had spoken over the last few weeks. She had come straight from the railway station, her brown port tucked behind her chair. She hadn't left his side since she arrived, her slender fingers pushing the hair back from his forehead, reaching out to take the washer from the nurse so she could be the one to wipe his face.

Shifts changed, doctors came and went, but Joanie sat by Michael's side. The cups of tea and food the nurses brought her sat untouched and the staff ignored the rules and allowed her to stay long after visiting hours finished. The robust matron, who everyone on the ward feared, had spoken to Joanie.

'Talk to him, my dear. He may hear you. A woman's words are soothing for a dying soldier.'

The doctor stood beside Michael's bed. It was the start of his late shift and he looked through the hospital window as the sun hung low in the sky, its dark orange hue visible above the buildings of the city. It sunk below the roofs, the cool night air sending a shiver down the doctor's spine. He had witnessed many men dying from this insidious war, but it never made it easier. They often slipped away at night or early morning, and the stilling of the air outside and the dimness infiltrating the room was a sombre mood for the last time these two young people would be together.

Here was a young man who had given up four years in the prime of his life. He had made it back from the war, and now it appeared to have been to no avail; a beautiful woman, so in love with him, and he with her, and for what? Darkness, disease, the evil tendrils of combat that had ended for the country but had not ended and never would for thousands of Australians and millions of others around the world. He sighed and pulled the curtains back so that Joanie could see a snippet of the outside world from where she sat.

'I'll leave you be, ma'am,' the doctor said gently to Joanie.

'Thank you, Doctor.' Her eyes were fixed on Michael's face.

* * *

The door closed behind the doctor and Joanie felt the tears she had tried hard to stop, falling on her hands. She bent over to stroke Michael's face, the woven grass ring he had given her in Rabaul scratching lightly on his cheeks. Her tears fell on his hands and for a moment she thought his fingers moved in hers. Her tears spilled uncontrollably. She had imagined that his fingers had moved before.

Through the window, she could see a sliver of the moon rising in the city sky. She stared hard at it, gathering herself, determined not to collapse in a heap but to gather up her strength to be with Michael to the end. The sky darkened, and the faint flicker of the evening star appeared in the night sky.

She thought about the journey, Rabaul, and what was supposed to be the adventure of a lifetime. The war had been so far away when they first arrived, and the mysterious jungles and ominous puffing volcanoes were such an exotic backdrop for meeting and falling in love. The last time she was with Michael, they had watched the sky above Rabaul and waited for the evening star—Elizabeth's star, so strong in all its lustrous brilliance.

Tonight, from the hospital window its sparkle was dull, and she drew a deep breath as a heavy dark cloud passed in front of it. She stroked Michael's hand as she continued to watch the sky, waiting for the star to reappear. A raspy voice, the sound so husky and weak she could barely hear it, spoke to her. 'It will come back out. The cloud will pass.'

Joanie could barely breathe, scared to take her eyes away from the night sky lest the voice be in her imagination. At that moment, the star reappeared, its light bright, in a gap formed by the bustling clouds that sailed across the night sky.

She looked down at Michael, his mop of blonde hair splayed out under his head, his brown eyes looking straight into her own. His face showed the hint of a smile as he pulled her hand towards him and pressed it against his lips.

CHAPTER 35

*J*oanie waited for a moment, enjoying the time alone with Michael. They gazed at each other for a long while as he held her hand weakly against his face.

When he closed his eyes again and let her hand drop down, she quickly pulled the cord attached to a small bell, calling for the medical staff. In the office down the other end of the ward, a doctor and nurse stopped writing up their records and looked at the light that signified the number of the room where the bell had been rung.

'I've been waiting for that call all night,' the doctor said, straightening his coat as he stood up. 'That beautiful young woman has not left his side. I thought that he would pass tonight.'

The nurse stood also, straightening her cap as they walked quickly towards the room where Michael lay. 'It's so unfair when he fought so hard to make it back here.'

They walked quickly to the room, slowly opening the door. Joanie's smiling face met them, and they were also rewarded when Michael once again opened his eyes. Michael looked at the doctor and ever so slightly nodded his head.

"He has rounded the corner," the nurse whispered.

The doctor gave a faint smile before patting Joanie on the shoulder. 'It is indeed a good sign.'

* * *

As the night progressed, hospital staff came and went, and by the morning everyone was talking about the young soldier who had fought back from the brink of death and turned the corner to recovery. By lunchtime that day the nurses had propped him up, his parched lips stinging as he took small sips of water and ate jelly, stating it tasted like the best thing he had ever eaten in his life. His words were shaky, and his hands trembled, but every time he looked at Joanie, he smiled and spoke a little more.

Joanie followed the doctor's stern advice to take a break and get something decent to eat. The nurse, Charmaine, who had written to Joanie weeks earlier about the seriousness of Michael's health, ordered Joanie to accompany her home for some food and rest once her own shift was finished in the afternoon.

The usually stoic Charmaine cried when she saw the difference in Michael. 'In all these years, I've seen so much misery and pain. Thank goodness someone was looking after the both of you and has helped your Michael pull through.' She wiped her eyes, grinning from ear to ear as she poured Michael a glass of water. Then she shook her body as if to straighten her thoughts, regaining her regimented bossy voice as she straightened the sheets on Michael's bed and barked out orders. 'Have your suitcase ready, Joanie. I won't take any arguments from you. There's a comfy daybed in the flat where I live with some of the other nurses. They would love you to come and stay. It's the least we can do.'

Joanie welcomed the offer of a place to stay, as she had only napped a little in the chair where she had sat for the last three days. Michael encouraged her to go. 'I'll only be sleeping. The doctor said I'd be like this for a few weeks before my strength starts to come back. You can't sit here for all that time. I promise I will only get better from here.'

* * *

Joanie grabbed something to eat from the hospital cafeteria and raced back to Michael, cherishing the hours they could spend together before she left with Charmaine.

The two of them had only spoken a little since he regained consciousness, any conversation draining Michaels' energy. He asked about Reg, but Joanie said there was no official news and they were still waiting to hear from him. Michael closed his eyes. 'You think you would have some news by now.'

Joanie cut the conversation short. 'We'll have plenty of time to talk about all of that once you're recovered. I don't want you to think about it. I know from listening to others that there was no way to get back into Rabaul once the Japanese invaded. Now Michael, no more. I want you better.'

Later that afternoon the doctor and Charmaine entered the room. They stopped as they walked in, both stunned at Michael's words. His voice was soft and still weak, but his words were audible to not only Joanie, but also to the doctor and Charmaine. 'I want to ask you again. Will you marry me, Joanie?' He held both of her hands in his. 'Will you be my wife?'

Joanie bent down and kissed him on the lips. 'I will, Michael, I will marry you!'

They both laughed as the doctor and Charmaine clapped loudly, their noise causing the buxom matron who strode up and down the hallways like a soldier, to pop her head into the room. A couple of junior nurses were right behind her, and the matron, along with the nurses, also clapped loudly, the room erupting into joyous laughter. Michael lay his head back down on the pillow to rest, the excitement of the moment draining him of some of his earlier traces of energy. The eagle eyes of the matron missed nothing, and she pushed her way to the side of his bed, tucking in the bed sheets again and ordering everyone out of the room.

'Now, out all of you, give this poor young man some time to recover. Goodness me, from the brink of death to a proposal! What a day it has been.'

* * *

Charmaine and some of the other nurses who lived in the small flat not far from the hospital fussed over Joanie while she stayed. They had all become good friends, sharing their own stories about lost loves, soldiers dear to them who had not returned and fathers who had survived prisoner-of-war camps or perished on treks in Borneo and Thailand.

The girls also showed Joanie the paper clippings about the Rabaul nurses who had survived four years in prisoner-of-war camps to eventually return to Australia at the end of the war. Joanie cried tears of joy and held her hands over her face after she was shown a photo of six skinny nurses, all laughing with their arms around each other when they landed back on Australian soil.

Until this point, she had always carried heavy guilt for being evacuated, leaving behind her friends Mi-Lee and her family, their house meri, Sissy, and her dear friend Jean. Joanie could only hope they had all survived the war years.

Now, in the photo in front of her, nearly unrecognisable but definitely her, was Jean. Her name, along with the five other nurses was printed below the photo, the article revealing the story of their resilience and endurance at surviving the atrocities and horrendous conditions that they were forced to live under, both in camps in Rabaul and then through the bitterly cold winters in Japan.

Jean smiled back at Joanie from the black and white photo, her body thin but her face still showing the cheeky grin that she was known for. Jean's sister Isabel, and husband Bert had owned a plantation further out from Rabaul and Joanie wondered what had happened to them. Perhaps, along with her father, Reg, they would eventually reappear and come back to their families.

There were some long and difficult discussions about Reg, in the weeks Michael lay in hospital recovering. It made it easier that Joanie knew first-hand the difficulties of the terrain and how dangerous the trail of escape would have been. 'He wouldn't have made it back out with you, Michael. By the sounds of it, you were near death when you made it to Port Moresby. You have to remember that he was double your age and not that well, even by the time I left. He wouldn't have gone with you anyway and he certainly would have wanted you to do what you had to.'

'I guess you're right, but it's still hard to deal with, leaving him and the other boys. I saw Andrew not that long before the invasion. We met in town while we were getting supplies. Do you remember that big tree on the corner at the end of the street where the store was?' Joanie nodded. 'We sat under it and shared a cigarette. Andrew talked a lot about Jean and how much she meant to him. I saw him one more time after that. George and I met him and some other men high up on the track, not that long after the invasion. They were headed to Tol Plantation. They reckoned if they could get there, the Australian government would have something in place to get them away from the area. They believed they would be safe there. I tried to get Andrew to come with us and I could tell he was tempted.'

'Why didn't he?'

Michael sighed. 'As soon as I mentioned crossing the water and that perhaps we might have to swim, he said no. There was no way he was swimming anywhere.'

'Why didn't you go with them, especially if they were so sure of Tol being a safe place?' Joanie was intrigued by the different paths for escape.

'Apart from the fact I had a bad feeling about Tol, I wanted to keep away from where there were larger numbers of people. When it was just George and me, the local people helped us. They were having trouble feeding their own, but with only two of us, they were more trusting and usually gave us something to keep us going.'

Joanie's voice was barely audible. 'What happened at Tol, Michael? What happened to Andrew?'

'You don't want to know.'

'But I do. Otherwise, I conjure up all different images in my head. The thought of what happened to the boys, let alone where Father is, fills my head.'

Michael took a deep breath, making sure that there was no one close by. It was challenging to tell Joanie the story. 'The details are just starting to come out now, as the soldiers who were up there make their way home. There were only a few survivors from Tol Plantation and it's a miracle they survived.'

'Go on.' For once Joanie didn't worry about him being upset or weakened from talking. She needed to know what so many others had hinted at, but no one would actually come out and say.

'I talked to a fella who had been at Tol. He knew Andrew. He'd been in the same barracks with him in Rabaul. This fella was one of those who made it out. He showed me his scars.' Michael stopped talking and stared out the window. 'Are you sure you want to hear this, Joanie? After this, I never want to speak of it again.'

'Please tell me, Michael. Those boys were like brothers to me. Wouldn't you want to know if it was your brother?'

He took a sip of water. 'This fella's name who survived Tol, was Patty. I guess his proper name was Patrick. He'd made it to Tol along with a large group of other men. They thought it was their best chance. But the Japs arrived and surrounded them, rounded them up and took them all prisoners.' He stopped for a long while, his voice barely audible when he continued.

'The Japs massacred them. The men never left Tol. They didn't stand a bloody chance. Patty showed me his stomach. He had been bayoneted eleven times. The Japs left him for dead, but he managed to crawl his way out from under the other bodies of Australian men who he'd been with.' Michael sipped the water again, his eyes cast down as he avoided looking at Joanie. 'The other men were all bayoneted and left to die where they fell. He's pretty sure there were only him and two others who made it out. Andrew had fallen near him. Patty lay like a corpse among the dead men for two days before crawling his way out. He thought it was probably February 1942 when he was at Tol.'

Joanie gasped, her face drained of all colour. 'But that was right at the start of the war. So long ago and yet we've been waiting for four years to get word. Four years we've been waiting for the boys to come home. All that time.'

'I talked to another fella, called Jack, who had been a prisoner of war at Rabaul. There were three of them from the 2/22nd Battalion, who stayed the entire war at Rabaul. This Jack, he was still there even after the war ended, thin as a rake but alive and healthy enough to help us with the clean-up. He said one night the Japanese guards came for all the Australian prisoners, rounded them up and loaded them on a ship moored in the harbour. He said he was made to carry luggage for the Japanese officers, but then they kept him at Rabaul as a labourer on the wharf.'

'What ship was it?'

'The *Montevideo Maru*. He was positive about the name and said there must have been over a thousand men who were marched onto it. He heard they were being taken back to Japan to be put to work in their camps.'

'That's the ship that they're saying Peter was on. His mother received a telegram saying he was on it and that all men had been lost when it sank. Nobody knows how it went down and there's no list of the men who were on it. There are women who I meet up with at The New Guinea Club, who are still trying to determine if their men were definitely on it.' Joanie's voice was raised and angry tears filled her eyes. 'There's no certainty with anything, Michael. All of us have waited all these years for a snippet of information, just a letter back, to let us know that they're alive. And now you're telling me that Andrew was killed right at the start of the war. In February?' Michael held her hand, his touch doing nothing to comfort her.

'I've dreaded the thought of telling you what I know. You deserve the truth. We all do, and God only knows why the Australian Government kept it quiet, because they also have known for years.'

Joanie continued, 'And Peter? When did the Montevideo sink? And how?'

'I tried to find out as much as I could when I went back up to the islands, but I'd always seem to end up back down in Cairns in hospital. It would either be this blasted malaria or scrub tick fever. The fella Jack, who I talked to, the one who carried the bags for the Japs, said that the ship left in July 1942. He said the word was, and he heard it back through some of the Jap guards he sometimes talked to, that,' Michael stopped, his chest heaving, his breath short. 'He said the talk was that it was sunk by an American submarine, halfway between Rabaul and the Philippines. The Yanks obviously didn't know that it was carrying Australian soldiers, a bloody thousand or more of them. The ship wasn't marked. To the Yanks it would have just looked like a Japanese freighter, running supplies and Jap forces.'

The two of them sat in silence, holding hands, watching as the light faded from the sky outside. The clouds were heavy tonight, blotting out the moon or any stars. A gloomy feeling pervaded the room and Joanie's chest ached. Both boys gone. So young and full of life. Peter and Andrew, her childhood friends. The boys she had played with, laughed with, danced with as they got older and even had romantic moments with.

They belonged back home in Woombye. Andrew would have married the nurse, Jean, and they would have had a tribe of unruly adventurous kids, who would have been just like Andrew. They would have grown up safely in the small town of Woombye, stealing the milk bottles and chasing snakes into tins, swimming across the river when it was deep and running hard.

She put her hand on her chest, feeling the pain inside, remembering that Andrew could not swim and that he hated the water. She remembered him telling her, 'I'll swim in that river or a dam, but never, never in the ocean.'

Peter also should have returned home, even if it was to marry one of the pious catholic girls from town and have ten perfect, little catholic children. He would have been such a wonderful father, a strong family man who would have always done the right thing by everyone. Now they were both gone! One was lying in the mud of New Britain, and the other was entombed in a Japanese ship at the bottom of the ocean.

Michael's eyes closed and his chest moved slowly as he tried to keep his breath steady. Joanie looked at him, her face scrunched up as she scrutinised his face.

'There's something you're not telling me Michael. I can read it on your face.'

There was no reply—just silence, heavy with expectation.

Her voice was a whisper. 'Tell me, please. That man, Jack, who carried the bags, did he know Father? Did he know what happened to him?'

Michael's eyes remained shut. He did not look at Joanie as he spoke, but his words came out softly yet firm. 'He knew your father well.' He paused for a long while before speaking again. 'He saw him in the line to board the ship. He said he got on the ship, the *Montevideo Maru*.'

CHAPTER 36

After the war, Michael's two priorities were to write to Joanie and locate his young daughter, Gracie, whom he had left behind in 1940. She had been nearly five when he signed up, and he wondered if she even remembered him. His story had interested Charmaine, who nursed him as he recovered, making sure he not only ate and drank what he was supposed to, but also ensuring Joanie got some well-needed rest and a break from the hospital.

'I swear Joanie would sit here for twenty-four hours a day if we let her.' Charmaine helped Michael back to bed, his body still thin and weak, but thankfully gaining strength as each day passed. 'She doesn't take her eyes off you.'

'She's been through a lot and now she's trying hard to track down my young daughter.'

'What's your story, Michael? I'm intrigued.'

'It's long and twisted, even before I left for the islands.'

'Try me. I have to sit here and make sure you eat all of this soup. It's quiet on the ward tonight. Entertain me with your story.'

Michael took a deep breath. 'Life sometimes takes turns you

could never imagine, not even in your wildest dreams. There has been a series of events that have taken me in a different direction than what I had intended to travel.'

'Joanie tells me you're originally from the bush. A drover. How very romantic.' She smiled and passed him a glass of water, placing another plate with bread next to the soup.'

'I was only seventeen. My twin brother Dan and I were drovers and taking a mob of cattle from Durham Station where we worked, down through the centre, to the town of Maree.'

Charmaine offered another slice of bread. 'Go on, I love a good story.'

He chuckled, 'Well, you'll love this next bit. When we arrived in Maree, the boss asked us to travel further and deliver horses to Wirth's Circus, the most famous in Australia.'

'Oh, my goodness. I've been to Wirth's Circus. They came to Lithgow once and my father took me. I still remember the elephants and the lions, the clowns and the crazy stunts they did on horseback. You know they even had a man they loaded up and shot out of a cannon. I'll never forget it.'

'Wirth's were well-known and travelled all over Australia before the war. Dan and I were so isolated where we came from and everything was strange and exciting. Dan loved it. He never left. But that's another story.'

'What happened next?'

'I guess I was naïve and unused to women.'

Charmaine's eyes were wide and fixed on Michael, the spoon dripping soup over the sheets as she held it high, waiting for Michael to continue. 'Don't stop now.' She hastily wiped the sheets, popping a spoonful of thick soup into Michael's mouth.

Michael teased and chewed the soft vegetables slowly. Charmaine's eyes narrowed. 'I'll tell the matron you're not eating if you don't continue.'

He finished eating, his voice low and guarded. 'My daughter, Gracie, was the outcome of one night of drunkenness with a worldly trapeze artist, Layla. I left Dan and the circus behind and moved to live in Melbourne with Layla. Those years were times of darkness. All I wanted was to return to droving, to see my family and to never live in a city again.'

'It would have been such a different world for you.'

'It was. We had hardly any money and I worked hard to provide a roof over our heads and food to eat.'

'You were so young.'

'It does sound strange when you say it out loud. Joanie was understanding about the situation right from the start. All she wanted was that once we were back together in Australia and married, Gracie would come and live with us. She would accept her like own daughter. We hoped that Layla will agree to those arrangements. She never wanted to be a mother and had no love for Gracie.'

* * *

The war had changed many lives and like so many others, Michael's soul was restless. The loss of men he had been with in Rabaul, particularly Reg, had left deep scars and memories that plagued his thoughts. The sights and sounds of men left to die in the jungle mud, the recollection of others riddled with malaria and dysentery and the nerve-wracking suspense of continually looking over his shoulder for the enemy, was something he was going to have to live with in his mind. There was also a gnawing hatred for an enemy who had destroyed millions of lives, both in Australia and across the continents.

The deep emotions were dulled however, when he thought of Joanie and the years they would have together as a married couple. They would find Gracie and bring her up together and hopefully also have children of their own. He had also been in contact with his parents who took some convincing that it really was him. They had received false information from the war office and official letters stating that he was presumed dead. Dan had also spoken to him and it was obvious that numbers and names had been mixed up with the translation of documents. It had only been a short conversation with his parents, but he promised once his health was restored he would come out and visit.

Those thoughts kept him going through the long weeks in hospital and now his dream was becoming reality. He was leaving hospital with Joanie on his arm, and they would take their marriage vows. He was indeed a lucky man.

CHAPTER 37

$\mathcal{A}$ small group of nurses gathered in the room usually assigned for meetings or staff functions. The matron and the doctor who had looked after Michael, along with Charmaine, were also there, as were a couple of other patients with whom Joanie and Michael had become friends. The room was decorated, and the table was full of food and drinks, with a colourful cake in the centre, as the group celebrated with the couple as they prepared to leave the hospital.

'Don't let us see you ever come back here now, young man,' the burly matron said, giving Michael an affectionate hug. 'You look so much stronger compared to only weeks ago when we thought we were going to lose you.'

No words could adequately express Michael and Joanie's gratitude for the care Michael had received. They shook the doctor's hand and said goodbye to the nurses, promising they would never forget any of them.

* * *

They had decided to get married quietly before returning to Woombye. 'We can have a bigger wedding later,' Joanie said. 'It will be easier for Mother, with Father not here. We'll wait and see if anything changes over the coming months. You never know.'

Michael smiled but his heart was heavy. Joanie was still not convinced that her father was not going to return, while he had resigned himself to the news that Jack had told him. Jack knew Reg and Peter and had seen both boarding the ship. He had told Michael that Reg had staggered along the wharf and gangplank, held up by Peter and one of the men from the post office whose name was Thomas. Reg hadn't looked well, and Jack suspected that he had malaria, to go with the malnutrition that they were all suffering from. 'He could hardly walk,' he told Michael. 'The lot of them were a bloody mess, even before they got on that boat. God knows what they suffered when it went down. They crammed them on there. I watched them board and then they all disappeared below the decks. It would have been crowded and there were many men like Reg who weren't well.'

'Do you believe the story that the ship was sunk?' Michael asked.

'There were plenty of rumours over the next couple of months. The Jap guards talked about what had happened and there was another Australian fella left in Rabaul with me, who knew a bit of their language. He said that some of the Japanese crew from the ship made it to one of the islands but were then captured by the Allies on the islands and killed. Another Australian fella with me in Rabaul, he had a different story. He reckoned the ship took all the men out to an island and they just did away with the whole lot of them. He seemed to think that the ship went out and then returned not long after without any of them. There were stories that they'd all been beheaded, that they weren't any use to the Japs, so they did what they always did. They got rid of them.'

'What do you think happened?'

'I believe that the ship was sunk by the Yanks. One day the

truth will come out. Those submarines have their own records. After everything calms down and war departments here and overseas get their records sorted, we will find out what happened. In my mind, the ship went down, and all our men went with it.'

Michael was gutted, his mind plagued by thoughts about how the men had died, either drowning or being slain like Andrew at Tol Plantation.

'It's amazing that any of us made it back,' Jack said. 'I heard stories about you fellas too. That you walked right down the coastline and over those bloody mountains. They say you were like the walking dead. Skeletons putting one foot after the next.' He shook his head. 'You're bloody mad, you fellas who came back up after escaping the first time. Returning to fight again, to put yourself back into the firing line of the Japanese.'

'If it weren't for the natives of New Guinea, we'd all be lying in unmarked graves up in those mountains. I could have come straight back to Australia once we'd got to Moresby. My mate George did.' He shook his head. 'Poor George, he was in a worse state than me. He was so convinced the bloody government was going to send help. Anyway, he made it back. My aim was always to get back to Rabaul. If I stayed up in the islands, I knew there'd come a day when the war would end and I could get back there. Perhaps some of the men might still be there. Maybe in camps or left to work for the Japs.'

'There was no one left, only a few of us. The nurses, the missionaries, all the officers, they'd all gone. They were all put on another ship and taken back to Japan. You can hardly believe they survived. Some of them are back home now. Those nurses,' he shook his head. 'it's unbelievable what they endured. The stories are horrific. The women,' his eyes filled with tears, 'they were stalwart, looking after the men and then surviving the ship journey only to be put through more torture and shocking conditions.'

'So much misery and the agony of not knowing for the families back home. It is a miracle that anyone lived.' Michael said.

Deep down, he knew that the men were lost.

Somehow, he had made it through. Not only from Rabaul and New Guinea, but also from the clutches of malaria. The despicable disease that took so many other young men who had lain in hospital beds next to him. He was one lucky man. There was only one thing left to do and that was to locate his young daughter, Gracie.

CHAPTER 38

*C*harmaine and the Matron had been witnesses to Joanie and Michael's marriage. They had gathered at the Registry Office at City Hall for a short and practical ceremony. To Joanie and Michael, it was perfect. They did not want to waste another second, and there were tears of joy as they were pronounced man and wife. Michael took Joanie in his arms, and the small group clapped and cheered as the bride and groom had a very lengthy wedding kiss.

Joanie hugged Charmaine. If it hadn't been for Charmaine, she may not have travelled to Sydney so quickly. Charmaine and the group of friends she had stayed with reminded her of Jean. She often thought of Jean, young, and so excited about taking up the position in Rabaul. Was she aware that Andrew had been slain at Tol Plantation, or was she, too, sifting through news reports and questioning others, hoping to discover his fate?

The paper clipping about the released nurses was tucked away in her bag and she often took it out, peering at their familiar faces. Her eyes always came to rest on Jean and her smiling face. She had been a good friend and they had shared secrets and their dreams about the men they had both fallen in love with. Her thoughts turned to her other friend, Vera, whose vibrant life was tragically cut short.

Just like Jean, she had been fun-loving, high-spirited, and mischievous. Above all, the two of them were caring and dedicated in looking after others.

One nurse had lived, and one hadn't. She pondered on that fact. How random life was. What made it that one man survived while the one next to him didn't? You would think that nursing in New Guinea would have been more dangerous than nursing on the Australian hospital ship, *Centaur*. Memories of others she had known jumbled her mind: those who had perished, who had given their today so that she and millions of others could live for tomorrow.

It was a miracle that the nurses had survived the conditions they endured in the POW camps. Joanie decided that once she had helped Michael locate Gracie, she would find where her good friend Jean was, and write to her. Perhaps she would know more about Reg and Peter. She may even have information on Mi-Lee and her family. There had been no news about the Chinese people who had been left to the mercy of the Japanese and Joanie feared what their fate had been.

Deep down, she tried hard to deal with the news Michael had told her about her father. The thought that he may not come home was starting to sink in. All the waiting, the years of listening to the prisoner's names, the hope that one day he would come walking through the door to resume his old life now seemed an impossibility. She questioned Michael further, suggesting different options for where he might be. But Michael was resolute about what he had told her. He had been kind, but firm, and she knew he was convinced from what he had heard, that her father, along with Peter, had both been on the Montevideo Maru.

It would be difficult to tell her mother the latest devastating snippets of news. Perhaps she'd keep it to herself for a while and not divulge the information when she wasn't completely sure of its accuracy. Edna might have heard more during the weeks Joanie had been in Sydney. Christmas was around the corner and service members were arriving back home all the time. Some had been evacuated from islands where they had been hiding, and others had been found in the jungles throughout the Pacific. But their numbers were small, and as the weeks passed it seemed that those who had made it through the war, were already home.

* * *

Joanie rang her mother to let her know she had married Michael and that they would be home after a couple of days staying on the coast south of Brisbane.

Edna understood their decision. Joanie did not want to walk down the aisle on anyone's arm except Reg's, so a civil service suited them all. 'Mother's fine with it,' Joanie told Michael. 'She said she's trying to stay positive and have the shop running for when father comes back. She'd spoken to some of the men at Burns Philp and they said there's a rumour that some of their men have been hiding at one of the missions for the duration of the war.'

Michael shook his head. 'There're stories going around every-where. You have to remember that Jack was positive he saw your father and Peter getting on that ship.'

Joanie hugged him. 'I know, Michael. But you never know, he might still be out there.'

* * *

The day before Joanie and Michael were due back, Edna busied herself, tidying the house and making sure the garden was trimmed and neat. She heard the postman come and go, and as usual she rushed to the mailbox. The container for the mail was a large milk can, and today she could see that whatever had been put in there was taking up the entire can. She grabbed the contents and pulled it out, not registering what she was holding.

A large rubber band held the bundle of letters together and she stared for a long while, confused by the parcel. She blinked and then closed her eyes, a clammy sensation creeping over her body, her hands shaking uncontrollably. She pulled the rubber band away, some of the letters falling to the ground as she frantically turned others over to see the back of them. Crouching down, she picked one up, and then another. The postmarks on the back and the dates showed when they had all been written. It was all the letters she had written to Reg over the four long years of waiting.

All of them were addressed to her Reg and all were from Joanie or herself. Now they had been delivered back to her letterbox – *RETURN TO SENDER*, stamped on the front of each envelope. For the last four years, she had written continually, filling him in on what they were doing and the home front news. And now, they were returned, unopened, back to her. She sank onto the steps, a tightness in her head blurring her vision. A heavy realisation pressed down and she clasped the letters to her chest.

CHAPTER 39

*E*dna tried to push the heavy sadness aside as she welcomed Joanie and Michael home. There was no need to tell Joanie about the returned letters at the moment. It would be better to rejoice that Michael had survived his illness and that he and Joanie were now married. It was the first time she had met the young man whom she had heard so much about, and his return and recovery from near death was something to celebrate. After so much sadness, the young couple's recent marriage was a shining point of happiness and for the first time in many years, they all had something to be grateful for. The three of them sat together, soaking in the moment.

The wedding was not the grand affair that Reg and Edna had once dreamed of for Joanie. As their only daughter, they had envisioned a large family gathering, with Reg proudly walking Joanie down the aisle of the same Woombye Hall they were married in. Or perhaps a simple service under the shade of the Jacaranda tree in the front yard. But Reg was not here and this new young man who Edna had taken to from the moment she met him, was now Joanie's husband.

Joanie, a beacon of resilience, deserved happiness in her life. She had endured the heartache of leaving Reg in Rabaul and the loss of her dear friends, Peter and Andrew. The presence of a man in the house, one who showed a keen interest in learning the business of the shop, was a welcome change. Edna couldn't help but feel a glimmer of hope for Joanie's future.

That night at dinner, they listened intently to Michael's story of endurance and escape. How he had escaped the Japanese and then the jungles of both New Britain and New Guinea, beggared belief.

'This war has left many families in tatters,' Edna said. 'What matters is that you are happy. I hope now that you have wed Joanie, your next step will be to find your little Gracie and bring her back here to live with us. The cottage next door is for you and Joanie. Reg always said that was what he wanted.'

The three of them chatted until late, Joanie and Michael finally making their way back to their new home. Edna had been busy over the last couple of days and had set it up with extra furniture, making sure that they were comfortable and settled in.

Today had been a big day and Edna also retired for the night; as she did every night, taking Reg's old shirt from under the pillow and tucking it up next to her body. The bed was big and empty without him, and the tears came just like they always did. She pictured him sitting on the verandah and serving customers in the store. She glanced over to the empty space beside her, remembering his soft voice and the way they would lie together and talk about their future, their life in Woombye and mostly about Joanie.

She wanted to tell him that she agreed with him, that the young man their daughter had fallen in love with was just as wonderful as Reg had written about in his letters that had arrived before the invasion. He needed to know that they were now married and going to live right next door to Edna and work in the store. She wouldn't be as lonely with them there and living so close to her would be a help with the business. She pushed her head further into Reg's shirt, the material wet from her tears.

Closing her eyes, she visualised his face, his kind eyes and tender hands.

The wine they had shared over dinner dulled her nerves a little tonight and she fell into a heavy sleep, salty tears drying on her face.

CHAPTER 40

*E*dna and Joanie's small piece of happiness was shattered the next day with the arrival of the telegram boy. He rang his bell on his bike, sending Edna and Joanie from next door, both hurrying down their respective concrete paths to the letterbox. The boy looked from one to the other, finally handing over the telegram to Edna. Michael was slower to appear, unused to the daily routine of waiting for the mail. He watched anxiously from the small verandah of the cottage that was now his home.

Joanie quickly unlatched the front gate and made her way to Edna, who sat on the rock wall in the front yard. She opened the telegram and held it out so that Joanie could also see it.

It is with deep regret that I have to inform you that the transmission of the nominal roll of the Japanese vessel, Montevideo Maru, which was lost with all personnel after leaving Rabaul in June 1942 shows that, Reginald Black, was aboard the vessel and I desire to convey to you the profound sympathy of the Commonwealth Government.

Minister for External Territories.

CHAPTER 41

Woombye to Bundeen Station - 1947

Michael was kept busy after his return to Woombye. Although some days he would have preferred to stay in bed and let sleep pass away the hours, he pushed himself to get up. He needed to be strong and carry on, to not allow himself to wallow in memories and regrets. He battled to keep the darkness from smothering him. The days weren't just about him, there was Joanie and Edna to also consider.

Thank goodness his health was improving, a fact he attributed to Joanie's good cooking and the fresh vegetables Edna grew in the backyard veggie patch. His arms and legs had filled out, and his strength had returned, allowing him to do the heavy work around the house and business. Daytime hours were occupied with learning the different practices of the store and implementing some new ideas of his own. Once life settled into some sort of routine, he started to talk to Joanie about Gracie, and how they could try to locate her.

She would be twelve by now and it was difficult to imagine

what she might look like, or how much she would have grown in the years he had been away. Numerous phone calls were made to try and track down anyone who might have some details about where the child's mother, Layla, had gone once she left Melbourne. Edna was also relentless in helping with his search. 'It takes my mind off Reg and I won't stop until we find your Gracie. She has to be out there somewhere.'

Edna had a knack for obtaining information, and it didn't take her long to find that Layla had died only four years after Michael left for New Guinea, not long before the end of the war.

Michael's gut churned when Edna relayed this latest information. It was not the sadness of her passing but the dread of what had happened to Gracie once her mother had gone. Layla had no family that he was aware of and no one she had been close to. The search for any family she may have ended in a dead end, and as much as they investigated, wrote, and phoned every department they could find, there was no trace of Gracie.

Michael contacted the adoption department, looking for children who had been fostered or adopted. He gave both names, Gracie De Souza and Gracie McTavish. There was no trace though, and he became more and more despondent, frustrated that his beautiful young daughter had disappeared without a trace.

Perhaps with his search stalled and while he waited for further information, it would be a good time to visit his parents and brothers in Western Queensland. He had not seen them since he left home as a young man, before the war. He would travel by himself and Joanie could stay with her mother to take care of the store. This was a trip he needed to make by himself.

* * *

Travelling by car was a much quicker mode of transport than the last time he travelled this way on horses. The roads had improved and in no time he was well on his way to Longreach, where he tracked down Wirth's Circus, still one of the largest in Australia. It wasn't hard to locate the big tents, the fluttering flags and colourful signs a strange sight after all these years of war. Michael's twin brother, Dan, was now the big boss, and along with his wife, Audrey, led a troupe of performers and a menagerie of animals that travelled the length and breadth of Australia.

The circus had been laid up throughout the war but was now back in full swing, doing the rounds of the country towns and cities, just like it had so many years ago. He reminisced; it had been fourteen years since Dan and he had been drovers, pushing a mob of cattle down through the middle of Queensland into South Australia and then delivering them to the stockyards in Maree. Further work with a mob of horses had led them to Broken Hill, and then onwards to the first circus they had ever seen.

His brother and Audrey—the beautiful bare-back trick rider— had met when the boys had first arrived. They had stayed together and married, not long after Michael had left.

It was an emotional meeting when the twin brothers greeted each other after so many years apart and Michael picked Audrey up, swinging her around, her squeals of delight, music to his ears. He fell in love with their five children, watching proudly as they performed tricks for him on their stout ponies that cantered obediently around the ring. Memories flooded back. The ponies they rode were much like the ones he and Dan had used, performing tricks in the dusty paddocks back home, their mother looking on from the doorway, waiting for them to break their bones or split their heads open. The memories were from another lifetime, a time in a different world.

Dan and Audrey wanted to know everything that had happened to him since they had last seen him. They listened to his story, amazed that he had lived to tell the tale and excited that it ended with his marriage to Joanie. Audrey ushered the children away so that the adults could talk. 'We've tried to find information for you about where Layla lived once she left the flat in

Melbourne,' she explained. 'The only record we could turn up was an old address from her parents, and I know you've already looked into that.'

Dan added, 'There's no trace of her once she left Melbourne, the only record being her death, four years later in Sydney.'

After a week of visiting, Michael left Dan and his family. He travelled by car back along the tracks that he had tramped over as a drover, following the roads to the small homestead where his mother and father still lived. There were tears for everyone when the three of them re-united, the hugs long, their smiles wide. It had also been over thirteen years since they had seen each other, and he was no longer the wide-eyed teenager they still affectionately called Kee Kee.

Over the week he stayed with them, Michael reminisced about the days growing up in such a remote area. As a kid he had loved roaming with the cattle. A simple life, with happy memories and what he had longed for, the peace and solitude of the outback. Through the years of living in the crowded streets of Melbourne and then the tropics of New Guinea, home was always this tiny house, set in the middle of nowhere and filled with an abundance of love.

His eldest brother Rory had never left and still lived nearby. He came to visit with his wife and their four boys and there was raucous noise and laughter as the two brothers re-united after so many years. It was a special feeling being surrounded by family. Rory's boys were boisterous and loud, reminding Michael of his own younger brothers. Sometimes he thought he could feel their presence, as if they were sitting on the chair near the stove, waiting for their mother's biscuits to bake or standing near the window, looking out as a line of storms thundered on the horizon. He rubbed his eyes and shook his head—memories and voices from the past recurring in his mind.

His mother, Edith, hardly let him out of her sight all week. One afternoon she stood with him as they looked at the army photos of his younger brothers, Frank, and Lachie. Their pictures took pride of place on her dining room wall and next to them were their service medals, the bronze stars and colourful ribbons they hung from, a reminder of their service to the Australian forces in World War II.

Edith sat on the couch. Her blonde hair had once been similar to Michael's, but now streaks of grey peppered it, her brown eyes lacking the spark they once had. He sat next to her and she passed him photos and letters from the two boys, some written not long before they had both been killed in action. Frank, the elder of the two, had trained down in the Adelaide Hills and then in Palestine before becoming part of the now well-known, 'Rats of Tobruk'. Edith had a photo that had been given to her that showed a wooden cross, one of hundreds of other crosses in the Tobruk War Cemetery in Libya. She pointed to a block monument with a large cross on it. 'That is a memorial that was built by the Australian forces. The cemetery is where the Australians were laid to rest.'

This was Frank's final resting place as far as she was concerned and where she imagined his body lay, along with thousands of other young Australian soldiers. 'They sleep together,' Edith said. 'He is at peace. That is the best thought I can keep.'

It pained Michael to think how much his mother had suffered in her life. She was only in her early fifties, but she and Hamish had not only suffered the loss of their tiny daughter, Elizabeth, before she had even turned one, but now both of their younger sons had not returned from the war. No wonder she hung onto Michael when they walked around the property, or sat close to him at night, her hand always on his arm.

Michael ran his hand over the photo of Lachie, the baby of the family. Bright eyes looked out from under the slouched hat turned up on one side, the rising sun badge pinned to the brim. He had only been nineteen when he signed up, and in the photo he looked more like a sixteen year old farm boy. 'He always had such a mischievous grin,' Michael said, wiping his eyes with the back of his hand.

'All you boys look similar,' Edith said. 'He has the same mop of blonde hair as you and those great long eyelashes.'

'He and Frank were too young to die, Mother. So many lost, both in Europe where Frank lies, and thousands of others up in the islands.'

'I know. Lachie was up in Malaya and then Singapore. Occasionally I'd get a letter or photo sent back.' Edith pulled out a couple of tiny black and white photos. Photos of Lachie with a couple of other men, the three of them standing together, smiling and smoking cigarettes. They all looked fit and healthy, their sleeves rolled up and their clothes dirty, just as if they had been working out in the paddocks here at home.

She closed her eyes. 'When Singapore fell, he was taken prisoner. They moved them to Changi and then the Thailand-Burma Railway.' Michael's body ached, his mother's torment almost too much to bear.

'Dan told me what happened, Mum.'

Edith straightened her shoulders and stood tall. 'They'll always be my babies. No one can take those boys away from my heart.'

Edith tucked the photos and letters back in a tin, closing the lid gently and resting it on her lap. 'I still have the two letters we received from you when you were in Rabaul. They're in a box under my bed with some other things that belonged to you. I never thought Lachie wouldn't come back. I worried more about Frank over in Africa, and I never slept, wondering where you were. But Lachie, he was so fit and strong, so young, and I just thought he would survive anything.'

'Michael put his arm around his mother's shoulder, her chest heaving with the difficulty of talking about her boys.'

'It's hard, Mum. For both you and Dad. It's bloody hard.'

Edith looked at him, her eyes sad, her face etched with lines of worry and hardship. 'My heart is broken, Michael.'

CHAPTER 42

$\mathcal{T}$he next day, Edith was in a lighter mood, and Hamish helped her dish out a big breakfast, with extra plates on the table for two of Rory's boys who joined them.

'These two young ones are hanging around a bit,' Michael said, playfully punching the youngest one in the arm.

'C'mon Uncle Kee Kee, we'll take you on,' the two youngsters said, jumping and climbing over Michael, who picked them both up and wrestled with them until they gave up. Edith's eyes followed the boys. It didn't seem that long ago that all her boys had been that young.

Hamish watched the young boys, too, and Michael knew his memories were the same: visions of a house filled with noisy, energetic boys.

Michael put the two young nephews back down in their chairs, ruffling their hair as they waited for breakfast to be served. Perhaps his own younger brothers would pop out from one of the other rooms at any moment, jump on him, wrestle and tussle one another until they were all exhausted.

Edith broke the silence as the adults grappled with their own thoughts and emotions. Her voice was shaky and she struggled to hold back her tears. She held up her cup of tea, in a toast to Michael. 'After all these years, Michael. We waited and waited for you. I knew you'd be here one day and we could talk and laugh, just like the old days.'

Michael clinked his cup with hers and his father's, laughing as the two youngsters also held theirs up to chink against the other cups.

For many years, Hamish and Edith believed Michael had been taken prisoner of war. Official letters from the war department had arrived, sometimes a month after being posted, but their information was clear. The first letter stated Michael had been captured, and a second round of communication stated he was presumed dead. They had mourned for him. Another son who wouldn't return, his loss hard to bear because they hadn't seen him since he had left for the town of Maree so many years earlier.

For years Edith had been unable to say Michael's name out loud or to look at the few photos they had of him. There were only a few belongings he had left behind when he left to work at Durham Downs, and she packed them away in a box and kept them under her bed. She had made herself a promise to never look at them, but just to let them stay underneath her body where she slept at night.

The loss of three sons was unbearable and Rory told Michael that Edith would walk for hours across the plains, not returning until the sun was low in the sky. Sometimes Hamish went to look for her and tracked her down miles from home, perched on rocky outcrops, sitting, staring across the vast plains to the west. A couple of times he brought her back on the back of his horse, her arms wrapped around him as she sat silently on the rump of Hamish's horse.

They all knew she was searching, waiting, watching for her boys, men who would never return. And then the day came when Dan was contacted by the hospital in Sydney. The information they passed on was that now the war had ended, Michael had returned from New Guinea. He was, however, gravely ill.

There was confusion over the information, and no one believed what they were being told until Dan investigated the situation further. He had managed to speak to a nurse called Charmaine at the hospital, who brought Michael to the phone. He was in a wheelchair and still weak, but he had talked to Dan and assured him that he had survived and was recovering, slowly but surely. Michael was saddened to hear his parents had been given false information. The fact was, he was alive and back in Australia.

Dan had hung up and yelled so loudly that his wife and children came running to see what was wrong. He jumped up and down, hugging them wildly. Another phone call to Rory had passed the information back to their parents. There was no doubt that it was their Michael, Michael McTavish. Edith had fainted, thankfully collapsing onto the lounge chair when Rory passed on the news. When she recovered, Hamish held her in his arms for a long while, her head nestled in his shoulder, her tears wetting his shirt. Hamish had found an old bottle of scotch and that afternoon the two of them sat on the verandah, watching the sun set as they celebrated the news about Michael.

When the excitement calmed down, Edith contacted the war office, stating that although they had received official word Michael had been, 'taken POW and presumed dead,' this was incorrect. In fact, their son was lying in a hospital bed, ill with malaria but alive. As soon as he was better, he would be visiting them.

Months later they received another official letter saying that Michael was presumed to be on the Montevideo Maru which had been sunk by an American submarine with all lives lost. Once again, they wrote to the war office, but there had been no reply, only more correspondence stating Michael's fate as before, but this time with Michael's war service medals attached. The whole matter was terribly confusing, and it was only once Michael had recovered and spoken to them on the telephone they were put entirely at ease. It had been a short conversation because the line was scratchy and kept cutting out, but there was no doubt for Hamish and Edith, their son Michael was well and now married, living in a small country town in Queensland.

Further communication with the department that handled the war records eventually revealed that Michael's service number had been written on a list for POWs. The number was his, but another name appeared beside it. The conclusion was that the war office had decided the number was the correct one and the name incorrect, so they had crossed out the other name and matched Michael's up instead. The lists were all handwritten and when Edith wrote and questioned the error, the official letter back stated there were some discrepancies and records were not always accurate.

The incidents at Rabaul had created confusion, the chain of events blurry, and reports differed depending on who you talked to. The lists of names of those who had been living in Rabaul at the time and those who were on the POW ship were even more complicated, with no one able to confirm who was or wasn't on the ship when it was sunk.

When Hamish and Edith searched for answers to Michael's fate and tried to find a reason for the mix-up with the names, they realised many other families, such as their own, were also searching for answers, scanning lists and looking for the true facts about their loved one's disappearance. Who knew which paperwork was legitimate and what wasn't?

What was important was that one of their sons had returned home to Australia and wasn't lying buried on foreign soil or entombed in a ship resting at the bottom of the ocean, its exact location unknown. Their Michael was alive and well, and sitting at the kitchen table just as he had as a child. He had come home.

CHAPTER 43

Over the course of the visit, Edith kept a close eye on her returned son. Although he said he had recovered and was well, something was wrong. There was a spark missing from his voice, and his eyes were full of anguish. When he talked about Joanie his voice became animated, and she glimpsed traits of the Michael she remembered. He told Edith he had married the love of his life and when everything settled down, his new wife was desperate to come and meet his family.

The visiting part sounded good to Edith and she was pleased he had found someone to share his life with. Still though, something was missing.

The letters Michael had sent from Rabaul before the Japanese invaded had filled the family in on what had happened at Wirth's Circus and why he did not return to the station but instead went to live in Melbourne.

Edith watched him as he stood in front of the pictures of Frank and Lachie, his fingers reaching up to touch their faces, in turn, from one to the other. He straightened the frames, stood back again and ran his hand across the bugle, resting on the shelf nearby.

* * *

One evening Hamish and Edith sat with Michael in the cooler air out on the verandah. Flocks of white cockatoos flew overhead, heading for the river area where they would roost on the weeping branches of the gum trees for the night. The sky turned from a vivid dark blue to orange and then pink, the last of its rays throwing a golden haze over the paddocks stretching out in front of them. To the east, above the horizon, the first star, Elizabeth's Star, twinkled brightly. The three of them stared in silence for a while, all lost in their thoughts.

Michael broke the silence, leaning back in his chair, his gaze still focused on the star. His voice was husky, his words slow. 'I've only been able to visit you now. For a long while it was too much to bear coming back when the younger two didn't.' He reached out and put his hand on his mother's, her fingers curling around to clench his own. 'I also had demons in my head I needed to chase away. There were many others who I left behind in Rabaul.'

Hamish puffed hard on his pipe, the aroma of the tobacco wafting through the still night air as he waited for Michael to continue.

'Joanie's father, Reg, never returned. The records note he is, 'presumed dead, taken POW in 1942 and drowned with over a thousand other Australian men on the Montevideo Maru. Joanie's mother still waits for him. I see her sometimes out in the front garden in the middle of the night, looking across the street, still waiting for him to return.'

Edith pulled out two handkerchiefs, one for Michael and one for herself. 'It's a terrible ache in your heart. I know how she feels. You just expect them to turn up and to hear those stupid tunes those two boys used to whistle in unison. She dabbed at her eyes, looking up to the star. 'The worst part is they had been gone from home for such a long time before they went missing. Now we don't even know where their bodies lie.' She blew her nose, trying to compose herself. 'The war will never end for us parents and those who are now widows.'

Hamish sat still, listening, not speaking, occasionally wiping his hand across his eyes, the tears falling on his weathered skin.

* * *

Edith took Michael aside before he left. 'Your father won't talk about it at all. He hardly mentions their names. It's like he's got a depression of sorts. He's never got over it and this is the first time in a long while I've seen him smile.'

'The war has changed all our lives forever,' Michael said. There are sights and sounds I can't get out of my mind. The scars on the outside are nothing compared to those I carry in my heart.' He held his hand over his chest, his dark eyes turning to Edith. 'But thank God for Joanie. I doubt I would have made it if it wasn't for her. She's a pillar of strength and supported me with such a determination, even though she has her own suffering to deal with.'

Edith took his hand in hers. 'She sounds like a beautiful girl. Are you happy? Can you find the peace in your heart now the war is ended?'

'It's never going to end for me. The Australian government left us there in Rabaul like lambs to the slaughter. It should be them who carry the guilt, but I still feel like I should have done more. I should have returned and tried to help Reg and the other boys escape.'

'There were thousands of Japanese there and the papers said that none of you had any chance. I read every article I can get my hands on; the mailman saves them for me. They're always months old but the news is about the events from years ago anyway.

Anytime there's something about Rabaul or New Guinea he brings the papers to me.'

Michael shook his head. 'They write about the invasion and all their theories about what happened to those men, be it at Tol Plantation or on the ship. There are many stories, but I always think, if there's that much interest in it now, why didn't they do something about it back then? Why did women like Joanie's mother have to wait so many years for the truth to come out?'

Edith got up from where she sat. 'You know there's been a few write-ups in the paper about how the nurses survived. I think one of them wrote the article for the paper. I have the paper clipping here; there's a photo of her.'

Edith went to the silky oak sideboard, the top covered in framed photos of her sons and grandchildren. She passed Michael a folded paper clipping from The Courier Mail, the heading glaring back at him. 'Japs starved nurses taken from Rabaul' The article was dated September 14th, 1945, and told the story of how the nurses had survived the camps and returned to tell their story. 'See that nurse at the back, Michael said, 'That's Jean.'

He read the article aloud.

'SYDNEY, Thursday — Stepping through the bomb-bay doors of the R.A.A.F. Liberator which had brought them from Manila, 16 nurses clapped by 150 relatives and friends and Red Cross representatives at Mascot Aerodrome tonight. The nurses had been prisoners of the Japanese for three years. Lack of food, heating, and news were the three shortages most complained of by the party, which comprised four Australian Army and 12 civilian nurses captured at Rabaul in January, 1942. They were comparatively well fed for the six months they stayed at a convent there, but 2 ½ years' slow starvation began when they were herded with 60 Australian army officers and taken in a ship's hold to Japan. The eighth of each month, 'Americans' Humiliation Day' to the Japanese, was marked for them by forced physical labour. They were sometimes slapped by the Japanese.'

'There's her name there.' Michael pointed to a name listed with sixteen others. He continued reading, Edith listening intently to the names she too had read over many times since the article had been given to her. Knowing Michael had been in Rabaul she had kept everything she could about the invasion, hoping one day to see his name or find him in a picture. Anything, just some sign he was alive and well.

Michael continued. *'Although tired and travel-stained, the nurses were in good spirits. They were wearing khaki cotton shirts and slacks, which were issued to them at Manila, and army topcoats, which arrived at their prison camp just before they were freed by the Americans. Sister Parker, who was also captured at Rabaul, said that the party was reduced to the stage where the entrails of cats and dogs were considered real delicacies. Mostly their diet consisted of three tablespoonfuls of watery rice for breakfast, a tablespoonful of cooked rice, carrot, and turnip tops for tea, and a piece of dry bread (if they were lucky) for lunch. She said that not once during their captivity did they taste sugar, butter, milk, or eggs. She lost nearly seven stone in weight, and the others lost from three to five stone. "Although most of the Jap guards were diseased, and had tuberculosis, we had to eat the leavings of their food to live," said Sister Parker. "We also hunted the buckets of food for the pigs to try to find something edible."*

The nurses were given a few clothes during their imprisonment. They made underclothes from some old sheets, which they took with them from Rabaul. Only other clothing received was a length of flannel material to make a winter suit, a fleecy-lined man's singlet, and two pairs of men's socks. They received no medical attention throughout their imprisonment, although a so-called doctor made several inspections. He appeared to have no real medical knowledge.'

Michael shook his head. 'It's wonderful she's well and back home. They must have been a tough lot of women to survive in those camps. When we knew her in Rabaul, she was a lovely young girl, lots of fun and high-spirited. She was a good friend of Joanie's and madly in love with one of Joanie's childhood friends, Andrew.'

'What happened to him? Did he come back also?' Edith asked.

'No, he didn't make it. I talked to him just before the invasion and then met him up in the jungle not long after. He also wanted to try and get back into Rabaul and rescue his brother Peter and Reg, Joanie's father. We discussed it at length with a few of the others, but we knew the situation and it would have been akin to committing suicide. The town, particularly where the Australians were, was heavily guarded and even to surrender was to run the risk of being killed.' Michael stopped, thinking how he had talked about Rabaul more to his mother than he had to anyone else in the last ten years. Often, he and Joanie would talk about her father and the two boys who she had grown up with, but he never went into detail about what he'd seen or heard when he was escaping, not wanting to upset her or conjure up images in her head. It was hard enough for her as it was.

'What happened to this Andrew; why didn't he make it out with you?'

'He was captured and killed at Tol with other Australians when they tried to surrender. They tried to convince George and me to go with them. But I had an uneasy feeling about it and knew I could survive in the jungle and somehow make our way off New Britain and back to the mainland of New Guinea.'

Edith placed her hand on Michael's arm. 'You had a natural flair for finding your way and surviving in the wilderness. I know it's completely different here compared to the jungle in New Guinea, but you always had a knack for finding food and water and getting back to where you were supposed to be. We never once worried about you getting lost when you were a kid.'

Hamish sat like a statue, puffing on his pipe, his only movement when he poked some more tobacco into the end of it. 'We always reckon you thought you were one of the Aborigines. The ones who can track anyone. Maybe those skills stood you in good stead.'

Michael looked fondly at his father. 'The Tolai people in Rabaul are just like our Aborigines. They took me into the mountains and showed me their villages. They shared their food and knowledge of the jungle with me. I owe my survival to them.' He stopped and took a deep breath. 'It was hard going and both George and I were very ill by the time we made it back to Australia. If it wasn't for Joanie, I'm not sure if I'd be here or if I would have made it through the last year.'

'What happened to George?' Edith asked.

'He left for Australia after we got to Port Moresby. He never went back. He's back down south with his family, doing well. He still writes to me every month. We shared a lot, George and I. We have a special bond.'

'Thank you for coming back to us, son,' Hamish said. 'We're proud of you and your brothers. You did what you had to for your country.'

'Those poor boys' mother,' Edith said. 'And what about the other brother? You said there was a brother called Peter.'

'Those two boys grew up with Joanie, they were like her own brothers, so it was very difficult telling her their fate.' Michael took a deep breath. 'Peter's gone also. He was on the ship with Reg, the *Montevideo Maru*. They say a couple of Japanese made it back and told the government in Japan what happened. There were no prisoners who survived. They were...' Michael looked up at his father, not able to meet his mother's eyes, 'they were all locked in below the deck.'

He stood up and walked over to the window, watching the dust swirl around the yard, a few brown hens scratching the ground, looking for that elusive bug.

'You know I longed for that dust in the yard there, when I was in New Guinea. I don't think I've ever yearned to taste red dust in my mouth, or to have it sting my eyes and fill my nose and ears like I did back then.' He opened the window, pushing the old glass casements so he could put his head out and breathe in the dryness of the land that he always thought of as home.

Turning back to his mother, his voice softened. 'I'll come and visit more regularly. I've spent many months trying to sort out my health and mind. Now I have a couple of things I still need to do but I'm on a good road at the moment. I promise you, I'll get out here more and next time I'll bring Joanie with me. You'll love her and she's dying to meet you both. I thought it best I come and visit alone this time. I guess, I wanted you both, just to myself.'

Edith came over, her arm linking through his as they both stared out the window. Cattle in a distant paddock shuffled their way to where a windmill spun with the breeze, its actions bringing up the precious bore water that would see them through the dry spell.

'Dan has made some good adjustments here for both of you,' Michael said. 'It's a lot more comfortable than what I remember. A new roof, screens and even fans. I'm guessing he also put in that brand new stove in the kitchen.'

'He did,' Edith beamed at Michael. 'You boys have always looked after us. We couldn't ask for any more from you. We just want you to be happy.'

'I can see Rory has also added onto the sheds and the yards look like they've had a lot of work done to them. It's great what they've both done, isn't it, Father? All the new improvements for you and Mum.' Michael tried to drag Hamish into the conversation, but he just gave a little smile and looked straight ahead, poking some more tobacco in his pipe.

His mother squeezed his arm, turning and walking slowly back to sit on the lounge. Michael gazed out the window for a bit longer, breathing in the air and watching as flocks of corellas landed in the trees down the far end of the home paddock. It was good to be home. He closed the window and turned to the piano, the top of it covered in a variety of family photos. The lid squeaked as he lifted it, his fingers pushing down on some of the notes, the noise echoing throughout the room. He pressed a few more before gently closing the lid.

'Do you still play, Mum?'

Her voice was soft, her Scottish accent still as strong as the day she had arrived in Australia. 'I haven't touched it since you boys went. I don't have the heart to play it anymore.'

'You know when we were the happiest, don't you?' Hamish eventually spoke, his words gruff. 'When we had nothing. When the rain used to come in through the roof and you kids collected it in buckets in the rooms. When the dust covered all the furniture because of the gaps in the windows and doors, and the wood fire in the kitchen made it so hot you boys would strip off all your clothes and run around the house naked. That's when life was good. We had nothing but each other, and they were the best years.'

'C'mon now, Hamish, let's give thanks Michael is here with us and try for one day to be happy.'

'He's right, Mum. They were the best days, when we were all tucked up here together. I loved it when you played the piano and we all sang along or when Dan tried to play the bugle or blew out a tune on that little tin sandwich of his. Before Dan and I went away and before this blasted war stripped us all of what we once had. We were content and a million miles away from any war. We were together. We had Frank and Lachie.' His voice wavered and he stood up, returning to the piano to look at the photos displayed on the top.

'We are happy that you are back, son, and it is indeed a blessing you survived against all odds.' Hamish was frank, his voice stern. He pointed to Michael. 'But you're not happy. I can read your mind and your eyes tell me a story. You're not, are you, son?' Hamish leant back and coughed, putting the pipe down on the small table next to him.

'Please don't spoil the day, Hamish.' Edith was well used to the moods of her husband since the war. He had never been the same since the days the telegrams arrived telling them their sons weren't coming home.

'It's okay Mum, I understand. I'm like Dad. Some days I can

find small pieces of happiness, but most days are difficult.' Michael said. 'And Dad's right. There's some contentment in my life and if it wasn't for Joanie I wouldn't be here today. But there's a big gap and I'll be honest. It punches deep in my heart and it won't go away.' He paused for a long while, clearing his throat before he spoke. 'I think about my mates left behind and Reg. Thoughts of Frank and Lachie consume me and every day there's a longing for a little girl called Gracie I said goodbye to before I went to war.'

Michael and his mother sat down again, Hamish re-lighting his pipe and sitting back in his chair, waiting for Michael to talk. Once he started it was difficult to stop and Hamish and Edith only interrupted a few times to ask a question, listening to him as he filled them in on what he had been able to find.

'I've even gone back to where we lived in Melbourne and talked to the neighbours to see if anyone knew where they went. Nobody knows anything. It's like she disappeared off the face of the earth.'

'If the mother died and there was no next-of-kin, she would have been put into a home.' Edith said.

Hamish muttered about the blasted war and Edith closed her eyes, upset for Michael, upset for Gracie and distraught about the effects of the war on her family. Her two strong healthy sons, plus millions of others weren't coming home, instead their bodies lay in fields, paddocks, jungles and oceans of distant lands.

'Such a useless waste,' she said, her soft tone and accent bringing back memories for Michael of when they were little and she would calmly talk to them, easing their worries and solving their problems.

Hamish shook his head and closed his eyes, the pipe still lit, hanging precariously from his mouth. If he closed his eyes and fell asleep, the pain would stop. It was easier to sleep and try and wipe out the fact that his family had been torn apart, not only two sons lost forever but now also a small child, Michael's daughter, missing, disappeared to God knows where.

After a long while he opened his eyes, his voice clear when he spoke. 'We hope with all our hearts, Michael, you find your little girl. When you find her, bring her to us. You hear me son, bring her out here to visit your mother and me. Don't stop looking. She is out there somewhere.'

It was a long speech from Hamish. 'I will keep looking,' Michael vowed, coming over to his father where he sat in his chair. They embraced, their strong arms wrapping around one another. Michael eventually pulled away, both men wiping tears from their eyes. 'I will find her and bring her here. I promise.'

CHAPTER 44

Brisbane - 1946

*B*ud married Ruby in the cathedral in Brisbane not long after the war ended. Never had a bride looked more beautiful, the long timber pews filled with family and friends, the organist thumping out 'Here comes the Bride' as she held onto her father's arm as they walked slowly up the aisle.

Bud wore his navy uniform, his shoes shiny, his hat in hand as he gazed at his young bride walking towards him. If only Beth could have been here to witness this moment. All those years ago, even before he had joined the navy, she had seen this moment in her visions, those eerie insights into the future that came to her at the strangest times. Her words came back to him. 'You had a beautiful red-haired girl on your arm. You introduced her as your wife. Flaming red hair, a few freckles, but very pretty.'

Ruby smiled at him, her auburn hair hanging in curls down to her waist, light makeup covering her freckles. He grinned back at her, thinking about those cute spots he loved to tease her about.

'They're adorable', he'd always told her, 'Those freckles are what I first fell in love with, well that and the breakfast you served me.'

She glided elegantly up the aisle, her green eyes meeting his as her father, Jack, passed her arm over to him. The minister's voice boomed through the lofty rafters of the church. 'And who gives this woman to this man.'

"I do,' Jack replied.

* * *

When they emerged from the church, the crowd waiting outside showered them with coloured confetti, their loud cheers a celebration of the union. Church bells rang out loudly and Bud gazed up at the vivid Brisbane sky above and thanked God for allowing him to survive and be here for this moment. He took Ruby in his arms, right there in front of everyone and swung her backwards, kissing her for as long as he could, her head nearly tipping back onto the ground.

Life was wonderful and as a couple, the world was their oyster. He watched her as she hugged all the guests, her laughter and smiling face bringing joy to his heart. He turned away and looked down at the crowd of kids who jumped up and down next to him, two of them hugging his leg and pulling on his jacket. The kids knew he always had a trick up his sleeve to play on them or a lolly hidden in his pocket to treat them. He picked up one of Ruby's nephews and spun him around. This was the best day of his life. He had another family now, new brothers and kids that he loved like they were his own. Ruby's parents had always been good to him, taking him in after his accident and treating him like he was their son. He placed his arm around them, squeezing both and telling them he was the happiest man in the world. The cameras flashed and a moment in time was captured. Ruby's eyes sparkled, her smile stretching wide as she kissed him. Life was continuing, love was enduring, and couples were marrying to start their own lives and families, free from the curse of war.

CHAPTER 45

Brisbane to America - 1947

*P*assengers lined the decks of the ship docked at the Brisbane wharf. It was bound for America, full of men and women who were either returning to their homeland or like Ruby, war brides, married to a Yankee sailor and saying goodbye to their homeland for who knew how long.

The ship's horn blasted loudly, signalling for those who weren't passengers to leave the decks and make their way back down the gangplanks. Ruby hung onto her mother, the tears streaming down both their faces. Her father hugged them both. It was the first time Ruby had ever seen him cry. 'Write to us. Tell us all your news,' he said, his hands clutching at Bud's as they shook each other's hands. Bud was lost for words. He had never envisaged it would be this hard. He and Ruby were in love. She would follow him to the end of the earth. Back home he wanted to start up his own ranch. Beth was waiting for him, his mother, his father, all of them who he hadn't seen for over five years.

He glanced around the decks at other families in the same situation. Mothers crying, fathers standing to the side, lost for words, their daughters bound for a distant land. When would they see them again? Would their new families take them in with open arms? A passage on a ship took over a month from one country to the other, so who knew when they would meet again.

He leaned over the rail, his arm tight around Ruby's shoulder as her hair flew across her face, her hand up in the air waving to her family. Tears streamed down her face and he held her even tighter. Her mother waved a yellow scarf, its colour bright against the crowds who gathered to say goodbye. He stood with Ruby, watching until the yellow scarf was no longer visible, the crowd a blur, the wharves a distant outline on the horizon.

Hours passed and still they stood at the rails, the ship making its way through the bay, past several islands and out into the open waters. Ahead of them the waves of the Pacific Ocean stretched out for as far as the eye could see. Bud breathed in the salty sea air, pleased he was above the water and not below it. Sailing craft raced each other on the leeward side, their bright sails brilliant against the blue of the sky, their crew hanging precariously from their sides. He smiled when Ruby rushed to the side of the ship, excited to watch dolphins leaping and diving through the waves. Australia was an amazing country with an abundance of unique animals and lush countryside that was perfect for raising livestock and growing crops. For a while he had been tempted to stay. But America was home and he needed to see his family. There were opportunities to set up his own ranch and Ruby would soon settle in. Perhaps they could sail back to Australia every few years for a visit.

She nestled into his shoulder, her tears no longer flowing, an excited smile on her face. 'It's just you and me now, Bud,' she said. 'Just the two of us.'

His big hands wrapped around her. 'I will look after you. I won't forget what you've given up for me.' They clung to each other, the sea spray lifting from the sides of the boat, its cool mist, invigorating. It would be the start of an entirely new life on a different side of the world. A world with no threat of war hanging over it and where anything was possible. 'Thousands sacrificed their lives for us. We have to grab freedom and liberty and make the most of it.'

'We will, Bud. We will make a new life and not forget what others have given.

CHAPTER 46

Woombye - 1950

When Michael returned to Woombye from out west, he threw himself into the business, working long hours and ensuring the shop ran as efficiently as possible. It was not a job he had ever envisaged himself doing and sometimes he longed for the vast plains of the west, the seat of a saddle and the dusty still air of the western trails. But life had taken a different direction once again and now his priority was Joanie and her mother.

While he had been away, Edna had discussed an idea she had been thinking about for a while. She wanted to swap houses. Michael and Joanie would move into the big house and she would move into the smaller cottage where they were living. It made sense. The main house had more rooms, and for her, it was empty without Reg. Sprucing up the cottage and making it her own would keep her busy and Joanie could change the main house and have it the way she wanted.

Michael agreed to the move. Edna was generous beyond belief

and had legally signed the main house and half the business over to Joanie and him. She calmed his worries that she was being too generous by explaining Reg would have wanted it this way and she was happy to step back from the responsibilities of the shop. The cottage suited her better now she lived alone.

Thank goodness their home offered Michael the slow pace of country living and plenty of space to roam when needed. The town of Woombye was pleasantly situated between rolling hills of green and the sprawling farms offered a quiet and peaceful place to walk when memories of the past overwhelmed him. If he could escape the streets of town for an hour each day and wander through the countryside, his mind would calm and his thoughts could focus on the days ahead, rather than what had passed.

Sometimes when he walked in the early morning hours, he spotted Edna sitting quietly on the bench seat at the lookout down the end of their street. Her body was upright, never relaxed and she sat on the edge of the seat looking out across the plains, staring, waiting.

The war years had left invisible scars on their souls and as much as he reminded himself how lucky he was, the memories continued to bubble to the surface. A myriad of recollections sometimes stopped him in his tracks, his head pounding, his body stiffening and tensing from the thoughts that plagued him. Once when an old truck backfired near where he walked, he had dropped to the ground, his hands and knees pushing into the rough stones that dug into his skin, leaving tiny indentations of blood where they pressed. Crawling on his belly along the gravel at the side of the road a roaring in his ears blocked everything; planes swooping low, their gunfire ricocheting in the dry grass growing in the paddock next to where he crawled.

When his mind finally cleared, he lay still on the ground, his breath heaving in short rasps as the fence and cow paddocks came into clear focus. A tan jersey cow chewing its cud, leant across the barbed wire fence, its wet nose pushing him where he lay. He looked up into its brown eyes, his reflection staring back at him, the absurdity of where he thought he was, forcing him to jump up and brush himself off. The cow swung its head wildly, snorted and turned away from him, flicking its tail before walking in the other direction. He rubbed his legs, the cramps clenching his calf muscles like a metal vice, forcing him to take deep breaths, to numb the pain and take a moment before moving on. His stiff legs moved in short steps and he hobbled to the bench seat at the look-out, only noticing Edna standing further down the hill, looking out across the valley, once he was seated.

She turned and made her way back to him. He wasn't sure how she knew he was there. An inner sense, a collective feeling of mourning or just intuition that he might pass this way. Perhaps she had seen him crawling along the ground like a frightened spider, cowering from invisible planes circling above, gunfire that strafed the grass where he lay, running from who knew what.

Edna sat beside him, her eyes empty, her hands clenched in her lap. He took her hand in his and rubbed it, as if it was cold. 'It's not easy, Edna,' he said, his voice husky, his words slow and hollow.

She turned to him, her lips curling up in the corners as she smiled. 'Reg came to me in my dreams last night. He left a message for you.'

Michael closed his eyes. 'A message for me?'

'Yes, my dear boy. Just for you.'

Michael placed her hand back in her lap, pushing his hair back from his face and picking out bits of grass that had collected when he hit the ground. 'What did he say?'

She took a deep breath. 'He said you need to move on and focus on your new life. That it wasn't your fault and there wasn't anything you could have done.'

It was rare for Edna to talk in this manner. The only time she talked about Reg was when she discussed what would happen when he came back. Michael sat silent, listening.

She stood up and straightened her dress, her hands meticulously pressing down where creases had formed. 'He said it twice. Tell Michael to move on from what happened and focus on life now.'

The two of them stood, staring across the valley, a line of cows meandering through a lush green paddock, a tractor chugging slowly behind them as they led the way to the milking sheds.

'Are you listening to me, Michael? It must be an important message because he didn't leave one for me or Joanie, just you.'

He pushed his shoulders back, lifting his face to the sun, taking solace from its warmth. 'He's right. I know what I should be doing and focussing on but,' he hesitated and looked into her eyes, 'you would know Edna, it's not easy. The demons in my head are sometimes stronger than what my thoughts should be.'

'I understand. But you and Joanie are young. Your best years are in front of you and if you let the memories of the war take over your soul, you'll stop living. You'll become an empty shell. I want more than that for Joanie and you, and so would Reg. You deserve happiness.'

They stood for a long while, neither speaking, the sun rising higher in the sky. Michael placed his arm around her shoulders, squeezing her gently. 'I'm a lucky man. Thank you, Edna, that means a lot.'

* * *

Joanie was cleaning the windows in the lounge room when she spotted her mother and Michael walking back up the street together. There was a faint smile on Edna's face, her step a little lighter than usual. Michael also looked happier than when he had left this morning and she wondered what the two of them had talked about. If only she and Michael could have a baby. Perhaps then he would regain the zest for life he had shown when she first met him.

When he was busy at the shop he was cheery, learning the ins and outs of the business, chatting to customers and ensuring everything was kept in order. The work was enjoyable and he was patient with the customers, always going out of his way to find something for them, delivering items when needed and often doing free maintenance for those who needed help. The locals loved him, and he had made friends who dropped in to see him for a chat or brought in some of their wife's homemade biscuits or cake to have with his morning cup of tea. To most, he appeared happy, calm and settled into his new life. She was a fortunate woman to have found such a man, who looked after her and her mother.

There were other days however when Michael didn't make it to the shop. The alarm clock failed to rouse him, or he would put the pillow over his head and ignore it. Joanie had learnt to read the warning signs and knew it was useless to try and talk to him when he was in one of those moods. Instead, she would get out of bed, making sure she was there to open the shop on time. On those days when the "black dog" chased him, he didn't get out of bed. When she came home at lunch, the curtains were still drawn, the doors and windows closed and the house filled with a gloomy silence. When she tried to talk to him, he turned away, a dark cloud cloaking his soul, his eyes forlorn, only a few words spoken when necessary and his movements slow like those of an old man.

This morning however there was a lightness in his step and she watched as he parted ways with Edna at the letterbox, a few more words exchanged as they each went their separate way. Joanie pretended she was dusting and hadn't seen them together. Edna considered Michael the head of the family, the household and the business and it warmed Joanie's heart that her mother and Michael not only got on but shared some moments together without her.

The French doors pushed open and she smiled as he came

through the doorway. His mop of blonde hair was unruly and needed a cut and she laughed out loud as he grabbed a rubber band from the top of the sideboard and pulled his hair back high on his head in a ponytail.

'You make a pretty lady,' she said as she approached him, his arms reaching out to hold her as he bent down to kiss her. His lips pressed hard on hers and she pushed herself up against him.

'I love you, Joanie. You're my reason for living.'

She stroked his face. 'And you are mine. Are you okay? You seemed upset or not quite yourself.'

'I need to concentrate on what is good. I'm sorry if I'm often distant or not happy.'

She sighed and pushed his hair down, pulling bits of grass from the back of it. 'It's okay. I understand. You don't need to apologise.'

'I threw myself down in the grass this morning. A truck back-fired and, well, I ...'

'You don't need to explain.'

He pulled her by her hands back towards the bedroom, his eyes full of passion and life. 'Today I don't care if the shop opens late. This morning is ours, just because it can be.'

She laughed as he scooped her into his arms and carried her back to their bed, closing the door behind them.

CHAPTER 47

$\mathcal{A}$lthough that morning was a turning point and Michael's demeanour improved, there were still days when he was down, his face grim with nothing bringing him any joy. He tried hard to remind himself of Edna's message, but memories of the past were ever-present and they pulled him in every direction. Joanie was also out of sorts lately and snapped back at him when he once again replied with another negative comment about something. 'For God's sake, Michael. Can't you see the good side of anything? Why are you always thinking the worst and never looking on the bright side? You're not the only one missing loved ones.'

With that, she stormed off, slamming the bedroom door hard behind her so hard that the brass bugle Michael's father had given him on his last trip out west, toppled off the shelf it was displayed on. It landed on a glass vase her friend Loreen had given her, the glass splintering over the floor. Michael came back inside from where he stood on the verandah, picking up the bugle and holding it for a long while in his hands. He brushed his hands over the surface, slowly feeling the familiar grooves and dents, as if tracing the memories it held.

His father had insisted he take it. Hamish's brother had been a bugler in the Boer War and the instrument had belonged to him. Somehow, he had returned alive, and the bugle was deemed to be lucky. It had travelled from Glasgow to Australia. Now it belonged to Michael, the only one in his family who had returned from the war, he reminded himself.

He started picking up the glass, his eyes meeting Joanie's as she also squatted on the floor, picking up the remnants of the vase. 'Loreen gave me that vase on my sixteenth birthday. And now, because of my anger, it's broken.'

'I'll buy you another one.'

She sat down on the floor, her back leaning against the wall. 'It won't be the same.' Her words came out shaky, and to her horror she started to cry, the tears streaming down her face as sobs racked her body. Michael rushed to her side and held her, his lips pressing against her cheeks, his arms strong around her as she wept like a baby.

* * *

For so long she had held everything together. Her shoulder was always there for others to lean upon, to cry on and because she was a good listener, many in the town came to the store for personal advice or for a chat. She was there for her mother and Michael, the men who bought hardware, who asked about her father, who shook their heads in sorrow when remembering those who hadn't returned. In the shop she consoled women; their sons were boys she had gone to school with, their missing husbands, family friends. They talked about injured brothers, mentally and physically scarred, and the unmarked graves where their loved ones lay.

Memories of Vera, Peter, and Andrew, ran through her mind

constantly. She worried about Sissy, Mi-Lee and her family. She couldn't bear to see her mother check the letter box one more time, or to wake during the night to watch her standing at a window looking out into the street. And then there was Michael. His moods were up and down like a yo-yo, his laughter rare and his outlook pessimistic, never hopeful. Sometimes there would be a glimmer of hope, like the other morning when he had thrown his responsibilities out the window and made love to her like when they were first married.

But those moments were rare and now her precious vase lay broken, the shards of glass shattered like her heart. It was all becoming too much to bear.

* * *

She rested in Michael's arms for a long while, her eyes opening and resting on the silken scarf hanging on the wall next to them. Michael followed her gaze. The scarf was made of the purest Chinese silk, its paintwork still as bright and detailed as the day it had been created.

It had been a present on her twenty-fifth birthday. Mi-Lee had given it to her as a gift, her husband Huan explaining that Mi-Lee was one of the most sought-after silk artists in the province where they came from. Joanie stared at the artwork, splashes of green and blue depicting the brooding mountains and tranquil oceans near Rabaul. The dark jungle covered the slopes, the beautiful colonial buildings of the town were detailed with great accuracy, and Mi-Lee's fine brushwork depicted an authentic view of what Rabaul had once looked like.

She could hear Mi-Lee's beautiful voice, her sing-song English the sweetest sound in the world. 'I am Mi-Lee, and eatery and trading store is best in all of New Guinea. Now what I need is pot that is very, very big.'

Michael's deep voice broke the silence. 'We must try and track

Mi-Lee down. That is something I will do this week. I will try and find out what happened to her and her family.'

Joanie regained some of her practical attitude, brushing her tears away and straightening her hair. 'Perhaps it is better not to know; the children, Li, Chun, and the baby, Ah Lam.'

Michael stroked her face. 'You know you grow more beautiful every day.' His words were rewarded with a smile and he kissed her softly. 'I have some letters to write to the officials in Canberra. There are a couple of places I am going to contact about Gracie.' He looked deep into Joanie's eyes. 'I know it's probably not going to bring me any information, but I have to try. I will also write to a contact I still have in New Guinea. Many of the Chinese survived and are still living on the islands. Perhaps Mi-Lee and her family are there.'

'Thank you, Michael,' she lifted her head and kissed him. 'Thank you.'

'It's worth a try,' he replied. 'Jean survived and now the letters you sent back and forth to each other are something you treasure.'

Joanie sighed. 'Jean's so strong and seems to find pleasure in everything she does. She says she can't waste any time, that she's missed enough because of the war. I'm so pleased she married and had children. She found happiness after everything she went through.'

Michael stroked her arm and held her tight. 'We must get through this. You and me.'

She leant back into him. 'We will. We will.'

* * *

Michael was serving a customer when Joanie rushed into the store. Coils of string were wrapped around Michael's hands as he measured the quantity the customer, Mr Butler wanted. She had known Mr Butler since she was a child, and he gave her a wink and a friendly hello when she entered. 'I've been trying to persuade

Michael that he should march in the Anzac Day Parade next month. We'd be honoured to have him with us and then you can all join us at the RSL afterwards. The two-up is always great fun and it's a good time to have some beers together and talk about the years gone by.'

'I'd rather not talk about it,' Michael replied. 'I'm sorry, but I won't be coming.'

'But it's a day for us all to remember together, commemorate those who didn't return. You should come.'

Joanie came around Michael's side of the counter and took the string from him, bundling it into a paper bag. 'Thanks, Mr Butler. We don't need a day to remember. It's with us every day. But thank you for your thoughts. The string is on the house.'

Mr Butler nodded and grinned, quickly exiting the store before Joanie changed her mind or Michael intervened.

'That was generous of you,' Michael commented. 'Thank goodness it was only string and not a lawn mower or something more expensive.'

Joanie jumped up and down, hanging onto Michael's arm. 'I just wanted him out of here. I have something to tell you. I'm pregnant!' She blurted it out loudly, staring at Michael, who stood motionless with a stunned look wrapped across his face.

Joanie shook his arm. 'Did you hear what I said? I've just come from the doctor and I'm three months pregnant. The baby will be born in September. Do you hear me, Michael? We're going to have a baby!'

CHAPTER 48

*E*dna's smile was so wide that Joanie thought her mother's face would split. 'I thought as much,' she said, 'because your dresses were tight, and sometimes you just seemed a bit off-colour. I didn't want to say anything, but it explains why you have been eating so much.'

'She's been a bit teary also,' Michael added, passing another plate of sandwiches her way.

Joanie piled her plate high. 'It does explain a few things. I thought I might have been pregnant, but there have been so many false alarms before that I didn't dare dream it was true.'

Michael nudged her playfully. 'Who is being the pessimist now?'

Joanie beamed as she looked at both of them. 'Michael, you will have to paint the spare bedroom and Mother, we'll have to find my old cot from up in the beams at the back of the shop. Michael, you can do it up and also we'll need new floor coverings and curtains in the spare room.'

Michael rolled his eyes. 'Sounds like you have a list for me already.'

'I do.'

Edna looked at both of them. 'I'm so pleased we swapped houses when we did. Now there won't be so many empty rooms. How about you stop calling it the spare bedroom. Let's call it the baby's room. After all, it was the bedroom you were in when you were a baby, Joanie.'

'I want the walls yellow, and the floorboards sanded and polished. And then the cupboard in there can be painted white and new handles put on. Mother, we'll need to go shopping in Brisbane. There will be clothes to get, nappies to buy and everything else needed for a new baby. My goodness, we'll need to get a baby bath, and Michael, my old wooden high chair is also stacked down in the back of the shed somewhere. You'll need to get it out and clean it up. I'd like it painted white also.'

Michael leaned back in his chair, sipping his cup of tea, watching Joanie, her eyes sparkling, her words coming out in between bites of her food.

He laughed out loud. 'Listen to both of you. I hope you're not going to spoil this baby.'

'Never,' Edna laughed also. 'A baby can never be spoiled by too much love.'

* * *

Edna travelled with Joanie to Nambour Hospital for her first check-up. According to her dates she was four months pregnant. Her stomach had swollen in the last week or so and she wondered how much longer she would be able to comfortably fit behind the steering wheel of the car. They talked non-stop all the way to Nambour, her mother regaling her with stories about when Joanie was little and how much joy she had brought to Reg and her when she was a baby.

'It will be sad your father will not be here to see your newborn.' Edna looked out the side window, the lush hills around Nambour dotted with cows, their heads lifting and watching them for a moment as they motored past. 'He would be impressed with your driving, Joanie. He always wanted you to do everything the same as a boy would.'

'I wonder what the baby will be. Boy or girl?' Joanie asked.

'Well, you won't know that until it comes. We can be prepared for either. Reg always said it didn't matter as long as it was healthy.' She sighed. 'I miss him dreadfully, but this baby will be a new start.'

'Michael has improved over the last year, Mother. He's not as up and down as he once was. He received a letter back from the organisation he contacted down south about his daughter Gracie, last week. But there is still no news, not a trace.'

'He may never find her. All he can hope is she survived and was well taken care of.'

'He says the same himself. There are no further leads to follow. There never really was, and as he says, she was only so young she probably wouldn't remember him anyway.'

'So many people all over the world looking for loved ones.' Edna took a deep breath. 'But where there is love, there will be life. And now a baby. We have been blessed and your father would be thrilled.'

Joanie guided the car into the hospital carpark. 'The doctor today will give me a due date and book me in for the delivery. Thank goodness we don't live far from the hospital.'

'I had no trouble delivering. I hope it is the same for you.'

* * *

Edna sat in the waiting room, which was full of expectant mothers, all at different stages of their pregnancy. New life, she thought, the world ticks on, not even wars will stop life from continuing, from couples loving each other and from babies being born. She watched some young children playing with blocks in the corner; post-war babies, born into a different world with no threat of war. She sighed. Hopefully, what they had been through would never happen again.

* * *

Joanie was in the doctor's room for a long time, and Edna started to worry about whether there were problems. She looked at her watch; it had been over an hour. She breathed a sigh of relief when Joanie walked through the door, signed a form at the desk and came over to Edna. 'All good, Mum. We can go.'

Edna knew Joanie too well. Something was not right. Her daughter didn't talk as they returned to the car, and her replies were short when Edna asked a question. Her chest tightened, and her throat felt dry. Whatever the problem, and why wouldn't Joanie tell her straight away?

She sat in the passenger's seat, waiting while Joanie stood by the side of the car. 'I'll be there in a minute, Mum. I just need a second or two to think. I need to gather my thoughts.'

Eventually, she opened the door and sat behind the steering wheel, pushing the keys into the ignition. However, she didn't start the car. Instead, she rested her head on the steering wheel, taking deep breaths.

'Please Joanie, tell me what is wrong.'

She turned to her mother. 'Nothing is wrong. Well, not really. The doctor examined me and then we had a long talk. She sat up straight and took Edna's hand in hers. 'I'm having twins, Mother. There are two babies. Michael and I are having twins!'

Edna's jaw dropped, her eyes wide. Her voice was a squeak. 'Twins? Two?'

'Yes, Mother. Two.'

* * *

Michael was mowing the lawn when Joanie arrived home. Her mother hugged Joanie briefly and gave Michael an enthusiastic wave. She turned and made her way back to her newly painted cottage. Michael turned the mower off. Joanie was starting to look pregnant and he watched as she walked carefully up the few stairs towards him. Her blonde hair fell softly onto her shoulders, her slender arms and legs tanned from the days she spent gardening. Her green eyes shone bright as she kissed him on the lips, her hand wiping away leaves resting on his shoulder.

'You've been under those bushes mowing. You have leaves and twigs on your clothes.'

He flicked some leaves and dirt from his shirt, looking at her as she stood in front of her.

'You have that look in your eye,' he squinted at her. 'It's that mischievous look you sometimes get when you're about to play a trick on me.'

'You know me too well, Michael. Everything is fine. I had a long visit with the doctor. What have you been doing?'

He grabbed her hand and led her over to the sprawling jacaranda tree. Hanging from one of the massive lower limbs was a swing made of rope with a timber seat. 'It's for you to sit on and relax. I made it wide and low to the ground so when you become fatter you can still fit.'

She sunk into the swing, memories of when she was a child coming back to her.

Michael pushed her gently and her feet lifted off the ground. 'I know you had one here when you were a little girl and your father used to push you in it. Your mother told me.'

"He did.' Joanie swung slowly and looked up into the thick growth on the branches above, the green fine leaves like intricate etchings, a blue Queensland sky stretching above. 'This was one of his favourite spots and it's also one of mine. Thank you, Michael, it's perfect.'

Michael halted the swing and reached for another smaller one lying on the ground. 'I'm just about to put this one up also. This is for the baby when it comes. That is when it's big enough to sit up and hang on.'

She smiled and looked at him without replying.

'What? You don't think that's a good idea?' Michael queried, the look on her face confusing him as to whether she was pleased with the second swing or not.

'It's a grand idea. In fact, it's one of the best ideas you've ever had. There is, however, a problem.'

'What? Too small? Too big? I can change it.'

She stood up and came to him, taking the swing out of his hands and placing it on the ground. 'The problem is, you are going to have to make one more.'

'That's easy to do. I can put however many you like up there. These lower branches are perfect for hanging swings from.'

'I said you need one more.'

'I don't understand what you mean.' He narrowed his eyes, confused even more when she started to laugh at him.

'Michael, we're having twins. The doctor says there are two babies in there.' She patted her stomach and pulled his hands onto hers, watching him blink and blink again, his mouth opening but no words coming out. 'It makes sense, Michael. You're a twin. We were so excited I was pregnant we never even thought about it.'

'My God. Twins. Like me and Dan.'

'Just like you and Dan, except we won't know what they are until they're born. Two. Two babies.'

Michael kept staring at her, shaking his head and touching her stomach. 'How will two fit in there? No wonder you have been eating so much. You're eating for three.'

'The doctor said everything is progressing normally and I will just have to visit him a bit more regularly as the months pass. Everything is fine.

'Everything is fine! Everything is bloody amazing. Twins. Who would have ever thought? We will be doubly blessed.'

Joanie led Michael back to the swing, wriggling herself into the seat. 'Push me gently, Michael. Push me slowly.'

CHAPTER 49

Canberra - 1950

Over the years Gracie's memory of her father had faded, and she no longer searched for his voice in the night sky. The evening star, or Elizabeth's Star as she still called it, continued to hold a place of importance for her and each night she looked to the sky, knowing the star was somehow connected to a father who had left her a very long time ago.

When she turned fifteen, her adoptive parents, Henry and Dawn talked to her about how she had come to them. They had given her love and everything she could have ever wanted in her childhood, since the day her mother, Layla, left without a backward glance. Now she was getting older she had started to ask questions about how they had become her parents.

'We have always thought of you and treated you like you were our own,' Henry said, the three of them sitting down to eat dinner. 'However, now you are older, perhaps there are things you may like to know, and we'd like to be truthful about those matters.'

Grace was curious but also scared. She didn't want anything to spoil her loving family life or disturb her friends at school. She attended one of the best schools in Canberra, went to a pony club on weekends, and had regular shopping holidays with Dawn in Sydney or Melbourne.

'I don't want anything to change.' Grace was adamant. 'If what you tell me is going to change me living here, or having to go somewhere else to school or to live, then I don't want to know. You're my mother and papa.'

Dawn spoke softly. 'We know that Grace, and we don't want anything to change either. There were papers filled out when we adopted you and nothing can change the fact that we are your legal parents. We just think in years to come you might have questions. This is a good time to see what you remember and get it out in the open.'

'I'll listen, but nothing is to change. I am your daughter and no one else's. I don't care what there was before, because if they loved me that much they would never have left me.'

'Well, Grace, when your mother, left you with us, she told us your father left before you were born. She said he hadn't wanted a baby, so had disappeared back out west where he came from.' Henry and Dawn watched the expression on Grace's face.

'What sort of lady was she? What did she look like?' Grace asked.

'She was a very attractive woman and had dark hair, just like yours.' Dawn hesitated. 'She looked quite poor though and you came with few belongings.'

Henry added in. 'We believe she was a showgirl, a dancer and actor in the theatres of Melbourne. From the little we know about her, we both came to the opinion that she, well...' Henry stopped talking.

'Go on Papa, it doesn't worry me. I think it's lucky that you both took me in. Now go on, your story won't upset me.'

Henry continued. 'Well, neither of us thought she was very caring. She acted like she was kind, but we could tell you feared her, and it was obvious she dressed you up for the occasion of meeting us. We could see right through her. She was after the money we paid her. She wanted no ties and asked that we never contact her again.'

'She told us your name was Gracie,' Dawn put her arm around her shoulders. 'Although as you know, we've always called you Grace. She told us she needed to work and she had married another man who wasn't your father. This new man didn't want a small child tagging along. There weren't any doubts for us when we adopted you. You were thin, malnourished and you may not remember, but when you first came to us you used to hide food, almost as if you were scared there wasn't going to be enough food to eat.'

'As for your father,' Henry's voice was husky, his tone serious. 'That is a different matter, and perhaps once you're older we could try and trace him if you want. It might be possible. I could look up birth certificates and find out his and your birth mother's details. That's if you wanted to look for them.'

Dawn butted in. 'The thing is Grace, often these types don't want to be found and when they are they don't want to know about a small child they gave away, or in your father's case, never wanted to have a part of.'

'Nothing changes for me then.' Grace wrapped her arms around Dawn. 'Thank you for telling me, but if she left me and he never wanted me, why would I want to find them? My life is here with you, my mother and father.'

Henry and Dawn breathed a sigh of relief.

'May I ask one thing though?'

'Yes, Grace,' they answered together.

'Why is Elizabeth's star so important in my life? Is it something you taught me when I was little? I have memories of it when I was younger, but I can't remember its story.

'Elizabeth's Star? Oh, you mean the Evening Star, the brightest and first star of the night sky,' Henry said.

Dawn shook her head. 'We're not sure about that Grace. When you came to us, it was already important and you looked at it every night before we put you to bed. You've always called it Elizabeth's Star, but we're unsure why. Sometimes we used to find you asleep, leaning on the windowsill as if you had been looking at it for such a long time and then fallen asleep sitting up. On cloudy nights when the star remained hidden, you would get most upset because you couldn't see it.'

Henry chuckled. 'You sometimes talked to the star. We saw you a couple of times ask it questions, and you also read your Black Beauty book aloud to it. I think lots of children have invisible friends. I wouldn't worry about it too much. Just a childhood imaginary story.'

Grace smiled. There was something about Elizabeth's Star, but she couldn't remember what. 'I don't talk to it anymore, but I still like to look at it. Maybe one day I'll remember why it's called that.'

CHAPTER 50

Canberra – 1950

Grace stood in line, craning her neck to see how far the queue in front stretched. The Civic Theatre was a popular outing on a Saturday night and she jumped from one foot to the other, impatient and worried they might miss out on tickets. 'What if it's sold out by the time we get to the front of the queue,' she asked her father, who shuffled forward as the people in front started to move.

'Be patient, Grace. There will be plenty of seats. We won't miss out.'

Dawn took Grace's hand, smiling when Grace squeezed it hard. 'Look Mother, the line is moving quicker now. I can see the man in the ticket box. Look at the poster over there. It's Black Beauty and that's a picture of the actress, Mona Freeman. I heard them talking about it on the radio. Can we sit right at the front? I want to feel like I'm right there. I want to sit between you and Father. Do you think it will be exactly the same as the book?'

The man at the counter handed the tickets over, passing one to

Grace. 'Looks like someone is excited to see Black Beauty. It's my favourite also.'

Grace felt very grown up in her swirling full skirt, a thick shiny red belt drawing it in tight at her waist. Her blouse was white, and she wore a pearl necklace, the beads hanging loosely around her neck. She smiled back at him, thankful she had dressed up, her black court shoes polished clean, new white bobby socks folded over neatly, their frilly tops sitting just the way she liked. Everyone was in their finest clothes and it was fun seeing what everyone else was wearing. 'It's my favourite story in the entire world,' she replied.

The man winked at her. 'Enjoy the movie. It's going to be a full house tonight.'

Henry thanked the man and the three of them continued into the theatre. The best part was that there were plenty of spare seats in the front row.

* * *

Grace sat on the edge of her chair, her eyes riveted on the huge screen in front, waiting for the curtains to open. Tears came to her eyes when the music began to play and she gasped as the black and white pictures flashed across the screen, holding her breath the first time Black Beauty emerged. She whispered to Henry. 'Black Beauty looks exactly like in the book. It's him, just like I knew he'd look. His coat is shiny.' She leaned into Dawn. 'Look Mother, that's Anne. Isn't she beautiful and her boots are lovely. She's just like I imagined. Look at the way she looks at Beauty.'

There was so much to see in every scene, and Grace tried to take in every detail. It was a bit different to the book but the main idea was the same and the characters came to life right in front of her eyes. When the movie finished and the credits rolled across the screen, recollections of other times floated in her mind, a memory of someone reading words out loud to her when she was a little girl. She bit her lip, trying to remember more but the memories were distant. People in the theatre started to move, the noise and the lights coming on waking her from her reverie.

She turned to her parents. 'We need to see it again. I want to watch it over and over. Did you see how Bill rescued Anne and Black Beauty? He's very handsome and he was so brave and then they fell in love.' She sighed. 'The ending is so romantic. Now they're in love and Black Beauty has a foal to look after. Did you see that, Father? Did you see how he kissed her and everything worked out in the end?'

* * *

The movie played over and over in Grace's mind, and she went to the theatre several more times to watch it. Henry had gone with her the last time, and the man in the ticket box laughed when he looked up to see them standing in front of him once again. 'You must be our best patrons for this movie. It will be gone at the end of the week.'

Henry replied, 'Yes, this is the last time. My daughter just has to see it one more time.'

'I know the words off by heart,' Grace added, taking Henry's hand as they once again entered the cinema and sat in the front row.

'You know it's better if you sit further back,' Henry advised, 'My neck gets sore when we sit here. Perhaps just this once?'

'No, I'm fine here. I feel like I'm right there with Anne and Black Beauty. It's almost like I could reach out and touch them.' She looked at Henry who was settled in and relaxing back in his chair. His moustache was neatly trimmed, and he looked handsome in his suit and tie, his hat resting on his lap, a neatly folded handkerchief peeking out of his suit jacket. 'Thank you for bringing me again. Mother said she couldn't possibly see it one more time.'

Henry chuckled. 'I'm only here because I know it's the last time. Just nudge me if I fall asleep.'

'How could you fall asleep, Papa? It's too exciting to take your eyes away from.' She clutched his arm. 'I have something important to tell you and Mother, but seeing it's just you and me here, I'll tell you first.'

His bushy eyebrows went up and down. It was one of the things she loved about him the most, that and the gentle way he spoke, even when he was trying to convince her to do something the way he wanted. 'What is it this time?'

She sat up straight, crossing her legs at her knees like Mother did. She was grown up now, fifteen years old and old enough to make her own decisions. 'I'm going to be a vet. I want to go to university and study. That's what I will do for a job and one day I'll have my own clinic, just like the one where we go. I'm going to look after horses like Black Beauty. That's what I'm going to do.'

Henry raised his eyebrows even further, his hand resting on her arm, squeezing it gently as the curtains drew back and the familiar music of the movie started playing. 'If that's what you want and you're determined, then, my dear Grace, I'm sure it will happen.'

'Do you think it's a good idea? One of my teachers said only boys can do those jobs.'

'That's rubbish, Henry muttered. 'You can do anything you like if you set your mind to it, and do you know what?'

'What?' she whispered.

'I know you will.'

CHAPTER 51

Bluegrass – Kentucky 1950

It had been three years since Bud and Ruby had arrived in America. When they had disembarked from the ship, they wasted no time travelling across the country to meet up with the rest of Bud's family who had moved to the Bluegrass region in Kentucky not long after he had joined the navy. His parents, along with Beth and her husband Chuck, had spent the past years anticipating Bud's return and developed a ranch they called, 'Bud's Vista.' With three houses on the property, there was plenty of room for everyone and they were delighted his beautiful Australian bride, Ruby, would be joining them. Bud and Ruby moved into a long ranch-style home that was only a short walk away from the other two homes, one occupied by Bud's parents, the other by Beth and Chuck.

The Bluegrass area was in the north of the state and known for breeding some of the best thoroughbred racehorses in the country. The countryside reminded Ruby of a beautiful landscape painting, with fertile rolling hills, padded with thick grass. Bud quickly settled into working life on the ranch, the lush paddocks and plentiful water a dream come true after the former ranch his family had owned in Oklahoma. This place was free of the dust of his childhood and working alongside his father and Chuck was a perfect situation after the years spent apart. The three families pooled their finances, skills and energy and already the ranch was noted as one of the best in the area.

The economy of the United States was growing at an unprecedented rate and opportunities were at every corner if a man was willing to have a go. Thoroughbred horses in Kentucky were the finest around and Bud dreamt of breeding the top racehorses in the state, if not the world. With the war behind them, the country offered everything for a young couple to prosper.

It was also a perfect time for having children. Luckily their new house had plenty of rooms for their sons. Jerry arrived nine months after their wedding and Wayne was born the year after in 1948.

Ruby tried her best to fit into her new life. She was close to Bud's parents and made friends with the other ladies in the district, her days filled with social activities, household chores and bringing up the two boys. The horses were already giving good returns and all three families were doing well, their bank balances growing solidly. Valuable connections were in place and rich clients travelled from all around the country to come to the ranch and make the most of the stock that the family had built up.

What more could she ask for, she thought, as she watched Bud walk a flighty stallion from the stables to the yard. There had never been anyone else for her. When she first met him, he had looked so tall and handsome in his sailor uniform, his words slow, his drawling Oklahoma accent washing over her when he spoke. He was romantic, always telling her how beautiful she was, doting on her and making her laugh even when she was cranky. She put her needlework down and gazed across the paddocks, the stallion rearing and striking out at Bud, who took it all in his stride.

Horses were his life and she watched him bring the stallion under control, his strong arms pulling the halter rope down, his arm wrapping around the stallion's neck as it calmed down. Bud looked up at her, blowing her a kiss before turning back to concentrate on the horse.

Ruby reached into her pocket and pulled out the folded paper, the last letter from her mother. Brisbane would always be home. She missed the café, the bustling streets of the city, her friends who she had grown up with and most of all her family. She closed her eyes and forced herself to fold the letter up and put it back in her pocket. She had already read it twice this morning. It had arrived last week and contained the usual news. Her brothers were both married, their wives expecting babies in the new year. Her father was busy in the café and her mother spent her days helping him or visiting friends. Nothing much had changed, and she could tell her mother kept the letters upbeat, glossing over her grandparents decline in health, leaving the part about their dog, Tasha, passing away to the end of the letter and assuring Ruby everyone was going well. Hopefully in the years to come it would become easier to visit. At this stage however, the passages by ship were long and expensive and Ruby was hesitant to take two babies so far away on holidays and without their father.

Bud was so tied up with the stud it would be impossible for him to leave for that long. He encouraged Ruby to investigate travelling herself, understanding her need to see family. It didn't matter how much it cost, money was no problem and he would cope fine while she was gone. She wiped her eyes. She couldn't leave him, not even for a short stint. It was so far across the sea and the boys were only little. They would all miss him too much. Perhaps when they were a bit older.

She gathered her thoughts as Bud came out of the stables and started jogging towards her. He jumped up and clicked his heels together in the air, a loud 'yeeha' echoing across the yard. A smile lit up her face as he bounded up the stairs towards her, his muscly arms reaching out to gather her up as he pressed his lips on hers. He eventually pulled away, his soft drawling voice making her heart race. She had always been madly in love with him and would follow him wherever he went. He smothered her face in kisses. 'My beautiful Ruby, why does it always feel like the first time I ever kissed you.'

She laughed and nestled in, her red hair falling across his chest. 'You are such a romantic. No wonder I fell in love with you.'

'It was one lucky day when I fell over on that footpath. We were meant to meet again.'

'Just as well I didn't listen to all those warnings about you Yankee sailors.' She tutted and rolled her eyes as Bud grabbed her backside, giving it a loving squeeze.

'Maybe it was all true that we were oversexed and overpaid. Whatever was said, we were definitely *over there*. And now, my beautiful bride, you're over here, and I'm mighty proud of the way you're settling in. I know it's not always easy.'

She tried to force a smile. 'I'd do anything for you, Bud.' She went to say more but stopped, her eyes downcast.

He cupped her cheeks with his hands, turning her face up so that their eyes met. 'It'll get easier. I know everything is so different. I don't want it all to be about me. You must be happy also. Sometimes I can hear you crying when you're alone in the bathroom.'

'It's just a bit of homesickness, Bud. It'll pass.'

Stroking her hair, he pulled her close. 'If only it weren't so far.'

'You couldn't get much further,' she sighed. 'We have each other and the boys. I'm sure it will get easier.'

CHAPTER 52

Woombye - 1950

win boys arrived for Michael and Joanie on September 9, 1950. The delivery had gone smoothly, and by the time Michael was allowed into the room to see his new sons, Joanie was sitting up in bed, a look of satisfaction on her face, a baby in each arm, fast asleep.

He kissed her gently, ignoring the glare from the nurse who told him in no uncertain terms the visit was only to be short. Mothers needed their rest and the last thing they wanted was a husband fussing around, bothering them. Joanie kissed him back, her words softly spoken. 'Twin sons, Michael. They're beautiful. Their weight is good, and they're healthy.'

Michael couldn't take his eyes off the babies, their tiny round faces, peaceful and angelic. 'Are we going to stick to the names we decided,' he whispered back, casting a quick look the nurse's way. 'I'm not allowed to stay long. I just had to make sure you're okay.'

'Yes. Robert Frank and John Lachie.'

Michael nodded, overwhelmed with the occasion, his fingers

gently stroking the babies' cheeks. 'They're so tiny. It's all over, Joanie. All those months, your body fed and protected them. You're amazing.'

She looked up at Michael. 'Two little Michaels. I'm in love with them already.' She giggled. 'I think it was that morning you carried me back into the bedroom.'

He leaned down to give her another kiss. 'We have been blessed.'

* * *

Looking after the twins kept everyone busy. Joanie spent her days either feeding or changing Robert and John, who by the age of five weeks were rewarding her and Michael with smiles and cute little noises as they started to recognise the different people in their lives. Edna spent most days with them, and there was a spring in her step as she bounded in through the front door each morning. 'I've put some freshly baked scones on the table and I just passed Michael on his way to the store and he said he'll make it back for morning tea also.' Joanie looked up from the lounge chair, holding out Robert for her mother to nurse, before picking John up from the rocker to take his turn at feeding. 'Thanks, Mum; I don't know what we'd do without you.'

Edna held the baby over her shoulder, patting his back gently as he squirmed a little before burping loudly, a plume of milk spraying over her. He gave her a little smile and she kissed the top of his head. 'Just as well, I have a spare blouse with me, Robert. I should have known you would get rid of that extra milk you gulp down.'

'He's a guts, that one,' Joanie said, peering down at John who looked back as he sucked noisily, his tiny hand hanging onto her blouse, his chubby cheeks pressed up against her breast. 'Baby John is not much better, though. Some days I feel like one of those jersey cows out in the paddock.'

'You're doing a great job feeding them both. Look how fat and healthy they are.'

'They're a good weight. Edna bounced Robert up and down on her shoulder. 'Look at him, Joanie. He's looking up at the photo of your dad. Watch him, holding his head up and staring straight at it.' She swapped him to her other shoulder. 'That's your grandpa. His name is Reg, but you can call him Grandpa. He's not here to hold you, but he will be looking down at you from heaven.'

'He's so strong already and he's really looking carefully at Father in that photo. He probably likes the colourful frame.'

Edna sighed and stared at the photo. 'The last ten years have not been easy for any of us, but Robert and John have brought a light back into our lives. Just like when Michael came home.'

'It seems like another lifetime ago.'

'Thank goodness for these two precious bundles.' Edna came back to sit next to Joanie on the lounge. 'I have a purpose in life now and feel like I am needed. My days are full, and at night I'm tired because these two have worn me out. I'm actually sleeping properly again for the first time since your father and you left for Rabaul.'

'It's worked out so well with living next door to each other. You will be part of these boys' lives as they grow up. Michael and I have no intention of moving anywhere. He's like a different person since the twins were born. The sadness has gone.'

* * *

Michael arrived back home on the dot of ten, the kettle whistling in the kitchen and the clatter of dishes bringing a smile to his face as he bounded in through the front door. He kissed Joanie and greeted Edna with a quick hello before peering into the cradles where the two boys slept. 'Are they due to wake up yet?' he asked Joanie.

'No, they are not and don't kick those cradles. I wasn't born yesterday. I saw you do that last week.'

He laughed. All he wanted was to pick them up, nurse them and look into their baby blue eyes and hear them make their little noises or perhaps be rewarded with a smile or one of them reaching out for his face. Today he would have to be content with just looking at them. They were both fast asleep.

Sometimes when they lay on their sides like they were now, he could see a resemblance to what Gracie had looked like when she was a baby. Yesterday Robert had grabbed his finger and made a cute baby noise, smiling as he looked straight up into Michael's eyes. It had caught him by surprise, a flashback, a memory of another tiny baby with blue eyes, looking up at him and making the same sound. Recollections of chubby arms hanging onto his neck, a little girl snuggling in close, the softness of her dark curly hair and the feel of her tiny body nestled into his own.

'We need to make sure they have lots of books,' he said, making his way to the kitchen table where Edna put out her scones, along with jam and cream. He touched her arm. 'Thanks Edna, you know they're my favourite.'

'We all need to keep our strength up. Twins are so much more work than just one.'

Joanie sat down next to him. 'Father always read to me when I was little. He used to fall asleep before the last pages and I'd wake him up to make sure he finished it.'

'I used to do the same with Gracie.' He looked over to the sleeping babies. 'Black Beauty. We always read Black Beauty.'

Edna poured Michael a strong cup of tea. 'I have no other places to contact about your daughter. I'm sorry Michael.'

He sipped slowly, staring at the cradles. 'It's okay Edna. I'm grateful for everything you've tried to do. I also have nowhere else to ask, ring or write to. She is in my thoughts every day and I can only hope she is well cared for. She would be fifteen now. I doubt if she would remember me anyway. I can't recall very much from when I was five.'

Joanie added in. 'I only have one or two memories from that age. One is when I cut my foot and the other is when our dog died. Apart from that, I don't remember anything else.'

'The war tore so many people apart.' Edna got up to check on the boys, turning back to grin at Michael. 'Robert is awake. He's lying here smiling at me, his eyes wide open.

Michael nearly spilt his cup of tea as he jumped up. Joanie laughed. 'You're obsessed. Just as well you were sitting here next to me, because otherwise I wouldn't have believed you didn't wake them.'

He picked Robert up and cuddled him close. 'My baby Robert. Daddy came home from work just to see you.'

Edna squealed in delight, placing her teacup on the sideboard. 'John is awake also. Finish your cuppa, Joanie. I'll nurse him while you have something to eat.'

Edna and Michael cradled the boys in their arms as Joanie relaxed back in her chair. A gentle wave of contentment washed over her, and she sipped her tea slowly, smiling as she watched them fuss over the babies. They all had each other—the five of them together—her family, a home, and the safety of a world without war.

It was indeed the lucky country, and deep down she had a calm feeling that the boys would be a blessed generation. The sacrifices by her generation and those who came before had been monumental and so many families had been torn apart with good people like her dad, Peter and Andrew and Michael's two brothers never returning. But life would continue, people would fall in love, widows would become grandmothers and couples would marry and have babies. The scars would remain, but life would go on.

~~~

ABOUT THE AUTHOR

 Rhonda Forrest is an Australian author who juggles writing and publishing, alongside teaching high school students. She writes captivating contemporary and historical/romance fiction about relationships, family life and social issues, set amidst beautiful and uniquely Australian landscapes.

After bringing up three daughters and traversing several careers, Rhonda went on to teach creative writing, English and history. Her passion for literacy, history and travelling around Australia fuels her novels. Along with her husband, she divides her time between Tamborine Mountain and a century-old cottage with a rambling garden overlooking the waters of the Whitsundays.

The history and personal connection to the events of Rabaul and the *Montevideo Maru* have always intrigued Rhonda and she has spent many years researching, reading and collating information about what happened to those involved, including her grandfather, James McGowan. She hopes that her trilogy, 'We'll Meet Again', will inform readers about the impacts and far-reaching effects that these events had on so many.

Other recent novels also bring to life the remarkable characters and settings that make up the unique Australian heritage and take the reader on a journey from bush to beach, with steamy romances, riveting history and eclectic characters.

Some books are available in audio and large print while other titles are available in Portuguese, Publisher- Leabhar Books Brazil.

If you enjoyed this book or any of Rhonda's other books, you can make a big difference by writing a review, or leaving a star rating on Amazon, Goodreads or Bookbub. A personal recommendation to family, friends, libraries and book clubs is another great way to share the books with others. You can also follow Rhonda on Facebook, Instagram, Goodreads and Bookbub.

Website - https://www.rhondaforrest.com/

Some photos from the family album -

My mother, Margaret Davey (nee McGowan) married Jack Davey in 1952. Jack had also served in New Guinea (1942-1945) and was at Rabaul for the surrender and clean-up at the end of the war.

Jack Davey (far right) with 2 other Wynnum lads - Rabaul

Margaret (right) with her friend Maureen - 1950

Jack and Margaret -Cloudland Brisbane 1940s

Jack Davey

'A dingo howls, a star falls.
Don't worry for me, I'll be home soon.'

We'll Meet Again trilogy is an epic World War II saga that will take you from outback Queensland to the jungles of New Britain, then back to the peaceful hinterland regions of the Sunshine Coast and Tamborine Mountain. Based on actual events that include the invasion of Rabaul, and the tragic sinking of the Montevideo Maru, these are emotional stories of love, survival, and the resilience of the families who waited for their loved ones to return.

*** For your pleasure - Sample chapters from, Book 1 (Elizabeth's Star) are at the back of this book. Happy reading! ***

SALTWATER ROMANCE SERIES

SALTWATER ROMANCE SERIES

From the wild freedom of 1970s Australia to the tangled emotions of the present day, the Saltwater Romance Series delivers three powerful love stories.

Set against the rainforests of North Queensland, the Whitsundays, and the golden shores of Stradbroke Island, these novels explore first love, rebellion, second chances and the journeys that lead us back to ourselves, and to the ones we can't forget.

SILKWORM SECRETS SERIES (Book 1 and 2)

Sample chapters are in the back of this book. Happy reading!

Growing up next door to each other in 1960s suburban Brisbane, Ruby and Bobby should have an idyllic childhood. However, Bobby's home life is vastly different than the loving security of Ruby's family, and not even the sanctuary of their shared treehouse set high in a mulberry tree can offer him the safety he needs. Emotional and layered, *Silkworm Secrets* is a moving story about the secrets children keep, the power of friendship, and a love that overcomes the hardships of the past. *Forever More*, continues the story of Bobby and Ruby and reminds us of the good and bad in people and that a loving family can come in many different forms.

ALSO BY RHONDA FORREST

OUTBACK QUEENSLAND ROMANCE SERIES

With a cast of eclectic characters and set amidst the rugged outback of Australia, the **Outback Queensland Romance Series** will introduce you to stories of friendship, resilience, and loving relationships that come together to triumph over obstacles defined by the past.

Two Heartbeats (Book 1) is followed by the sequel, *Time Will Tell* (Book 2)

Turn Left (Book 3), *A New Start* (Book 4), *Outback Magic* (Book 5) and *Echoes of the Outback* (Book 6) are stand-alone books with some links to the other books in this series.

WHITSUNDAY ROMANCE - YOU MAY NEVER WANT TO LEAVE!

Love by the Jewel Sea - Book 1

Summer by the Jewel Sea - Book 2

The Lure of the Jewel Sea - Book 3

BINDARRA CREEK ROMANCE

BEYOND THE GATE - Mystery Romance at Bindarra Creek

CHRISTMAS AT FORREST GLEN - A Bindarra Creek Romance

A MAGICAL SUMMER - A Bindarra Creek Small Town Christmas Romance

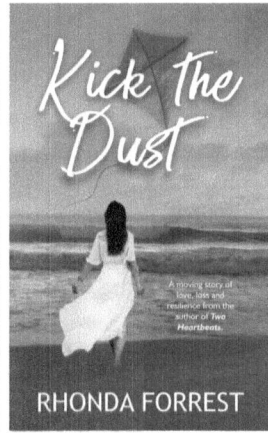

THE SHACK BY THE BAY - Whitsunday Historical Romance

Romantic and purely Australian, *The Shack by the Bay* captures the pristine beauty of the Whitsundays and the wartime memories of older Australians while introducing an eclectic blend of friends and family.

ALL MY HEART - A Tranquil Bay Romance

A small town and school - She only had to last six months.

KICK THE DUST - Contemporary Romance

'If I close my eyes, it's easier to hold onto a memory. When I open them, I think it might really be there in front of me.'

SILKWORM SECRETS

SAMPLE CHAPTERS

'*The ancient trees with their rough bark wrap around me like silk cocoons. Their solid trunks and tendril roots grip the ground as if to say, I will hold you, I will not let go.*'

CHAPTER 1

There had been great excitement the day the silkworms first came to the treehouse. Walking knee-deep through the dense covering of ferns and bushes beneath the mulberry tree, Bobby had announced that he had a surprise for Ruby in his satchel. It was dim and cool under the tree, the knotted branches and canopy forming a shady, secluded area, only a few frilly-necked lizards and the occasional brown snake sharing the space with the two of them.

She had tried to get him to stop and open his bag, the suspense almost too much, but he kept walking, determined for once not to let her win.

'Wait, Ruby Rose. Just wait until we climb up and then I'll show you.'

'But what is it? Can't you tell me? I'll die of curiosity.'

Ruby liked to be in charge and know everything. The suspense made her climb erratically, stopping and starting,

continually looking down at Bobby climbing steadily below her.

'Just get up there and I'll show you,' he said.

Standing on her toes, she balanced on the rungs leading up the tree. He noticed the bottoms of her feet, dark purple colours mixed with dirt from the earth below. Her flowery cotton dress was also stained purple from where she had sat on some of the thousands, perhaps millions, of berries that had dropped from the tree during the fruiting season.

Above them, the trail of timber blocks, like steps, wove their way up into the darkest reaches of the tree. Nails that had long ago been hammered into the rough, textured bark held the timber secure, and as they climbed higher, tiny glimpses of the sky became visible; a blue backdrop to the thick branches that reached upwards, their tops covered by the dense canopy of weeping smaller branches and leaves.

Perched amongst the thick foliage of the massive mulberry tree the treehouse was obscured, a safe haven, a place no one else bothered with, tucked away in an overgrown corner of Ruby's backyard. The two best friends considered the spot to be the best place in the world, and its location among other large trees—figs, mangoes and a towering pine tree—provided them with their own secret corner, a safe house with no adults, just the two of them, talking, laughing; conspirators.

'Hurry up.' Ruby used her bossy voice as she held up the canvas for Bobby to enter the treehouse.

Once inside he had reached into his satchel and presented Ruby with a number of pieces of cardboard, all covered in multitudes of silkworm eggs. She was ecstatic and caused him great embarrassment by continually hugging him and then jumping up and down, making the treehouse creak and shake a little.

It had been school holidays and they had watched every day, Ruby recording in her notebook when the tiny, grey eggs stuck to the cardboard had lightened in colour.

Finally the day they had both waited so patiently for: tiny silkworms, hundreds of them, wriggling, squirming and climbing over each other, filling an old school port, safe in their new home.

Although Ruby had only been eight, she was fastidious about keeping records of events that occurred in and around the mulberry tree. She left her small notebook in the treehouse, only removing it when she needed to record major incidents. Today she wrote: *143 healthy silkworms. All eating leaves.*

The silkworms grew quickly, fattening on the never-ending supply of leaves from the mulberry tree that seemed to be at its best, the thick canopy dripping with the heaviness of its foliage and fruit. The job of picking the greenest leaves from the tree and making sure that all the worms were fed had been allotted to Bobby. Bobby's other job was to clean the droppings from the boxes so the silkworms would have enough room to move around.

They had found extra boxes, the original school port now overflowing with fat silkworms that quickly ate through the leaves. Their droppings were bright green, an indication, Ruby told Bobby, that they were happy and healthy.

Once, when Ruby was not around, Bobby had carried the largest container, the school port, down the tree and into his bedroom at home. Plugging in the vacuum cleaner, he had tried— just using the pointy end of the vacuum and not the brush part as he later explained to Ruby—to suck up the droppings and give the container a really good clean.

Ruby had not been impressed and had efficiently recorded in her notebook:

September 24, 1968, 54 large fat silkworms. Now only 12 surviveing. Bobby and vacum encident.

Now she needed to make more notes regarding the latest incident. Bobby stood beside her as she recorded in her neat handwriting:

March 4, The accident, 1970.

School port moths, 17 healthy moths, now only 7 surviveing, 2 of those are injared becous of falling from tree.

Bobby and Ruby falling over encident acident.

' What?' Ruby said as she looked up at Bobby, his mouth opening as if to speak.

Perhaps it 's not the best time to point out her spelling mistakes, he thought, as he closed his mouth, instead smiling and shaking his head. ' You're the best club president,' he said, 'and at least we still have some moths, even after the accident yesterday.'

The small girl rolled her eyes at him, an indication that she was not impressed with the situation.

He had long ago decided to ignore Ruby's habit of eye rolling, as well as to go along with most of the ideas she came up with. The time he spent with her was his only sliver of happiness in amongst the misery of home and school, and he would do anything to keep the peace between them, whatever it took to stretch out the time before he had to return home. Even though the happenings of the day before had been calamitous to Ruby, they hadn't even rated in his own list of personal disasters.

Ruby was oblivious to the situation at his house. Although he sometimes longed to tell her what was really happening, he had decided that for now it was better to keep it that way, to keep it all to himself. Just try not to think about it, he told himself.

CHAPTER 2

The accident had happened the day before, on what had started out as a typical afternoon but had quickly gone wrong; a disastrous chain of events resulting in their moth tally decreasing to just seven.

As usual, they had both rushed home after school and made their way up into the treehouse as quickly as possible. They lay side by side, enjoying the cool of the rough timber flooring in their meeting area.

Bobby was happy to lie still and listen to Ruby as she chattered on about making a new area that she wanted to call the sitting area. Although there were many sections to the treehouse, designated and specified, it was, after all, not such a big structure. They had drawn boundary lines for the different areas on the floor with white chalk, the faint lines invisible in places where their bare feet or bodies had rubbed over them.

Now they sprawled out with their heads in the spying area, feet pushed up against the stump of the activity table, their bodies stretched across three areas—spying, meeting and activities.

Bobby, being the elder and taller of the two, lay contorted, with his knees bent high and his neck twisted slightly so he could fit across the largest flat area of the treehouse. He tried to stretch out his long legs, sinewy from years of school sport and running, before resigning himself to the cramped conditions. Turning his head, he looked through the slits in the timber walls. His intense brown eyes were set deeply, and his tousled dark hair, springy with the Queensland summer humidity, framed his squarish, still boyish face.

Ruby was stretched out fully beside him with her shoulder jammed up against his, her bare feet nowhere near the stump-table that hindered the comfort of the taller Bobby. Conspirators; two sets of eyes flickering back and forth, lying deathly still as if their lives depended on invisibility.

'I told you it was a good idea,' Ruby whispered, indicating the rolled-down canvas across the doorway. ' There's no way anyone can see in now.'

'You're smart for a girl. Sometimes.'

Bobby's chuckle was cut short by the cutting look, a savage glare as the small girl turned towards him, glinting green eyes scowling, her scrunched-up face willing him to remain silent. They stared hard at each other and Bobby concentrated on her face as he counted the biggest freckles, a smattering of cute brown spots across her nose that faded into each other as they ran across the top of her somewhat chubby cheeks. There were a couple of gaps in her teeth where adult incisors had failed to come through quickly enough to mask the fact that she was still young enough to be losing baby teeth.

Knowing better than to tease Ruby about still having teeth like a baby, he kept his quick words to himself rather than incur the wrath and sharp retorts that would flow forth from her; so young but already more than capable of sticking up for herself.

Wavy blonde hair spread out beneath her, so long that it reached below her red cotton shorts. Her thin brown legs were stretched out beside him as she tried to match the length of his own. Ruby didn't like to be far behind Bobby in anything, and she was always measuring her height, telling him that one day they would be the same size.

'But you'll never be as strong as me,' he would say, flexing his muscles, thinking that one day he would have muscles as strong as Popeye in the cartoon pictures.

'My dad says that I can do anything a boy can do,' Ruby said. 'Just because I'm a girl doesn't mean I can't do stuff. He reckons I can do whatever I want, and if I want to be the strongest person, well, I can be.'

'Girls can't do some things that boys can.' Bobby looked at her, suspicious of her confidence and confused about her ideas, so different from what was promoted in his house.

'Of course they can. I can be whatever I want. If I want to be a doctor, well, I can.'

'That's not right. Girls should be nurses or mums.'

'My dad says if I want to be an astronaut like Neil Armstrong then I can be. He says I'm really smart, and when I grow up I can be whatever I want.'

'Bet you can't be a concreter like him.' 'Bet I could.'

'Girls are supposed to get married and have babies. They look after the kids and cook, clean the house.'

'I don't like cooking and cleaning. I hate cleaning the bathtub. I'm going to do something else when I'm grown up.'

'Like what?'

'I'm going to be a lawyer.'

' You mean like on *Homicide?*' he said, referring to the popular television show.

'Yeah, you know, they solve crimes.'

'I thought you weren't allowed to watch those shows. How do you know what a lawyer is when you aren't allowed to watch it?'

'Silkworm secret,' Ruby said. 'If I lie in bed with the door open, I can see the TV screen reflected in the big mirror on the sideboard. My dad's a bit deaf so he has it up pretty loud. I get to see most TV programs, but you can't tell him or Mum.'

'Lawyers are always men.' 'I watch *Matlock Police* too.'

'Your dad would be really angry if he knew you were watching those programs. You'll get in trouble if you get caught.' 'Bobby, I won't get caught. Besides, they're really scary, so most of the time I put my hands over my eyes.'

'You're so lucky that your mum and dad care about you. I wish my parents were like yours. The other day Theresa asked me how you get a new mum and dad. She's tired of all the trouble at home and the way Sally doesn't get looked after properly. I didn't know what to say. I wish I was older, then I'd run away and take them both with me.'

The two best friends stared hard at each other as they talked. It was a game they often played: who could go the longest without blinking. Both blinked sharply, however, when a loud voice bellowed up from under the tree.

'Ruby, you climb down here this minute. I know you're up there. I wasn't born yesterday.' Footsteps scuffed through the thick layer of fallen leaves, moving closer, the voice booming out again. 'You get down here *now*. I've got jobs for you to do and you're not supposed to play until your homework's done.'

The two conspirators, who had no intention of moving or answering, pulled faces at each other, imitating the adult face below.

'Your father will clip you across the ears when you come down and there' ll be no ice cream for you tonight.' Mary, Ruby's mum, waited for a reply. ' You're wasting my time, Ruby. I've got better things to do than look for you. I'm telling you now, though, if you didn't change and you've got mulberry on that school uniform there'll be hell to pay.'

The exasperated voice faded away as Ruby's mum made her way back to the house.

'She's not really mad,' Ruby whispered. 'She just likes to sound like she is, making out she's the boss.'

Bobby looked worried. 'Are you sure your dad won't thrash

you?'

The small girl's laughter resounded off the rough timber walls. 'Are you joking? My dad loves me too much. He would never hit me.'

'Does your mum ever hit you?' Bobby was trying to manoeuvre his neck, which was starting to feel like it would be attached sideways on his body permanently.

Ruby's little face scrunched up, her eyes narrowing. 'She loses it sometimes, especially when I keep going on about something. Because I'm more stubborn than her, she knows she can't beat me. I can always tell when she's really mad because her face goes red and her eyes … it's like she's a dragon and there's flames coming out of them, red flames licking out of her green eyes. And sometimes her lips go real thin and mean, like this.' Ruby sat up and gave a demonstration.

' What does she do? Does she use a belt?' ' Worse than that.'

'A cricket bat? A broom handle?' 'Don't be silly.'

'I know,' Bobby said, 'the whippy wire out of the curtains.' His curiosity was aroused as he imaged the horrendous punishment her mother might inflict.

' Way worse.' Ruby loved having Bobby's full attention. 'She goes all quiet, then she starts whispering all the angry things she wants to say to me.'

'You mean she doesn't scream or yell?'

Ruby rolled her eyes. 'No, she goes quieter and quieter, telling me off, saying she's going to tell Dad all the bad things I do.'

'Then what?'

'She snaps off a branch, a thin little branch from the wattle tree out the front. She sort of tests it in the air and then real quick, before I can run away, she twitches me with it.'

'Across your face?'

'No, stupid, across the back of my legs, and it stings like crazy and sometimes it leaves a red mark. If I rub it really hard I can make it stay there until Dad gets home and then I tell him that she whipped me with a thick tree branch.'

'Is that it? A bit of a whack from a wattle twig across your legs?'

' Well, it stings.'

'That's nothing, a little wattle twitch.'

'If I put it on real good and make out it hurts a lot,' Ruby said, 'when I sit with Dad at night he rubs it for me. Then he sort of lectures me, tells me how to get around Mum, how not to annoy her. You know the sort of stuff: "Your mother loves you, you need to be nice to her, don't bite the hand that feeds you." Dad reckons she's the boss.'

Bobby lay without speaking, staring up at the patchy tin roof. 'Bobby, are you listening to me? Do you reckon your mum's the boss?'

A lengthy silence followed before he spoke. ' There's no way Mum's the boss. You know my old man; you've seen what he's like. He's not kind like your dad.'

'Your dad's always nice to me,' Ruby said, 'and he gives me a little sausage when we go to your meat shop, and sometimes he makes Mum laugh. He always chats to her, tells her she has a pretty dress on, says he can smell her dinners cooking and that she must be the best cook in the street.'

'Ha.'

'Mum says that your dad has done really good to have such a big shop, and Dad reckons your dad is a good butcher giving us the meat cheaper, and he says that your sister Theresa works hard, she does really good at school, and Mum and Dad think you're smart, and your Uncle Mike, well, Mum says, "Fancy having an uncle that knows the prime minister, real high up in the govern-ment he is, and he has so much money and—"'

Bobby cut her off, wondering how she could speak for so long without a breath. 'You know things aren't always what they seem to be.'

'Like how?'

'Just … never mind.' He stretched out his stiffening muscles. 'What do you mean? Don't start something and not finish it.' 'I mean sometimes things look good to other people, but

they're only seeing what's on the outside.' ' Well, what's on the inside?'

'Forget it. I'm going to get your stupid records book so you can write up the tally.' Bobby sat up suddenly, signalling an end to the conversation.

'Hey, I'm the boss.' Ruby grabbed Bobby as he tried to stand up, his long legs wobbly and unsteady after lying cramped and still for so long. 'Just because you're older—'

And that was when, in a split second, it happened: 'the accident' as Ruby liked to refer to it.

It was like watching a slow-motion movie. Ruby gasped out loud as Bobby's legs became tangled, his body twisted, and he lurched unsteadily towards the table in the centre of the treehouse. The piece of fibro that made up the top of the table rested on the stump of a huge branch. Apart from the way the tabletop crumbled a little around the edges from time to time, it made a perfect flat surface for many of their activities.

That day a number of containers were lined up neatly across the table: an old school port with broken hinges, its stickers peeling; two shirt boxes, the colours on their sides faded and blurry; and two smaller shoeboxes. All the lids on the containers had been punched with multiple holes, providing air for the tiny creatures within.

Ruby's eyes widened as Bobby stumbled and fell forward, one arm reaching out to steady himself and stop his face smashing into the boxes on the table. His hand made contact and he grasped wildly at the closest object. Before their eyes, the largest container, the school port, turned over, the lid going one way, and the rest of the port flipping forward and landing upside down in the reading area.

'Shit.' Bobby gathered himself, standing steady, looking from Ruby to the school port.

They both knew. They knew that below that port, which was now lying lidless in the centre of the reading area, were gaps in the timber floor that opened to the ground far below. This was serious. Bobby registered the fact that Ruby hadn't reprimanded him for swearing; rule number five on the list of Silkworm Club rules.

Ruby crawled slowly over to the port and waited for Bobby. Together they lifted it, cautiously moving it straight up and not sliding it, or allowing it to have any more contact with the floor than necessary.

'Uh-oh.'Bobby pursed his lips and waited for Ruby's response. 'They've nearly all fallen through the gaps,' Ruby said. 'They won't live, they can't fly.' Her voice was shaky as she carefully tried to pick up the contents that had fallen from the container. Bobby pressed his face to the openings between the floorboards, one eye closed, trying to spy any survivors of the fall. Ruby's voice took on the steadiness and authority of the Silkworm Club president. 'I'll pick these ones up. Can you please go down and see if you can find any on the ground?'

She scooped up the mulberry leaves scattered on the floor, a few silkworm moths gripping to their surface, their delicate wings flapping wildly, their eyebrows furrowed. 'It looks like there are about five here. That means twelve are missing. This morning there were seventeen.Hurry up, Bobby, they only live for a few days so we need to find them and put them back in the box. Then they can lay their eggs.'

As usual, Bobby followed her instructions. Even though he was older by three years, Ruby was the club president, and besides, she was good at organising everything and everybody. It was easier to just follow her directions and do what he was told.

He scrambled down the tree trunk, hanging onto the timber steps and hand guides that wound their way down to the ground. The thought of looking for white moths that had probably drifted off on the wind made him smile. He knew that the heavy leaf litter and dense ferns growing wild under the tree would envelop and hide a free-falling silkworm moth that had no sense of surviving in the wild.

But he would try; he would do anything to please Ruby because she was, after all, his best friend.

CHAPTER 3

Dad says you've just got to get on with stuff,' Ruby said as she tidied the treehouse. 'Step forward and don't cry over spilt milk. I'll bring a mat up and put it over the gaps in the floor.'

The boxes on the table were now lined up straight. Everything had to be in its place and she cast her eyes over the timber boxes, squinted and then rolled her eyes when she noticed the ice-cream tin with a few large mouldy mulberries left in it. 'Got it.' Bobby tipped the few remaining mulberries out the window, replacing the container in its correct position on the shelf. Amused at how neat she had to have everything, he watched her move the crate chairs so they were even and straight.

They both ran their hands over the boxes that were full of cocoons. When the moths hatched, they would hopefully add to their now decreased tally.

'See you in the morning,' Ruby said to the silkworms.

Bobby held up the canvas for her as they made their way out of the treehouse and into the real world below.

When they reached the bottom of the tree they sat for a while, balancing on the huge protruding roots that were covered in the same rough bark as the trunk; sections of the roots smooth however, due to the continuous movement of bare feet across them over the years.

'I have to go in,' Ruby said eventually. 'It's nearly night. Even Dad will go mad if I come in after dark.'

'I better go home, too. I still have to do all my jobs before Dad gets home. I'm sorry about the moths, Ruby Rose.'

'Best friends don't get mad with each other. It was sort of my fault, too.'

Emerging from the cover of the trees, they turned in the direction of their houses, both looking up at the horizon as the fading light threw an orange hue over the backyard. Ruby saw the light flick on over the back veranda and knew her dad would be starting to look at the clock, wondering if he should call her in to clean up before dinner.

'See you tomorrow.' Bobby sounded despondent, sad.

He never wants to go home, Ruby thought. He must really like the silkworms, and me, better than his own family.

The darkening light separated them, the clicking of the side gate indicating that Bobby was in his own yard.

Sure enough, Ruby's dad Francis was sitting out on the back steps, his work boots and socks kicked off to the side as he enjoyed a smoke in the balmy evening light. She ran towards him, her small legs going, as her dad would say at a million miles an hour. Placing his cigarette down on the brick stairs beside him, he held both arms out as she jumped onto him. Chubby arms wrapped around his neck, her kisses smothering his face.

'My Ruby Rose, my little mulberry fairy,' he said, squeezing her tightly, his face nuzzling into her blonde wavy hair.

'I'm never going to let go of you.' Ruby clung to him, her mulberry-stained face squashed into the hairs on his chest, her legs drawn up so she could nestle in, snug and secure.

' What have you been up to today, little one?' He moved her to one side so he could puff on his cigarette.

'Dad, Dad, you'll never believe what happ—'

Her mum's voice interrupted them. 'Right, you two, the pair of you, grubs. One covered in mulberry, the other in concrete dust. You need to clean up before you come in for dinner. Stop your story right now, Ruby. We'll listen while we have dinner and then I'll decide if you get dessert.'

Ruby recalled the earlier incident, when her mother was looking for her, calling out. It seemed so insignificant now. Wait until she told them about the moths, and how Bobby had rescued two of them, then surely she would get dessert.

Francis picked her up and she wrapped herself around the front of him, her arms around his neck and her legs wrapped around his waist. They looked at each other and laughed together.

Ruby's mum put on her cranky voice. 'Clean up, both of you, or else there'll be no dinner for either of you.'

Steam rose from the hot water as Ruby bathed, only her head above the water as she lay back in the old claw-foot bath. She loved the bathtub. It was deep enough for her to float in, and the warm water closed in over her, softening the mud and mulberry stains. Her dad would be in the outside shower now, scrubbing hard, removing the dried concrete and dust, the remnants of a day of hard work. She knew he would wait until she had run the bath water, letting her get the hot water first in case it ran out. After he finished, her mum would send him in to get Ruby moving.

She hated getting out of the tub. Instead, she always drew out her time, leaving it until the last moment to take the small scrubbing brush from the wire basket hanging on the wall. Then she would scrub as hard as she could, removing all of the dirt and stains from her hands and feet. She knew her mum would inspect her cleanliness, and if she had missed any marks, Ruby would have to use the bucket and cold water outside to finish off after dinner.

The door rattled as her dad banged on it. 'Hurry up, dinner's out.'

Ruby emerged scrubbed and refreshed. Her dad hugged her, one hand ruffling her hair, both revelling in the freshness of feeling clean.

The three of them sat around the small dining-room table and ate their evening meal, her mum smiling and relaxed now, her dad talking about his day. It was the usual steak and mash, carrots, and of course the greens—beans and peas. This was their favourite time of the day. It was quiet, just the family, all tucked up together, ready to chat and catch up with what each other had done during the day.

Her dad beamed at both of them. 'Righto, Ruby Rose, now tell us what exciting things you did today.'

***

Silkworm Secrets - Dark Secrets from a Distant Past

www.ingramcontent.com/pod-product-compliance
Lightning Source LLC
Chambersburg PA
CBHW050023120726
47903CB00006B/1885